THE CRUELEST QUESTION

One thought comforted Anne as her arms went around Buckingham's neck. He would not think her a wanton. He surely would know that she succumbed because she found him irresistible.

Which was the truth. She wanted to hold him, to feel him, to taste him. The thought of spending all of her life wondering forlornly what it might have been like to lie in his arms was suddenly insupportable. Fire was licking through her, sending her spinning off into a world where she could not get enough of him. She wanted to run her hands down his back, feel his sleek skin, feel the hard strength of him. Her breath came shallow and fast. She felt heated everywhere he touched and yet, when they lay together on her bed, he pulled back and looked at her with heavy-lidded eyes.

Then he asked the question she feared he would, the question that would put the weight of what they did upon her alone, the question there was no escaping now.

"You want me, Annie . . . ?"

A Certain Reputation

by
Emma Lange

A SIGNET BOOK

SIGNET
Published by the Penguin Group
Penguin Books USA Inc., 375 Hudson Street,
New York, New York 10014, U.S.A.
Penguin Books Ltd, 27 Wrights Lane,
London W8 5TZ, England
Penguin Books Australia Ltd, Ringwood,
Victoria, Australia
Penguin Books Canada Ltd, 10 Alcorn Avenue,
Toronto, Ontario, Canada M4V 3B2
Penguin Books (N.Z.) Ltd, 182–190 Wairau Road,
Auckland 10, New Zealand

Penguin Books Ltd, Registered Offices:
Harmondsworth, Middlesex, England

First published by Signet, an imprint of Dutton Signet,
a division of Penguin Books USA Inc.

First Printing, April, 1995
10 9 8 7 6 5 4 3 2 1

Chapter 1

Anne de Montforte noticed the man the moment she stepped to the doorway of her aunt's rooms. Even from the corner of her eye, she marked how he seemed to fill the landing. He was a stranger. She'd no question of that. Though he stood in the shadows, she knew she had never seen him before.

"Well, Cuz, I'm off, then."

Anne smiled at the young man before her, the tall stranger forgotten. By birth, Robin Godfrey was her cousin, but in truth, he was like a brother to her, and having him in London with her for the last weeks had been the brightest spot in Anne's homecoming. For all the years she had been in Italy, she had not had anyone to whom she was so close as she was to Robin. Her father had been so changed there, he'd been almost a stranger, and as to her husband . . . but it wasn't the time to think of Peter, nor even of the four people in the rooms behind her who had only her upon whom to rely. Rob was sailing off that very day.

"May the wind be at your back, as the Irish say, Rob. That's an appropriate wish for a sailing man, is it not?"

"It is, indeed, though I'll admit there is nothing like a storm to get one's blood flowing."

Rob's grin was as cocky as he was young, and Anne chucked him on the chin. "You will have a care for yourself, young man. No reckless calling up of storms for the love of adventure!" His grin as intact as if her words had gone in one ear and out the other, which in fact they had, Rob took her slender hand in his and pressed something into it. Anne's smile faltered as she looked down at the leather pouch he'd pressed on her. "What is this, Robbie?"

"The bonus my Uncle Reed promised me, if I saw the stout *Dora* repaired in good time. It's to tide you and the children over until I return with my earnings from this trip."

"But . . ."

"I'll hear no 'but,' Annie." Robin cut her off with a finger laid firmly across her lips. "You and Aunt Betsy and Uncle Dick made me one of you after I was orphaned. I'm delighted I have the opportunity to do something in return."

"Rob! You owe me nothing." Anne tried to shove the pouch at him, but Rob caught her hand and curled it around the warm leather.

"I'll hear nothing about 'owe,' Annie. You would do the same for me, and don't deny it. I can hear you now, you know. 'Of course, you will take it, Robbie Godfrey. Don't be more absurd than you can help.'" Anne couldn't help but smile, for Rob had imitated her at her older-sisterish best too well. The young man grinned back, smugly pleased. "There now, you see. You've as good as admitted you would push the pouch on me, if you were the one who had it. Think of the children, if you please. And that with this you'll not be obliged to find work in some gloomy little shop before I return with the profit Reed and I will make on the coal we sell in such abundance to those cold countries around the Baltic. And you will take a portion of that purse, too," he went on, warming to his new, self-appointed position as family head. "I could not bear the thought of you drudging about some shop waiting upon arrogant witches who are not half so good as you."

Anne wasted no time disputing her relative worth. "This money is yours, Rob. You must use it to start the fortune you mean to make."

"Will make," he corrected with the breezy confidence of

youth. "And will share with you, for you are my closest family, Annie. My Aunt Peg and her trade-tainted but wealthy husband, Reed, have been generous to me, but they have never been to me what you and your parents were. It was a bitter thing for me, Annie, that I was too young to go with you to Italy and had to stay with them."

Anne squeezed his hand. "And I missed you, Robin. Indeed, I cannot say how much I longed to see you at times." But Anne did not mean for either of them to dwell on the difficulties she'd encountered in Italy. Even as Rob's eyes darkened, she shook her head. "But you have already done so much for me, sending me a goodly portion of what it took to get us home. You owe me—"

"All I would owe a sister," Rob firmly insisted. "You must realize I'll worry about you, Annie, if you don't accept my contribution, and you must realize as well that you do not want a sailor to have anything on his mind but his sailing." When Anne made an inarticulate noise of frustration, he grinned triumphantly. "I thought that might convince you! Now then, no more arguing. Tides have a way of not waiting. God keep you, Cuz." He leaned down to kiss her brow. "Look for me in two months or mayhap three, if the Baltic's rough."

From the shadows of the stairwell, Trevelyan de Montforte observed the little scene with cool, cynical, but not unappreciative eyes. He couldn't see her face well. There was only one small window at the far end of the hall, but what light there was lit her hair. Trev traced the thick, dark, satiny spill of it down to her full breasts, where his gaze lingered. Though the bells had chimed the hour of eleven some time ago, she had obviously just risen from bedding with the boy, for her hair was not yet pinned up and she was dressed in only a satin robe. Belted at her slender waist, the thin wrapper flowed closely over nicely flaring hips and those full breasts.

Though he gave little sign of it, Trev was amused. He had had no relish for this particular errand. The quarrel was not his, but his uncle's, and he rarely had patience for other people's quarrels. Perhaps he would learn to cultivate patience in the future. He had always thought it a tedious virtue, but it did seem, from the look of it—or her—that this particular errand, at least, would not be tedious after all.

She was clearly still the lightskirt John had said she had been before her marriage. Trev had not missed the undoubtedly disappointingly thin pouch the boy had pressed on her. She'd protested prettily but as predictably pocketed it in the end.

Young Red Hair was kissing her now. She squeezed his hand touchingly, and then her visitor departed by another set of stairs at the far end of the hall. Trev never gave the boy another thought. Before his cousin's widow could close her door, he stepped forward.

Anne gave a start of surprise. She had forgotten the dark stranger completely and to find that he had been waiting, silently watching her parting with Rob, sent an unpleasant chill through her. Pulling the front of her wrapper close against her, she arched a sharply inquiring eyebrow at him.

"Mrs. Peter de Montforte?"

His voice was low and well modulated, but his tone was clipped, as if he were accustomed to authority and saw no need to pretend he was not. Anne's eyebrow lifted a fraction higher, but if she did not care for his tone, she cared even less for his size. In order to meet his eyes, which were difficult to see in the dim hallway, she had to arch her neck, but Anne did not do it meekly. She thrust up her chin and replied curtly, "Yes?"

"I am Buckingham, Peter's cousin."

The Duke of Buckingham. Had he pulled a knife out of his pocket, she could not have felt any more shock or, almost, any greater thrill of alarm. He had not put himself out for a condolence visit, of that she was certain, for in the four years since Peter had died, he'd never put himself to the lesser trouble of writing her a note to express his sympathy.

"May I come in?" he asked, mocking amusement threading his voice.

Gathering her scattered wits, she stepped aside, and said in a determinedly assured voice, "Of course, your grace."

He displayed the casual, unconscious grace of an athlete as he strode by Anne, entering her Aunt Hetty's tiny entry hall, filling it as Robin had never done. But Robin was not so tall or well built. Nor was Robin her enemy.

Buckingham, nephew to the man who had disowned his son for marrying her, almost certainly was. Anne strove to ignore the knot forming hard as a rock in her stomach as she took the lead, proceeding through an open door into a narrow, gloomy sitting room that echoed with the raucous sounds of the crowded street below.

Anne shot a glance at Hetty's aged couch. A pillow covered the fray in the cushion, and so she gestured toward the couch and the small fire the sunless room required though it was mid May. "Please make yourself comfortable, your grace." She glanced up then, getting her first look at him in reasonable light—and had the presence of mind to look away at once. "I will have tea brought to you while I change," she heard herself say, as she stared at the faded burgundy pillow.

What she saw was the face of the man beside her. He looked nothing at all like Peter. There was nothing boyish or merely pleasant about him. His features were chiseled, every line stamped with self-assurance. Even his hair was more dramatic than Peter's, for it was black as night. And his eyes. Dear heaven, though they were blue like Peter's, they were of a different hue altogether. The lightest blue, they made a striking contrast to that black hair, and might have prompted Anne to make pleasant comparisons to a summer's day had they been warm. They were not. Cool, decidedly cynical, and uncomfortably penetrating, they seemed to lay her bare with a single glance.

"Perdone, signora?"

Anne whirled around in the direction of the door. It was Alberghetta, her maid, come just in time. Anne had been about to make excuses for her dress, or lack of it. She had been up most of the night with Alex, who had an upset stomach. Come morning, Hetty had taken her place, allow-

ing her to sleep until Rob had come, when she had had to
rise hastily to bid him farewell. It was all perfectly innocent, but she didn't owe this man—cousin by law and duke
though he was—any explanation, particularly one that in-
volved admitting one of her children was not in perfect
health. She had the grim intuition that the reason the duke
had stooped to visit Shipner's Lane, had to do with the children that were the only real link, beside a shared name, that
Anne had with his family.

"Yes, Betta?" she replied, and was inexpressibly relieved
that she did not sound as breathless as she felt.

"The tea, signora." Betta held up the tray, as she darted a
furtive glance at the duke.

Poor Betta was right to find him fearsome, Anne
thought, though not in the way she likely did. The gentleman dominating her aunt's sitting room was not interested
in a servant. He did not even spare a glance for Betta. Anne
knew it, for she could feel his eyes raking the length of her.

"Very good, Betta," she said, deliberately ignoring that
insolent look before she betrayed herself by pulling her
wrapper even more tightly over her bosom. "As you can
see, I've a guest. The Duke of Buckingham will take the tea
while I change.

"If you need anything, your grace, call for Betta, but I
won't keep you waiting long." There was no help for it.
She couldn't avoid his eyes forever. Anne lifted hers, a
thrill of something, likely fear she thought, rushing through
her. Their eyes did not so much meet as collide, hers flashing defiance and, though she was unaware of it, a clear
challenge. "If you will excuse me, your grace?" she said,
although the phrase was the merest courtesy. Anne did not
wait for Buckingham's permission to follow Betta out of
the room.

Trev watched her depart, his blue eyes drifting down to
the softly flaring hips swaying beneath the satin robe. He
could have told her that she needn't change for him, that he
was accustomed to seeing women in dishabille, but he had
missed neither the challenge nor the defiance in her eyes.
However receptive Peter's disreputable widow might be to

other men, it was obvious she was on her guard against him, a de Montforte.

Uncle John had expected as much. "Of all my nephews, you're the only one will do for this business, Trev," he'd said, his voice weak and raspy from illness, but as emphatic as ever. "I don't doubt she loathes even the name de Montforte. Bound to after I exposed her for what she is and denied her the position and fortune she wanted. She is a strumpet, Trev! My agent got the sworn testimony of four men when I sent him to Italy to find out about her, but he was too slow. She had already gotten herself heavy with a bastard, and Peter, fool that he was, had succumbed to that old wile and married her, breaking the marriage contract I'd made with the Pendergasts—breaking my word to them! Ah, but that is old history. You are a different kettle of fish from Peter, Trev. You know all there is to know about women, strumpets particularly. I'm counting on that vaunted experience of yours. Seduce her, compromise her, buy her—whatever it takes! I can't leave my heir to the likes of her to raise."

Trev agreed there. Whores didn't raise gentlemen. But they did pleasure them. Particularly if they were beautiful. A swift smile curving his well-formed mouth, he strolled to the window. Privately, he had always questioned his uncle's contention that Peter had been trapped into marriage by a pregnant whore. He had not thought Peter so foolish as that, nor had he thought his younger cousin imbued with so strong a sense of responsibility. Now the question was settled, and to Trev's satisfaction, at least. Peter had not made his mésalliance on account of some bastard child. No, he'd wanted the woman, her richly polished, mahogany hair, that soft, pouting wanton's mouth, those full, rounded curves.

She was an enticing prize, as she must know. Men had paid for her favors, Peter paying the ultimate price. Trev grimaced absently at the inadvertent comparison he'd made between marriage and death, but he was not distracted from his original train of thought. If she had had takers in Italy, and by sworn testament she had, why had she come back to

England—to this? He glanced around the unappealing room with its worn furniture and faded curtains. Surely she had had wealthier customers there.

Or had her eyes put off the Italians? Were Italian men superstitious about green ones? Or had they been put off by the sparkling challenge those eyes contained? Had she been too much for southern men, accustomed to more subservience? A slow smile lit his face. Was the earth flat? But no matter, whatever Italian tastes might be, he knew his own. And he had a distinct preference for a succulently shaped challenge.

Chapter 2

Anne paused outside the sitting room to smooth the skirt of her dress. There wasn't a wrinkle in it, of course. Betta had seen to that, and even were Anne to beat the skirt, there was no hope she could transform her old bombazine into anything matching the elegance of the duke's clothing. Every article he wore screamed of the finest tailors, not to mention the costliest materials. Not that he looked like a fop. No fop would have presented himself in mud-splattered boots, even were his boots so obviously from Hoby. Nor would he have worn such drab colors. The duke's coat was a rich chestnut brown, true, but brown nonetheless; his breeches, the standard buff. No, he was carelessly elegant. Anne grimaced again, more resentfully, seeing in her mind's eye the superb fit of his not really so drab coat over his strong shoulders. Well. She straightened. She didn't have his daunting figure or his wealth, but at least she was dressed respectably now, and perdition to his insolent blue eyes, anyway.

Buckingham was not warming himself by the fire, as she'd expected, but standing at the window, staring into the crowded street below. Perhaps he was fascinated by so exotic a scene, Anne thought, knowing she was being defensive but feeling unable to help herself when she thought of the street before his palatial house. There, all would be quiet, stately, elegant. . . .

Anne straightened her shoulders sharply. She was only sapping her confidence. "Did you not care for your tea, your grace?" she inquired, stepping into the room, her chin as high as her shoulders were squared. Her question at least had the effect of forcing Buckingham to turn his back upon the dismal view.

Trev swung around to find his cousin's widow dressed in a long-sleeved, gray bombazine dress that was so sober it made him want to laugh, given what she'd been wearing earlier. It could not quite hide her slender figure with its courtesan's curves, but it certainly made as little of her charms as possible. Her hair was tamed, too, with only a few strands left to curl about her face and the rest of the silky mass pulled sleekly back and pinned in a simple knot at the nape of her neck. The knot looked heavy, but she carried the weight well on a neck that was long and graceful.

Next to the dull gray of the dress, her creamy skin glowed. She had calculated the effect nicely, for the gray did not diminish her eyes. They were, still, a vivid green lit with challenge.

"I was not thirsty, thank you."

"A shame," Anne said lightly. "Betta makes an excellent cup of tea. But if I cannot offer you refreshment, what can I do for you, your grace?"

At the sudden gleam that flared in his eyes, Anne caught her breath. It mocked her. Yes, it certainly mocked her, but it was heated, too. She'd seen that kind of heat often enough before to know it. If he was her enemy, he was the most dangerous kind—an interested one.

She flushed, despite every resolve she'd made not to be affected by him. Anne did not generally disappoint herself so, and the flush deepened. He saw it, flicked his eyes down to the line of color on her high, round cheeks, and then looked back at her, another light in his eyes now. She'd have liked to slap his face. That would erase that amused gleam, but already the infuriating light was fading, his blue eyes becoming cool, even inscrutable, once more.

"Actually, I have come on behalf of my uncle."

His voice was neutral now, but Anne's stomach clenched, and she had not another thought for the interest that had flashed so briefly, if distinctly, in his eyes. It meant nothing to her compared to this.

"I see." Striving for calm, she thrust aside a piercing regret that she'd returned to England. She could not have lived the rest of her life in Italy, rearing her children on foreign soil. And besides, there was Hetty. Her aunt had no one to nurse her when she suffered one of her breathing spells. "Well, whatever your reason for coming, won't you have a seat, your grace? We may as well be comfortable."

Anne took the end of the couch with the fray, but she needn't have worried Buckingham would see it. He didn't take a seat at all, instead propping a fine shoulder negligently against the chimneypiece, so that, she thought sourly, he managed to look both casually comfortable and distinctly intimidating all at once.

"You may not know that Peter's brother, my Uncle John's eldest son, died some months ago," Buckingham began without preamble.

Anne had not known. The news had not reached her in Italy, nor, of course, did she correspond with Lord John de Montforte. It was the worst possible news she could have heard, and if there was not much sympathy in her voice when she replied, there was certainly sincerity. "I am sorry to hear it."

If Buckingham guessed at the alarm he'd roused in her, he did not betray it. Calmly, he observed what she knew already. "Uncle John has no blood heir now." Anne could make no response, silent or otherwise, only stare fixedly up into his cool, blue eyes and hope against hope that she did not betray her increasing panic to him. When she did not speak, Buckingham went on as dispassionately as if he had no notion he was threatening what was dearest to her in the world. "He wishes to make Alexander his heir. The estate is a considerable one. Upon Uncle John's death, the boy would come into several, sizable pieces of property. He would be secure and would, of course, move in the best circles. Naturally, Uncle John wishes to see the boy has the training necessary to assume the inheritance properly."

For the space of a moment, hatred tore through Anne. How calm and assured he was while he used those smooth, guileful words to disguise that he meant to rob her of her child! Yet at least she was certain now precisely what threat he presented. It helped to clear her head. "Which all means what, precisely?"

She was cool, Trev thought. Her voice was level and her gaze steady. Only the tautness of her jaw betrayed hidden emotion, and he did not know her well enough to know what the emotion might be. Was she greedy for some sort of personal recompense, perhaps? If so, his task would be made easier.

"At six, Alexander would go to live with his grandfather at Uncle John's principal estate in Sussex."

"At six! That is next year!"

Anne lost control of her voice. It rose shrilly, and Trev finally read her panic. So . . . she was reluctant to give up the boy. Perhaps that was to her credit, but she surely understood that Peter's boy would prosper far better with his grandfather than in the meager circumstances she could provide.

"It is not uncommon for boys of six to be sent off to school."

"For boys of the best families, of course."

Trev's eyes narrowed. He was not accustomed to being mocked. It was on the tip of his tongue to inquire caustically if she could enlighten him on the customs prevalent among penniless gamester's families, but he caught himself. He'd an end to achieve, and it would not be as easily accomplished were he to indulge himself by reminding the vixen of her dubious place in society.

In the end, he conceded her point with an indifferent shrug that galled Anne far more than any derision could have. "As you say, boys of the best families often go to school at six. During the long holiday, Alexander will come to you for a month until he reaches the age of ten. Then he will choose for himself where he spends his holidays."

"He would choose by himself?"

Anne made no attempt to conceal her skepticism. She was beyond caring whether she caused the duke's keen eyes to narrow. God rot him and all his arrogant condescending breed! He probably believed she ought to be grateful for what he offered. The thought so incensed Anne that she swore all the more fiercely that he and his uncle would not get their unfeeling hands on *her* son.

"As I said, the boy would choose for himself," Buckingham repeated, a definite edge in his voice. "As to you, ma'am, you would, of course, be comfortably settled."

"In the Americas, perhaps?"

Two could play at that game. His reasonable tone contrasting mightily with her snappish one, he drawled smoothly, "If you so choose, of course."

Anne's green eyes flashed. "Well, I do not so choose, nor do I choose to sell my son to the cold, tyrannical wretch who disowned his own son!"

"I take it those are the terms in which Peter described Uncle John?" When Anne nodded emphatically, Buckingham inquired with strained patience, "And you consider Peter a reliable witness in relation to his father?"

"Peter was not a scoundrel! I think any reasonable father could have made an accommodation with him."

"What accommodation did Peter allow?" Buckingham demanded more levelly than might have been expected. "He never protested the marriage agreement his father had contracted for him years before. He simply begged a year for a grand tour, and then, some weeks after the marriage, got around to informing his father that, by the by, he had made a *mesalliance* with a complete stranger. I am sorry to be so blunt," he remarked when Anne's mouth tightened into a stiff line, though he sounded more curt than sorry. "But you judge my uncle unfairly. He acted as any other man in his position would have done. He is no ogre."

Anne forced herself to breathe deeply. The important thing was to concentrate on her legal rights in regard to Alex, not on any presumed right she might have to a fair hearing before the de Montfortes. There was no use pursuing phantoms. "Perhaps Lord John is not a demon, your grace, but I know that I will never put my son in his hands."

"I see. You would prefer your son to forgo wealth, education, refinement in favor of . . ." As his voice trailed away, Buckingham glanced derisively about the uninviting room. "Living in splendid rooms like these? And let me see, I think becoming a clerk would be a likely career. How fortunate he will be with his ink-stained fingers, cold bones in winter, and half a dozen children to feed."

"At least he would love them!"

His pitiless, bright blue eyes lanced Anne to her core. "If you would do me the favor of sparing me female hysterics and sentimentality, I would much appreciate it."

Hysterics! They were speaking of her son—of his life, of hers. But Anne forced back the furious retort that rose to her lips. She was speaking to a man who had no children, a man who had likely never been contravened in his life. "I may not sound reasonable to you, your grace, but I believe I am doing what is best for my son. I intend to provide him an education, and I fully believe he will amount to more than an overworked clerk."

Trev did not ask her how she thought she'd come by the money to educate the boy. He knew she would not admit the truth, and he lacked the patience to listen to lies. "I said you would be comfortably settled. Is it that you wish to know the particulars of the settlement?"

"*No!*" Her effort at control did not last beyond the question, for though she had expected something of the sort, actually having the question put to her galled her fiercely. "I will not sell Alex for any price! What kind of men are you and your uncle that you believe I would tear Alex from everyone he loves and send him to a cold stranger for a little silver?"

Anne could have bitten her tongue the moment she saw the muscle leap in Buckingham's jaw. It was the only indication he gave that her question had affected him, but it was enough to make her heart race with alarm. "My uncle and I are reasonable men with an understanding of the world," he said coldly, eyes narrowed. "And I can assure you that anyone of reason, upon hearing the particulars of this dispute, would declare you mad for refusing your son the future Uncle John proposes."

Given the degree of anger Anne sensed in him, and the power he most certainly possessed, it was not entirely surprising that she should leap to the worst possible conclusion. Despite all her cautions to herself about holding to some modicum of calm, she shot to her feet. "Are you threatening to have me sent to Bedlam, your grace?" Her voice shook with emotion. "If you should try anything of the kind be warned that I've a weapon, too. I've the letter your uncle wrote to Peter when he disowned him. If you bring any kind of suit against me, I shall have it published far and wide for all to read, and everyone in England will be able to judge who is the worthier candidate for that place."

Despite her temerity in threatening him, Trev felt a glimmer of admiration for her, albeit impatient admiration. She looked unexpectedly valiant with her chin thrust out at him and her hands balled into fists as if she meant to fight him herself, and yet she was clearly terrified. They were standing close together, toe to toe almost literally, and he could see the stark fear behind the fire in her eyes.

"Calm yourself," he said, but not so curtly as he might have. "I am not in the habit of resorting to such means to achieve my ends. Sit," he insisted, when she continued to stand there, her breast heaving distractingly while she regarded him as if he might grasp her in his talons and drop in among the Bedlamites at any moment. "I had no thought of Bedlam at all, I assure you. I would not have my worst enemy sent there, and I think you are not quite that."

Anne bit her lip. She wished mightily she had not overreacted and played the hysterical female in earnest, but neither could she seem to find the words to accept the duke's assurance. She did believe him, if she didn't know quite why, but she didn't know the extent to which he could speak for his uncle.

Trev watched her try to regain her poise, relaxing her

fists and taking calmer breaths. He hadn't expected her to
be so fiercely determined to keep her son, and he could not
be certain that it was devotion that drove her. Every day
mothers sent their sons away to school without a qualm, offering them up to masters who were far harsher than his
uncle.

Perhaps she really had been turned against his uncle by
the letter she'd mentioned. Uncle John would have been in
a rage when he wrote, and he was known for being a devil
when in a rage. The other possibility was that she was a
conniving and excellent actress, positioning herself to de-
mand a princely settlement. If so, time and wealth were on
his side, and they would arrive sooner rather than later at an
accommodation. However, if she really were as intent upon
keeping her son as she wished to appear, she could make
things difficult. Not that she would keep him from the end
he desired. Trev had yet to meet the man or woman, in
court or out, who had dared to deny him something he
wished. But she could turn a family matter into a public
one, dragging up old stories that could only hurt Uncle
John and make him a subject of gossip, something he'd
abhor.

Whatever her motives, one thing seemed paramount. To
carry out the commission he'd accepted, however grudg-
ingly, he must keep her—and her son, of course—near him.
Otherwise, it was possible she'd run off and put him to the
trouble of finding her. Also, near him, she'd get a taste of
the world she meant to deny her son, if indeed she really
did mean to keep him. If not, they could bargain as easily in
comfortable circumstances as in these grim ones. Either
way, he would win, as he did not for a moment believe she
would hold out once she had actually experienced the com-
forts and luxuries provided by wealth such as the de Montfortes possessed.

But, should she prove to be unlike anyone he'd ever
known, he could do as his uncle had advised. And, he had
to admit, the thought of seducing the widow de Montforte
to his way of thinking held considerable appeal.

His thoughts must have shown in his face, for the widow

gave him a wary look, prompting him to call his thoughts to order. He wanted her acquiescent, not suspicious.

"We've gotten off on a bad footing," he said, his smile deepening at his statement of the obvious. She did not warm, but he had not expected a quick capitulation and continued easily, "And I've behaved as if you must decide what I do concede is a large issue at once. But that is not the case at all. Of course, you may take all the time you need, and while you decide, you may as well be comfortable. I am sure you will agree that these rooms are not the ideal place for a child to live. You will come to my home." He softened the order by bending upon her a smile he knew from experience had its own persuasive power with women. "Spring and summer are particularly lovely times of year at Sisley. Alex will have all the room he desires to run and play, and, after all, it is only right that he come to know Peter's family."

Anne did not trust him, his invitation—if his command could be so termed—or the singularly powerful smile that had curved his mouth so pleasingly. She did, however, whether she trusted him or not, have overwhelming reason to consider his invitation.

"You are very kind to think of us," Anne said, allowing herself the luxury of irony in place of the luxury of refusal. Gratified further when she saw his brow lift at her tone, she continued far more serenely than she felt, "I must give your invitation some thought, however, your grace. There are several factors to consider, but I should be able to send a reply to Buckingham House by tomorrow afternoon."

Trev kept his expression even. She really was cool, making him wait for his answer as if he were an importuning schoolboy. But he was not furious. He knew he had her. He'd seen her eyes flicker when he'd mentioned the boy having room to run. "Until tomorrow, then, Mrs. de Montforte. I look forward to hearing from you."

Chapter 3

Trev had read Anne accurately. It had been precisely when he mentioned the benefits to her children that she had realized she would not refuse his invitation.

Hetty's section of London was grimy and crowded with all manner of people, some perfectly nice, many not at all. Anne did not dare take the children outside unless Betta was with her, and then it was a tiring walk's distance to the nearest park, a small square only a little larger than Hetty's sitting room. Not that they had gone often. It had rained almost every day since they'd arrived. Cold, foggy, and unrelievedly gray, London had come to seem almost a malignant force to Anne. Both the children had had colds, as had Betta. And poor Hetty had suffered one bout after another of wheezing and gasping for every breath. Surely, Anne thought, in the country, where the air was clean and fresh, her aunt would do better.

In reply to the note of acceptance she sent around the next morning, Buckingham's secretary, Mr. Beddowes, a spare, meticulous man, had appeared at her aunt's to organize their removal to Sisley, his master's principal estate. Since he also brought a troop of maids and footmen with him, the packing went quickly. Almost too quickly. Anne was still wondering what she had done when the comfortable carriage the secretary had put at her disposal rolled to a stop before Sisley's gray-stoned magnificence.

She could, however, thank heaven that Buckingham had elected not to accompany them. In fact, she had not seen him since that morning he had descended upon her without warning. She didn't know why he had not come, nor even if or when he would follow, but at least he had not been on hand to watch her shiver with mingled awe and dread, though she had warned herself his ancestral seat could be nothing short of palatial.

To Anne's considerable relief, the duke's servants, or his principal servants—the butler, the housekeeper, and the steward, Mr. Beardsley—received her with reserved courtesy she could not fault, and though they put her in the wing of the house opposite from the family wing, she took no offense. She was pleased, in fact, that she would be so removed from Buckingham's private rooms, should he come to Sisley.

Anne thought he had come only a few days after she arrived, when Barrett, the butler, approached her. In his grave, careful way, however, Barrett announced not his master, but Rob.

Having thought her cousin halfway to the Baltic by then, Anne found it an effort beyond imagining to keep to Barrett's dignified pace as she followed him down to the drawing room where he had left Rob. She feared her cousin had come to tell her his ship had gone down, taking with it the small investment that meant so much to them both.

But Rob assured her at once that nothing more deadly than contrary winds accounted for his presence. When he had gone to her rooms to advise her of his delayed start, her aunt's landlady had bustled out to tell him that she had gone, and where.

"Mrs. Bates was shocked to her core to think you knew the likes of Buckingham, but she was not half so shocked as I was to learn you had come to his home, Annie. Whatever prompted you to come here? Did the man force you?"

"No, no," she hastened to assure him. "Nothing quite so

bad, though Lord John de Montforte does wish to make Alex his heir and raise him far from his sullying mother."

"The devil!" Rob clasped Anne's hand in his. "You don't mean to let him take the boy, surely?"

"Of course not. I've seen the sort of parent he was with his own son."

"Then why did you come to this palace? Surely it will be harder to resist the de Montfortes here."

"I cannot see why," Anne said reasonably, and proceeded to give Rob her reasons for coming to Sisley. At the end, she added Buckingham's point that her children had a right to know their father's family. "If it is at all possible, I should like them to be on reasonably good terms with the de Montfortes. They'll have nothing of their father else. And, while they are coming to know the de Montfortes, perhaps the de Montfortes will come to know them, and realize that it would do Alex more harm than good to be removed from those he loves."

Rob nodded slowly. "You hope Buckingham will then intercede with the old grandfather? Perhaps you are right, Annie, but what of little Nell? If Lord John wants her, too, you've no legal claim to defend."

"But he doesn't know that!" Anne looked half amused, half scornful. "He believes I am Nell's mother and that I used her to trap Peter into marriage."

"No!"

"Aye," Anne insisted, smiling a little at his consternation. "You needn't look so outraged, Rob. In my eyes, Nell is my child, and as long as Lord John and the duke believe the same, they will leave her to me." Discreetly Anne forbore to mention that Buckingham was not aware yet that Nell was with her, as there was no reason to unsettle Rob any further.

"And what of you?" Rob asked, going off in another direction without warning. "Buckingham's reputation is as famous as you are attractive, Annie."

Although Anne could see Rob was embarrassed at what he implied, she couldn't help her surge of anger; and though strangely, the sharpest part of her fury was directed at his grace, the Duke of Buckingham, it was Rob who stood handily before her. "I don't doubt that Buckingham does have a reputation, but it does not follow that I shall fall on my back for him!" Anne's hands settled on her hips as she continued, forcefully, "Do you think I have not dealt with hot-eyed noblemen before, Rob? In Italy, Papa brought home any sort of man to dinner as long as he was entertaining and willing to play cards until all hours of the night."

"I understand your life in Italy with Uncle Dick was not sheltered," Rob returned, his jaw as stubbornly set as Anne's. "But you were not alone in the home of any of those men, and though I know Uncle Dick was not the most attentive of fathers by then, he would never have let a man take advantage of you. Here—"

"I did not then and will not now allow any man to take advantage of me, Robert Godfrey! Not any man, be he duke or serf! And I am not alone here. Hetty has come with me, as well as Betta."

"Betta would defend you to the death, Annie, but she's only a servant, and your aunt may be a dear woman, but she's no fighter. She'll fold like paper before a man like Buckingham."

"I won't! But I doubt you truly fear Buckingham will force me to anything. You fear I will lose my head over him."

Anne was right. It was what Rob feared, but he had not stated his fears so plainly, even to himself. Hearing her bald words, he winced. "No! It's not that! It's—"

"Yes it is," she said curtly. "You think my head will be turned by his practiced charm, or if not that, by this place." With her hand, Anne gestured around the drawing room. A portrait of an attractive, elegant woman, perhaps Buckingham's mother, clearly done by Joshua Reynolds, hung over the fireplace, while on the facing wall Turner, the great water colorist, was represented by not one but two works. Near the window there stood a small, exquisite statue of David, and overhead, to please the eye of those chancing to look up, there was an intricately wrought plaster ceiling.

Underfoot, a priceless Turkey carpet stretched the length of the not inconsiderable room. Even without considering the numerous gilt chairs and settees scattered about in conversational groupings, or of course, any of the other seemingly endless rooms in the house, the overall effect was spectacular. "I grant it is all very grand," Anne conceded, her eyes lingering on the half-naked figure of David. She had a suspicion its creator was the Italian master, Donatello, it was that fine. "Actually," she said, smiling despite herself, "he has exceedingly lovely things. But nothing here is worth my self-respect or Alex. I would lose him for certain, you know, if I allowed myself to be overcome by all this."

"I hope you'll remember that when he's telling you that mayhap you can persuade him to your point of view with your charms," Rob returned gruffly, then, seeing Anne's eyes flash again, he put up his hands in the age-old gesture of placation. "Very well, perhaps I go too far, but only because I am concerned for you, Annie. You don't know his reputation as I do. And because I do, I shall take the risk of angering you further by mentioning our cousin Charles. Would you not be wise to go to him until I return?"

"Charles?" Anne echoed, a wealth of disgust in her tone as she thought of the cousin to whom her grandfather's title and estate had gone. "I had a letter from him, you know, when Peter died. He included a draft for fifty pounds and said that was all the assistance he could give me, as he'd his daughters to consider. He did add, though—gratis—that any difficulties I might be experiencing were of my own making. 'It is not done to push oneself where one is not wanted,' was the way he put it, I think. Of course, he never offered to speak to the de Montfortes on my behalf, though he must know them. I suppose he did not want to risk offending them on the chance that Buckingham might still be unmarried when his girls come out in a few years. No, Rob, I'll not go to Charles unless I am truly at the end of my rope."

Rob ran a hand through his unmistakably red hair. "I can't say I'm surprised. He read me a most tedious and angry lecture when I decided to go into this shipping business with Uncle Reed. Said it was bad enough that my aunt should marry into trade without my becoming a tradesman myself, but he declined to say how he expected me to support myself, when he has never offered a penny. Still, Annie, you can at least tell these de Montfortes that the Earl of Edgemoore is your cousin. Surely they'll get off their high horses a bit then."

"Surely they won't," Anne replied at once. "It was Papa with whom Lord John found fault. And that I lived in the home of a man of such dissolute habits as Papa exhibited in those last years blackened me in his eyes as well. Mama's antecedents would make no difference to him."

"But can you not just mention them?" Rob persisted.

For his efforts, Anne gave him an exasperated look. "I could, but I won't. And it isn't misplaced pride that keeps me from it," she went on, anticipating his next argument. "I have taken a risk by coming here. Though I have good reasons, it is always possible that Lord John may try to take Alex from me by force. I do not believe even he would do anything so gothic, but I must be prepared for every possibility. If I do need a bolt hole, I've got nowhere to go but to Charles, and if the de Montfortes know of my relation to him, they'll know where to find me."

"And Charles would hand you back to them?" Rob finished her thought, frowning. "Damn! But I think he would, if he thought doing so would gain him and Helen an entrée to Buckingham House. But Lord, Annie! You are so unprotected."

It touched Anne that Rob would worry so about her. She had not had anyone do so in a very long time. "I've my wit and spirit; they should do." She deliberately gave her young cousin a cocky grin. It had the desired affect, for he began to smile, too, and she breathed a sigh of relief. She did not want Rob to know that she felt as alone and vulnerable as he'd described her—and as for Buckingham, well, it would truly give Rob cause for alarm if he knew she could describe the duke as clearly as if she had seen him only moments before.

"Do you intend to tell his grace that upon my return you

will be a somewhat wealthier woman?" Rob asked, interrupting her thoughts.

"No." Anne shook her head, shaking off the precise and clear image she had had of waving black hair and heated blue eyes. "I can't see the advantage in Buckingham's knowing that I shall soon have the funds to be modestly independent. He might double his efforts to persuade me that I am all that stands between Alex and a satisfactory life."

Rob shook his head, though something of his smile still lingered. "Lud, but you are sailing close to the wind, Annie, and that's a fact."

"Aye, and there are shoals all about: accusations and omissions and half-truths and powerful lords and small children. But I can look after myself, Rob. You may sail off to the Baltic assured of it." She took his arm, and patted it affectionately. "Only get back as quickly as you can, and the children and I shall do very well in the meantime. We'd be fools if we did not. We've the finest roof, or nearly, in England over our heads and acres of tended gardens and parklands in which to romp to our hearts' content. In fact, Alex and Nell are racing about a delightful reflecting pool at this very moment. Come out and see them. We can walk around some of the park, too. I saw deer yesterday. . . ."

Anne led the way outside, where they soon found the children and spent a very pleasant afternoon. The servants duly noted how friendly they were together, and having seen much as the servants of the twelfth Duke of Buckingham, it was not surprising that they should assume the two were lovers. When Rob decided to stay the night, Barrett, after a consultation with Mrs. Goodwin, the housekeeper, put the young man in the room directly adjoining Anne's. Anne, oblivious to the placement and its meaning, wished Rob a good night and went happily to sleep thinking what a pleasant day it had been with her amiable cousin and without the duke.

The next day Rob left feeling far more heartened than when he had come. After all, there was still no word on when Buckingham would arrive, and Rob was young enough to believe that if a man did not follow posthaste after a woman like Anne, it was because he had other fish to fry. Even after Anne's assurances, though, Rob still felt slightly uneasy about what might happen when the other fish had been thoroughly savored.

For her part, Anne refused to dwell on the loneliness Rob left in his wake. She had been alone before, and at least now she had hope that when he returned, she would be able to provide security, if not luxury, for her children.

They were the light of her life, and she would do much for them. She would marry Peter all over again, even knowing this time how august his family was, and what a bitter reaction her entry into the family would provoke. Between them, they had seen Nell cared for and given at least the appearance of legitimacy. And later, Peter had given her Alex, whatever else he might have failed to do. Both Nell and Alex, actually. He had given her both blessings.

And she was in a setting that lent itself to considering blessings, Anne admitted, smiling wryly. The gardens at Sisley were in bloom, while the park afforded one lovely, carefully designed vista after another, and when she and the children tired of the grounds, they had the house itself to explore.

After a full week of pleasant, lazy days had passed, Anne began to hope that Buckingham had forgotten her and her son. It was the Season in London, after all, and she reasoned that he had been distracted by other interests,

Feminine interests, likely. She remembered more clearly than she cared admit the way his eyes had appraised her in her robe. He was accustomed to women. And he would attract them effortlessly.

Anne did not allow herself to muse on what sort of woman Buckingham would prefer by custom—that is, until one warm, lazy day, as she and Alex and Nell and Betta were returning from a visit to the river that meandered through Sisley, one of the grooms driving them. The excursion had been so pleasant and carefree that she'd relaxed her self-control, and, before she knew it, her thoughts had landed on the duke and even, speculatively, upon his preferences in women. The images were unexpectedly intense.

And so when the children shrieked suddenly that he had arrived, Anne wondered in dismay if her thoughts had been so vivid that they had affected Alex and Nell somehow.

But nothing so fanciful had occurred. Following the direction of their pointing fingers, she realized that the duke's gleaming black carriage was, indeed, pulled up before Sisley's elaborately carved stone entryway. Immediately, she gathered herself and instructed Tucker, the groom, to take them to the back of the house, saying they were all too mussed from their afternoon at the river to meet the duke and any company he might have brought with him.

But the truth was that though Anne did certainly wish to look as well as she could, she simply could not consider facing Buckingham, however she was dressed, so long as her heart was beating in its present frantic, staccato rhythm.

Chapter 4

Anne was given an hour to calm her nerves. Mrs. Goodwin, herself, relayed the duke's request that Anne and her family join him for tea in the south drawing room at four o'clock.

Though they required the assistance of several maids and Betta as well, Anne's little party arrived in the drawing room first. The room was a favorite with her children, because it contained a painting in which a group of children were depicted at play. It was a great relief to Anne that they could amuse themselves by making up stories about the fictional children. She felt nervous as a cat and utterly incapable of entertaining them herself until Buckingham deigned to show himself.

Trev was not late intentionally. Arriving at Sisley unannounced, as was his habit, he had not found Barrett at the door to greet him, and he wanted to know before he went down how Anne de Montforte had comported herself during the time he had allowed her to settle in at Sisley.

Had she played the grand lady, curtly ordering the servants about? He would not have been surprised. Those not so far removed from being servants themselves could be the worst tyrants. Or perhaps she had been overawed by Sisley and, feeling grossly inadequate, had secluded herself and her child in her rooms? He'd not have wagered on it, somehow, but one never knew. Not that he'd been unduly distracted, wondering how she had fared. His mistress had not found him inattentive, nor had his friends. Still, Anne de Montforte was new game, and new game not only conveniently lodged in his own home, but also new game with a hostile spark in her eye. The combination was, Trev sardonically admitted, irresistible, and a full four days before the ten he had intended to stay away, he had informed his mistress not only that he'd business that called him to Sisley, but that, alas, their time together had come to an end. He had sweetened the blow with a pretty diamond bracelet, and if she had pouted when he kissed her for the last time, she had, happily, spared him her tears.

At a discreet knock on his door, Trev called out a summons. "Ah, Barrett, here you are," he said, shrugging into the coat Simms, his valet, held out for him, and causing the punctilious little man immense frustration by moving away before he could perform the unnecessary ritual of smoothing the coat's nonexistent wrinkles from his master's enviable shoulders.

"Your grace! I was detained by other duties! I apologize—"

"Nonsense, man." Trev accompanied the curt words with a brief smile. Barrett had been butler at the Hall when he was a boy. "You cannot sit by the door all your life on the off chance I might take it into my head to arrive. I trust my guests have settled in?"

"Yes, your grace. I put them in the east wing as you suggested, which has suited Mrs. de Montforte nicely as she is close to the nursery. Mrs. Teasdale has professed herself pleased, as well, as did Mrs. de Montforte's guest."

Buckingham went very still. "Her guest?" he echoed, any thought of inquiring about Mrs. de Montforte's habits or her manner with the servants quite forgotten.

Barrett, of necessity, knew his master and knew, therefore, what the sudden stillness signified. Trev noted his butler's almost imperceptible hesitation, but however Anne de Montforte's beauty may have affected the old retainer, his loyalty was to his master. "Yes, your grace," he said. "A Mr. Godfrey stayed for a night."

"Describe him," Buckingham commanded, his eyes narrowing.

"A young man, your grace, with a Scotsman's red hair. Of medium height and well formed."

"Thank you, Barrett." Trev's expression gave no hint to whether he recognized the young man his butler had described. His next coolly approving words indicated however, that he had some image in his mind with which to compare Barrett's description. "I daresay you could make a name for yourself with the Bow Street Runners, if you should wish."

The old man inclined his head with great dignity. "I am pleased to have accommodated you, your grace, but I fear my running days are long over."

Trev smiled at that, causing the atmosphere in the room to ease somewhat. "All the better for Sisley, Barrett. We could not do without you, you know."

Barrett flushed with pleasure, but Trev was departing the room before he could do more than mumble a "You are too kind, your grace."

Simms, a neutral if avid observer of the scene, released a long breath. "Kind he may be, but only when he chooses. 'Tis the worst, when he goes still like that. Lud! I'd not want to be in the lady's shoes just now."

Barrett agreed, but he would not stoop to gossip with the Londoner, whom he considered an upstart, and so he said loftily, "I am certain it is only a minor misunderstanding. Nothing more," and gave Simms a small, quelling smile before he departed.

Trev's eyes were blazing as he strode into the drawing room. The thought that her lover had bought another night with her here, in his home, in one of his beds . . . when he had been half worrying that she might be so overwhelmed by the luxuriousness of Sisley that she would flee. . . . He would not again allow himself to forget what she was.

Anne, who had been sitting quietly in a chair by the window, trying to calm her furiously beating heart, felt scalded by the fury in Buckingham's eyes. He'd thrown open the door without warning, sweeping into the room like some irate potentate. She'd have liked to fly to her feet and say something scathing—anything, she knew not what—but she could scarcely make a scene before the children. Particularly as one of them was, she assumed, the reason he was in such a fury.

She could, though, speak first, and forced herself to do it, lest he direct his formidable anger at the children. "Your grace, good afternoon. May I present my aunt, Mrs. Teasdale?" Anne hoped she appeared unruffled, but felt too agitated to judge, and sent up a fervent prayer that Hetty might be able to lance a little of his anger. The closer he came, the darker and larger and more furious he seemed.

Hetty, mercifully, did prove to be the distraction for which Anne had prayed. Trev had all but forgotten that he had other guests, and with effort, he called himself to order.

The aunt merited none of his anger. He could see at once she was a gentle creature, and neither a match for her vivid, wanton of a niece, nor anything like the earthy, robust, even garish creature he had expected. Quietly clad in a soft, lavender-colored dress, she had rather delicate, quite pleasant looks. Her pallid complexion gave the impression of less than perfect health, but she was certainly not at her last prayers. Trev found the gleam in her eye engagingly lively.

Mrs. Teasdale could also, like most women, be pleased to have her hand saluted gracefully. Though Anne was startled by the faint blush that colored her aunt's cheeks, Trev was not. His attentions regularly had that effect. It came with being a duke, and an inordinately attractive one at that.

"I am most pleased to meet you, your grace," Hester replied a trifle breathlessly to Buckingham's words of welcome. "And to thank you for the honor you have done us by making us welcome in your quite magnificent home."

Honor he had done them by making them welcome? Anne thought sarcastically. He'd all but forced them to his "magnificent" home. Anne saw Hester beam her sweetest, most sincere smile up at Buckingham and reminded herself, before she cried out something about betrayal, that Hester, who was blessed with a natural optimism, believed the de Montfortes to be reasonable people who simply knew too little of her niece.

"The honor is mine, Mrs. Teasdale," Trev replied, his low, lazily assured voice exactly suited to him. He smiled, too, the intense white smile that Anne remembered well from their first meeting. "I've two lovely ladies all to myself. Well, not all to myself," he appended, as he caught the uncontrolled movement of a small foot out of the corner of his eye. Still smiling, he straightened away from Mrs. Teasdale, and found himself regarding two children.

She had insinuated her bastard into his home. Trev's features became curiously still in a way that Simms and Barrett would have recognized, but he did not show any other sign of this fresh surge of anger. It was not the delicate girl before him who deserved to bear the brunt of his fury. But her mother did, and she would.

"This is Alex, your grace. And this is Nell."

Trev flicked his eyes to Anne. She had come to stand protectively by her children as they respectively made a credible bow and curtsey to him. While the children were distracted, he allowed her to see, just for an instant, the fresh fire in his eyes. She understood, for she flushed, but he had to admit that she held his gaze, nonetheless.

Hetty's voice broke into their silent exchange. "Come now, Alex and Nell, and sit by me, and tell his grace how much you have enjoyed yourselves this week in his home."

The children went dutifully to their great aunt, while Trev found a comfortable seat across from the three on the settee, and Anne returned to her original chair beside them.

It was the girl, Nell, the widow's love child as it was quaintly put, who spoke first. Her voice was so soft, Trev had to strain to hear her murmur the rote words her aunt had given her. "I have enjoyed myself very much at Sisley, your grace," she said, and then lifted her curly auburn head to regard him with wide, solemn, chocolate-brown eyes.

Trev had a sharp, completely unexpected sense of recognition, but little Nell allowed him only the briefest glimpse of her face. Before he could do more than register the impression, Trev was regarding the top of her head again.

Peter's son then pulled his attention away altogether. Entirely different in nature from Nell, he spoke up animatedly the moment his sister went quiet. "I have enjoyed myself, too, your grace! Nell and I have chased all around the gardens. And we've driven down to the river, where Mama said you must have gone boating when you were a boy. And we've admired all your horses! Tucker says you have bang-up horseflesh."

Trev heard Anne say, "Alex!" in despairing tones, but far from objecting to the cant, he found himself grinning at the enthusiastic child, who had his father's blue eyes and his mother's thick, glossy, dark hair—as well, it seemed, as her spirit.

"I am glad you appreciate good horseflesh, Alex. Perhaps we can see about mounting you while you are here." Alex fairly leapt from the couch in excitement, but Barrett came then with the tea cart, and Trev returned his attention to Anne. "Will you pour, Mrs. de Montforte?" he asked silkily, wondering if she could carry out the task without embarrassing herself. As to how gracefully she would do it, he would see for himself in due time. In the meanwhile, he allowed his gaze to drift back to the shy little girl, who bore so little resemblance to either Peter or the woman he had supposed her mother.

To prompt her to look up at him, Trev asked, carefully softening his voice, "And you, Nell, is there anything in particular that you have enjoyed at Sisley?" He smiled at her, which he found was something of a mistake, for peeping up at him through her lashes and seeing his smile, Nell immediately dropped her eyes and blushed. "Yes, your grace," she said in her small voice, "I, I have enjoyed—"

"I know!" Alex interrupted, smiling upon his sister with all the irrepressibility she lacked. "You liked the trap because Tucker let you hold the reins, Nellie. He said I get to do it next time! And you liked feeding the ducks until that goose ran at us. We'll find a stick next time to whack him."

Trev chuckled to himself at the boy's bloodthirsty spirit, but he was content, relaxing in his chair with his long legs stretched comfortably before him, to observe the little group across from him. And the first thing he had to allow was that he found it an unexpected pleasure to watch Anne de Montforte pour a cup of tea. Her hands were slender and pale, and quite sure in their movements. Nor was she giving the ritual all her attention. As she poured, she also went about the business of gently reining in her son, observing to him that it was to Nell the duke had addressed his question, and therefore it was for her to answer.

Brightly, without the least defiance in his tone, Alex noted that Nell did not *like* to talk. His mother did not dispute the point, merely saying that there were often things in life that we did not care to do, but that honor and courtesy nonetheless require of us, and that one of those was to reply to conversation made by a host. "Nell will learn to acquit herself very well at conversation if we allow her the opportunity to practice. As her brother, you've the responsibility not only to curb your generous impulse to save her difficulty, but actually to encourage her. Now Nell, is there something else you have enjoyed here at Sisley? His grace would like to know, I am sure."

When Anne flicked her eyes to him, it was impossible for Trev to mistake the appeal in them. Knowing how duplicitous she was, he wondered briefly if she was trying to make a show of being a concerned mother, but it did not matter, for she appealed on behalf of a particularly defenseless child.

"Yes, I would, indeed, like to know what you've enjoyed, Nell," Trev said, as per his cue, and then continued with sudden inspiration, "but perhaps you will let me guess before you tell me. Let me see, I would say that you have devoured Cook's aspic, but have turned up your pretty nose at her tarts, particularly her lemon tarts."

Although Trev had had little experience with children, he did know women, and so he was not shocked when he saw Nell's mouth turn up in a grin even before she lifted her head to look shyly, at him. What did stun him, though, were the beguiling dimples that creased her full cheeks, for at the sight of them and her liquid-brown eyes, he placed the elusive memory.

Trev had met the woman only once. Passing near his uncle's estate in Sussex, he'd decided to visit on the spur of the moment, and though Uncle John had not been at home, Peter had been, and had confided with the swagger of a young man that he was having an affair with the wife of a neighbor, an older fellow who generally guarded his wife closely but was away for a time, Trev could not remember where or why. Trev had only stayed the night, but Mary Redvers had come to dinner, and though he had never heard of her again, nor even thought of her, for that matter, he now remembered her soulful brown eyes and engaging dimples, and even the bashful manner that it seemed she had passed on to her daughter.

He would write to inform Uncle John that he'd gotten the girl's parentage wrong, though in truth Trev didn't believe he would much care that she was his granddaughter. Uncle John was not overly enamored of women for one thing, and for another, it was, specifically, an heir he wanted, and he wanted one now. As to Anne, though Nell's obvious parentage would exonerate her of the charge of trapping Peter into marriage, there were yet too many other, more damning charges against her for Uncle John's attitude toward her to be affected.

For his part, though, Trev found he was a bit curious. Nell was surely Mary Redvers's daughter, but Peter had never mentioned the woman and now Anne claimed the child. What had happened? Where was Mrs. Redvers, for instance? His sister Maddy would know, or at least would be able to discover the particulars—for Maddy, it was the stuff of life to know everything about anyone who was a member of England's privileged Ten Thousand.

And why not ask the widow? Trev flicked his gaze to Anne, though he didn't expect to find emblazoned on her face the reason she called another woman's child her own. It was a mystery, but not so urgent a mystery that he must get to the bottom of it immediately. Quite the contrary, he decided that it would be far more interesting to play a waiting game and see when and in what circumstances she would choose to reveal the truth.

"But what of you, your grace?" Alex's direct question prompted Trev to look at the boy, whose head was cocked as he inquired with friendly curiousity, "What do you like best at Sisley?"

Realizing he had entirely missed whatever Nell's soft answer had been, Trev trod carefully. "Well, as I have lived here since I was born, I've too many things I like to pick a single favorite, but I can say that just now I find I like very well indeed having both my cousins to stay with me."

He had put an emphasis on both and, as Nell blushed with pleasure and Alex grinned, Trev slanted an interested look at the children's mother. She was watching him, and she understood. He knew it because there was such relief dawning in her green eyes that they seemed to glow.

She looked away almost at once, but not before Trev had noted that befriending her children did appear to turn her up sweet. And that, sweetened, she was enough to take a man's breath away.

Still, he surveyed her coolly. However radiant she might look, the witch had been free with her favors in his home. With someone else.

Though he bid the others adieu at the end of the tea, Trev asked her, courteously enough, if he might not have a moment of her time when she had settled the children. She hesitated, obviously aware that his pleasant tone was solely for the benefit of Aunt Hetty and Nell and Alex, then bowed to the inevitable. In a tone he thought justifiably strained, she said she would be happy to meet with him as soon as she was able.

"Come to my study, then," Trev said. "Barrett will show you the way."

Chapter 5

When Mrs. Goodwin had conducted Anne on a tour of the house, she had not taken her to Buckingham's study. Apparently, it was an inner sanctum entered only by the duke's permission. He gave it when Barrett knocked to announce her arrival, and she stepped into a masculine room, redolent with the scents of wood and leather. Her gaze went first to a heavy, surprisingly cluttered desk. Behind it bookshelves lined with leather-bound volumes stretched from the floor to the ceiling, but the comfortable chair that stood between the desk and the bookshelves was empty. He was not by the fireplace, either, and then she found him on the opposite side of the room by the windows. His arms crossed over her chest, his tall, well-made body outlined by the light, Buckingham was not enjoying a view of his park but was watching her with narrowed eyes.

He gestured toward a couch and some chairs. "Have a seat, Mrs. de Montforte. We've several things to discuss," he said, his voice was no warmer than his look.

Anne chose a straight-backed chair, thinking a little wildly that he could not trap her in it. In her calculations, however, she had not taken into account that Buckingham would seat himself upon the nearest arm of his couch. It would have been better by far to have been hidden in the depths of the wing chair, she realized, for he was not even an arm's length away—and, as usual, was looking down on her.

Buckingham did not speak. He simply studied her, his legs stretched before him. The tip of his boot nearly touched her toe, but Anne would not give him the satisfaction of seeing her retreat even so insignificantly, and she left her foot where it was, while she concentrated on returning his gaze as unflinchingly as possible. The steel was there in his eyes, but there was, unmistakably, derision as well. And it was that that brought Anne's chin up and prompted her to take the offensive.

"You wished to see me, your grace?"

"Which is why you are here," he affirmed, mocking her in a voice that was so soft the hairs on Anne's neck lifted. "I'll not tolerate your playing your games here at Sisley, Mrs. de Montforte."

Anne believed he referred to Nell, and her mouth went dry. She thought he had accepted Nell. "I . . . I don't understand, your grace," she said.

He flicked his gaze from her eyes to her mouth and back again. Anne had no notion what he was thinking, though she had the oddest sense her mouth had settled some question for him. Then he said, his voice soft as silk, "I'll not have you entertaining gentlemen—or rogues either, for that matter—while you are at Sisley."

For a long, disbelieving moment, Anne stared at him, fighting an urge to laugh aloud, out of sheer relief. His fury had nothing to do with Nell! Perhaps he was looking as if he could slice her in two without a care, but he wasn't threatening what she held most dear.

Inevitably though, that feeling of relief subsided, and when it did, Anne was still staring into eyes that were hard as stones, eyes that accused and condemned without a hearing, without even naming the charges. What had he said? That she could not have visitors, whether gentlemen or rogues? "Am I a prisoner, then, that I may have no visitors?"

At the cool righteousness in her voice, Buckingham's features tightened. Seeing the response, Anne felt a nameless thrill similar to what she had felt at their first meeting. Having never felt anything like it before, she could only guess it was fear.

"You will not entertain another man while you are at Sisley," he snapped, obviously seeing no need to explain himself.

"Why?" she demanded, her anger rising.

"In the first place, because this is my home, and I dictate the rules here, and in the second . . ." Trev's mouth curled in contempt as he made her wait for the second reason. "I shouldn't think I would have to tell a good mother not to whore under the roof where her children sleep."

"I am not—" Anne gasped, unable to stoop to say more. Damn him! She hadn't comprehended what he had meant by "entertain." And now he'd made her face flame. "Blast you!" she cried, her eyes flashing daggers at him. "If you are referring to Rob, he's my cousin!"

Anne could see no sign that she had taken Buckingham aback, much less that he felt remorse, for he continued to study her in the same flat, narrowed, insulting way.

"Perhaps he is your cousin, but if he is, he is the kind of cousin you receive with your hair down and dressed in a thin robe with only a night rail beneath. You will not behave so at Sisley, nor accept pouches filled, or half-filled, with money, either. While you are my guest, you will behave like a guest of this house should, like the lady Peter's wife should have been."

Anne had thought he'd already made her as angry as she could ever be, She'd been wrong. The blazing fury that swept over her consumed all that was left of her caution. She sprang to her feet. "And what of you, your grace?" she challenged, spitting out his address contemptuously. "Are you exempt, as host, from acting the gentleman Peter's cousin should be?"

Anne saw the light that blazed in his eyes and knew she had pushed him beyond his limit, but she could not have guessed he could move so quickly. Even as she was drawing back, moved by a caution that returned too late, Buckingham came off the couch to catch her wrist. She resisted, trying to pull her arm free, but he tightened his grip steadily until she fell still.

"You are a brazen witch."

It was so softly said. Anne was panting, and it took her a moment to register the threat in his voice. Her eyes flew up to his, but his gaze had settled on her mouth. Suddenly and unexpectedly, Anne became aware of how close they stood. He held her arm almost to him. Had she twisted her wrist about, she could have raked his chest with her fingernails. Had it been bare.

Suddenly, there did not seem to be enough air in the room, only his eyes making a feast of her mouth, his chest, so hard and broad, inches away, and the heat of his body flowing out to dizzy her, and his mouth . . .

It was madness! Anne jerked hard against his hold. "Release me!" She had meant to scream if need be, but her voice emerged low and shaky.

Perhaps that was why Buckingham paid her no heed. "Why should I?" He shook her arm to bring her eyes back to his. "I'd have put a bullet in a man for what you said, yet the punishment I would mete out to you would be a good deal less . . . painful than that."

"For pity's sake!" Anne felt weak as a kitten. The light flaring in his eyes was so hot and ruthless it made her knees sag. "You insulted me," she said, summoning every scrap of composure she could. "And I gave you tit for tat. I lost my temper—foolishly, I freely admit. However, I do not believe I deserve to be assaulted for that."

"Ah, but would it be assault?" he queried, his eyes, heavy lidded with his interest, dropping slowly back to her mouth.

With a supreme effort, Anne fought a terrifying urge to lick the lips his searing gaze seemed to have made dry as kindling. "I wish you to let me go, your grace. Please."

For the sake of her pride, Anne tried simply to be firm, but her voice emerged heavy with plea. She regretted it, even, unthinking, bit hard on her lip. Why, she could not guess, but it seemed that unmindful gesture affected him, for he abruptly relinquished his hold on her. Anne bowed her head and shakily sent up a prayer of gratitude as she rubbed the place his long fingers had held.

"Did I hurt you?" He had not moved. Through her lashes she could see the threads around the buttonholes of his lawn shirt.

"No." She didn't know why he'd asked. His low voice had been curt, without any concern.

"If I did not hurt you, then why are you rubbing your wrist?"

He was simply too close. Anne caught an elusive whiff of bay rum. "For comfort," she said almost angrily. "If that is all . . ."

"It is not."

Anne looked up at that. She wanted to get out of the study. She felt weary and battered, and she'd not be comforted if she laid her head on his chest, though it riveted her awareness in a way that dismayed her. "If it is that you desire some formal proclamation, then I give it to you, your grace. I shall agree to abide by your decree that I not lie with any man while I am at Sisley." It was more than he had said, precisely speaking, and Anne couldn't keep a sudden flash of triumph from the green eyes she'd lifted to him, nor resist adding, "It shouldn't be a difficult promise to keep."

The moment she had said it, she could have bitten her tongue. She had no idea why she risked taunting him—she truly did not—and she braced herself to fly if he reached out for her again.

But he did not. She thought him entirely unmoved, in fact, until she saw the gleam in his eyes. It was amused. Disquietingly so, really. "How chaste you will be, Mrs. de Montforte," Trev said softly, his mouth curving slightly at one corner. "Consult me if your resolve wears thin. Exceptions can be made."

She went pink, caught off balance by his transformation from dangerously overwhelming rake to dangerously charming one. Still, despite her confusion—or possibly because of it—Anne's tone was stiff. "I'll not be wanting any exceptions, your grace. I am in the habit of being chaste, though you won't believe it."

"If I did, I would think it a waste."

It was there still, the lazy, teasing note in his voice. That it affected her again, Anne considered a sign of actual madness. He had, only moments before, all but called her a harlot—he was still doing so even then. It was his looks. It was not fair, she thought, looking up into his face, with its strong but elegant, even beautiful, masculine lines, that he should be so damnably attractive and have, to boot, charm to spare when he chose to use it. In an unsteady voice, she spoke the first words that came to mind. "I think it is time I go, your grace."

The oddest expression flickered across his face. Anne thought it might be regret, but it was gone before she could be sure. "One more moment," he said with a ghost of a smile. "You needn't look so uncharacteristically irresolute," he murmured, apparently sensing her confusion. "I vow I'll not ravish you this afternoon, Mrs . . . but that is one of the things I wanted to discuss. I realize I find it awkward to use my own family's name so formally, and I mean to call you by your given name, Anne. Do you object?"

Anne, who had risen in hopes of leaving the room, lowered herself just to the edge of the straight-backed chair. "Would it matter if I did?"

"No," he admitted, a smile playing around his strong mouth.

Anne shrugged and, keeping her eyes steady upon his, resisted the infectiousness of his softened humor. Not that she'd have smiled back, but she might have admitted to him that she had never become accustomed to her husband's lofty family name and, particularly since his death, had felt almost like an imposter using it.

"Well, Anne," Buckingham said, obviously teasing her and as obviously enjoying himself, "now we are on such a friendly footing, may I ask whether you ride?"

The completely unexpected question caused Anne to blink, but hard upon her surprise came a feeling of deficiency. All the gentry rode. Determinedly, she fought to keep her chin from lifting defensively, but nevertheless, Buckingham seemed to know what it cost her to say the simple, likely expected, "No, I do not." The lines at the corners of his eyes crinkled. Her chin inched up a little further, but then he undid her completely by saying equably, "Well, then you may have the pleasure of learning, if you wish."

For a split second all Anne could think was, "I am going to ride!" Then she remembered who offered her the lessons, and that he might very well charge a price too high for her to pay. Framing a cautious reply, she said, "I should like that very much. Thank you."

But once again he seemed to read her mind. "You needn't go all wary, Anne. I'll exact no repayment for the lessons except that you help me with the children. I have decided to acquire ponies for them."

He hadn't asked for her approval, Anne noticed, but she didn't care. She was too glad. Alex, particularly, would be beside himself. "Thank you again, your grace. That is very kind of you. They will be in alt." Anne smiled, unaware that her pleasure brought a warm glow to her eyes, as if a candle burned softly behind them.

"Hmmm," was the extent of Buckingham's response, and when he said nothing more, only observed her with a veiled look, Anne thought the interview done.

"You'll need proper riding clothes, I should imagine," he said abruptly. "You may elect either to ride soon, and alter whatever clothes Mrs. Goodwin can find in the attic, or to wait until new clothes can be made up for the three of you by someone in Melbury."

Anne shook her head at once. New clothes were too personal. She could too easily imagine the rights he would believe outfitting her gave him. Aloud, however, she pretended to consider his first alternative. "I am certain the children would want to ride as soon as possible, as, I admit, would I. I'll speak to Mrs. Goodwin. Aunt Hetty and I can make the necessary alterations."

"You needn't. We've maids to occupy."

"Very well," she said, and then watched in astonishment

as her amenable reply caused his handsome face to split into a broad, truly amused grin.

"I thought that you would go mulish and insist upon your independence," he said, answering her surprised look. "Don't you sew?"

Buckingham was truly beguiling in that friendly mood, Anne thought. She smiled back before she knew what she was doing. "I do, in fact, but with so little pleasure, I would be delighted for someone else to do the alternations on my habit and Nell's."

"Not Nell's," Buckingham contradicted decisively. "Riding sidesaddle is difficult enough for a grown woman; she will begin astride so that she may learn control. She can wear breeches and a coat as my sister did."

Lesser beings might be shocked by a girl in breeches, but obviously Buckingham was not concerned with the opinion of lesser beings. For once, Anne agreed with him. "She'll think it's a treat to dress up like Alex. I'll go now and tell them."

As she rose, she gave Buckingham a sidelong glance to see if he meant to object. But though he did rise, all he said was, "I hope they'll be pleased," until she reached the door, when he called after her. "Oh, and Anne, I expect you and Mrs. Teasdale to dine with me tonight."

Her hand on the door handle, Anne dared much. "Is that an invitation, your grace?"

To which he replied ever so blandly. "No, not at all." Then, as all her indignation toward him came storming back, he added in the same tone, "It is a plea to be rescued from my own company."

Startled, Anne glanced at him over her shoulder and saw that his blue eyes were dancing beneath his strong, black brows. It occurred to her that the Duke of Buckingham did, indeed, know how to get what he wanted. "Very well, your grace," she said, knowing he could force her, if his teasing did not prove effective. "We shall see you this evening."

Trev studied the door she had shut behind her. He did not think of the evening ahead, but of the first part of their interview, specifically that part in which she'd said Red Hair was her cousin. Now that she was gone and the sparks that flew between them with her, Trev admitted he might have misread what he saw.

So, she had not taken another man to her bed at Sisley. She had, however, nearly provoked him beyond his control. Not that she would not have yielded in the end. She would have. There was too much charge between them for there not to be attraction on her side as well as his, but he had never forced a woman to anything in his admittedly reckless and even occasionally heedless life. He had not had to, but he had found in watching her worry her lip in her anxiety that he had not much taste for it, either. He wanted those provokingly pouty lips whole and soft and freely offered up to him. And they would be. That he did not doubt. Only it would take more time than he had thought. Rather than feeling annoyed at this prospect, Trev found himself smiling ever so lazily.

Chapter 6

"Mama! Are you ready? What a tall hat!"

Anne smiled at Alex and gave the beaver hat Mrs. Goodwin had found for her a light tap on the crown. "My hat was once all elegance, I'll have you know, young man. And yes, I am ready. Are you excited about meeting your pony?"

The question was rhetorical. Alex was hopping from one foot to the other, unable to contain himself. Mr. Beardsley, the duke's steward, had been most efficient. Though less than a week had passed since Buckingham had given him the commission, he had already found two suitable ponies, and Anne and the children were to have their first riding lesson that morning. Mrs. Goodwin's maids having been equally industrious, they were all three dressed in the riding clothes Anne and the housekeeper had selected from the trunks in Sisley's attic.

With Alex tugging at her and Nell skipping about almost as excitedly, Anne and the children made off for the stable-yard. She did not expect Buckingham to be there. He generally reserved his mornings for business, meeting with Mr. Beardsley or riding out onto the estate to see to some matter for himself. His industry had surprised Anne—disconcerted her, even—for she had, she admitted, been rather pleased to dismiss him as a useless pleasure seeker.

A faint frown drew her brow down in an unhappy V. She was thinking that if she knew a little more about Buckingham, he likewise knew more about her, though less of it to her credit. She and Hetty had dined with him every night, and Hetty had acted upon her belief that Anne's difficulties would be resolved if only the de Montfortes knew her better. Anne had tried to quell her aunt with sharp looks across the dinner table, and with pleading afterward, but Hetty, for all that she was a dear, could also be stubborn, particularly where she deemed the welfare of a member of her family at stake.

To Anne, the worst had come when Hetty had taken it into her head to laud Anne for her dealings with her parents, calling her niece brave and loyal for the way she'd nursed her mother. Had Hetty stopped there, Anne would have suffered only mild embarrassment. But Hetty had not stopped. Ignoring Anne's incredulous expression, she had been frank with Buckingham about Anne's father. Even then, three days later, the memory had the power to tinge Anne's cheeks with mortified color. Hetty had omitted nothing as she had described how her brother had seemed to come unhinged after his wife's sudden death. Other people might face the trial of a loved one's death bravely, but Buckingham now knew that Anne's father had not. He had bitterly cursed the brevity of life, and subsequently thrown himself into the pursuit of pleasure with such a vengeance, he'd had to flee to the continent to escape his creditors. Keeping to the point of her story, Hetty had praised Anne as the staunchest of girls for having gone at sixteen years of age to look after her father in Italy. Anne, however, knew very well that Buckingham was thinking not of her loyalty, but rather of what he believed she'd had to do to support herself after her father died. Hetty did not know the worst of what the de Montfortes believed, or that Lord John had denounced his daughter-in-law as a lightskirt. Anne had sat there rigid, shamed somehow, knowing what Buckingham thought, though it was not the truth, and terrified that he might betray that ugliness to Hetty. He hadn't, though. He'd done no more than murmur something proper about being sorry about her parents. Not trusting herself to speak, and avoiding his eyes, she had accepted the sympathy with nothing more than an inclination of her head.

Anne had not, of course, been able to avoid looking at Buckingham all that week. She had deliberately held herself aloof from the surprisingly easy flow of conversation between him and Hetty. She often caught him looking at her—sometimes thoughtfully, sometimes with amusement—the most disturbing times were when he'd studied her with a certain gleam in his eye. She resented that intent, interested gleam mightily and even more, its disturbing effect on her. Every night she had reminded herself he was a rake, whose raison d'être was to seduce women. He'd have perfected that look as a boy, and as a man would know from experience its effect. She vowed that uninvited look would achieve nothing with her and that soon, surely, she would become so inured to it, she would not even notice it.

"Oh look, Mama! There's his grace."

Startled back to the present, and feeling as if her thoughts had somehow conjured him, Anne followed Nell's gaze. She was aware there had been a distinct thrill in Nell's soft voice, and wondered if her daughter were not more excited about seeing Buckingham again than about riding for the first time. Yet, when Anne saw the duke herself, she realized she could not in good conscience blame Nell for being awestruck.

He was speaking with his head groom, an Irishman named O'Neill. The man's short, wiry frame was the perfect foil for Buckingham's tall, broad-shouldered one. He wore no hat, and Anne somewhat sourly wondered if he knew that his hair gleamed like polished ebony with the sun upon it, or that the simply tied cravat at his throat appeared all the whiter in contrast with his hair and the dark chocolate brown of the riding coat he wore. The coat fit him to the inch, of course, as did his buckskins and tall, black riding boots. And yet for all his expensive clothing, she had to admit that the master of Sisley looked at home in his stableyard. He was as well-muscled as any of his grooms. Oh, perhaps one or two had thicker shoulders and necks, but

none were taller or any more powerful looking than Buckingham was in his lean, loose-limbed way.

When Alex called out a greeting to his cousin, Buckingham left O'Neill to cross the yard, moving toward them
with the easy saunter Anne had to count as another of his
assets. It had to do with his long legs and athletic grace, but
Anne sharply cut off her study of him. She would not have
him see her appraising him, however dispassionately, and
approved the uninviting line into which she felt her mouth
settle. None too soon either. He was already greeting the
children.

"Good morning, Nell and Alex. You both look as eager
to meet your ponies as they are to meet you. One is named
Merry and the other Daisy, and you may decide for yourselves who is to have which pony. If there is a dispute,
however, your mother and I will settle it. Agreed?"

As the children eagerly nodded an affirmative answer,
Buckingham looked over their heads to Anne, making a
leisurely inspection of her costume from the tips of her
leather-clad toes to the top of her beaver hat. He allowed
his gaze to linger at her chest, making Anne all too aware
of the snug fit of the habit above its tight, high waist.

Quite unthinkingly, Anne took a deep, indignant breath.
The immediate result was that her bosom swelled. The ultimate result was that she was doubly assaulted when Buckingham's eyes met hers, for they were alight with both
laughter and the lazy heat that could unsettle her so. "Good
morning, Anne. I must say, I doubt those riding clothes
have ever been worn to such advantage."

After a breathless moment in which she thought her heart
had stilled, Anne regained control, furiously reminding herself what she had planned to do in such a seemingly inevitable situation. She broke the contact of their eyes.
"Thank you, your grace," she said, her voice soothingly
brisk. "Your maids are skillful sewing women, as you can
see from Nell's costume, which though it had to be greatly
altered, looks as if it were newly made."

Her determined diversion worked, perhaps because Anne
looked steadily at Nell and gave Buckingham to understand

she would not look at him again until he had remarked on her daughter. When a rosy blush washed over Nell's expectant face, Anne knew Buckingham must have given the little girl a bright smile. "In fact, Nell," the duke remarked, "you look quite enchanting. Indeed, you look so fine that I believe you'll set a new fashion for young girls' riding clothes."

Nell dropped her wide brown eyes to the toes of her riding boots, though the corners of her mouth turned up in a pleased smile. "Thank you, your grace."

If Nell's response was that of a shy child suffering an almost unbearable amount of attention, however pleasing, Alex's response was quite the opposite. He held himself straight and said proudly, "I am wearing your clothes, your grace! Mrs. Goodwin said they fit me excellently."

Trev chuckled, ruffling the boy's hair. "And so they do, Alex. You look every inch the young gentleman going for his first ride. Come along and we'll see how you like your ponies."

The ponies were reverse images of each other, one dark brown with a light mane, the other light as Buckingham's buckskin breeches but with a dark mane. Alex immediately took a liking to the darker one, named Daisy, and Nell was pleased to have the lighter Merry. Once the children had made their choices, Buckingham showed them how to hold out a lump of sugar in their hands, precisely where the ponies liked to be scratched behind the ears, and how to be mindful of their ponies' hooves. When finally he thought them enough at ease with the animals, he showed them both how to mount themselves, how to sit properly, and how to hold their feet in the stirrups. He did not show them how to hold the reins, however. That lesson would come later. For the time being, until they were accustomed to the ponies and Buckingham was assured they would have control of them, the grooms would lead them around the paddock.

Alex took to riding as a duck takes to water. If given the chance, he probably would have taken the reins himself that first day and galloped confidently to the horizon. Nell, though, was not nearly so fearless as her brother. She gazed at her pony with solemn eyes that held more than a little apprehension, and Anne immediately stepped forward as she had not with Alex, promising Nell she would stay near her.

She wondered briefly if Buckingham would think she was coddling Nell unduly, but he made no criticism. Indeed, he added encouragingly, "In fact, Nell, if you wish, your mother can hold your hand while Tucker leads you about the paddock."

Nell allowed in a small voice that she did wish to hold Anne's hand, but when Tucker led her into the paddock and she saw Alex riding without assistance as O'Neill led his pony about, she quietly relinquished Anne's supportive hold.

Buckingham, walking beside them, nodded approvingly. "You are being very brave, Nell," he said, "like a true de Montforte. Very soon, I daresay you will even be winning races over me."

Nell giggled at his teasing, her dimples peeping out. "Well, perhaps I shall beat Alex one day," she offered instead, with a shy but distinct eagerness that made Buckingham laugh aloud.

Anne observed the play between Nell and Buckingham with some bemusement. She had not expected him to come for the lesson at all, much less to give it with such patience and care for the differences in the natures of the two children. She did not need O'Neill to tell her, though he did, that his grace had ridden as naturally as a child as Alex did now. She had guessed as much, and was all the more surprised that his own ease did not make him impatient or condescending with Nell. He gave her a bit more of his attention and was very gentle with her, but he held her to the same high standard as he did Alex.

The result was that by mid-morning both children were well on their way to idolizing him. They looked to him for approval, beamed when he gave it, and concentrated the more determinedly when he had some correction to make.

Anne was pleased to see them establishing good rapport with their noble cousin. After all, it was one of the reasons she had come to Sisley. Yet she found herself worrying. He was putting himself to a good deal of trouble, and she did not know why. Might his attentiveness be a whim? Would he forget them when it became clear Alex would not stay with the de Montfortes? If they continued to regard him so highly as they did now, Alex and Nell would be crushed.

After an hour, Buckingham told the children they'd have to dismount or they would be too sore to ride the next day. "Besides," he said after he had lifted them down, "I am sure you would like to watch your mother take her first lesson. You do still want it, do you not, Anne?"

Even though Anne had had the week to become accustomed to hearing Buckingham use her given name, it still took her by surprise. The effect was something like what happened every time she looked into his startlingly blue eyes—she had to fight a bewildering fluttering of her nerves.

Buckingham seemed to read her discomfort, too, for he used her name at every opportunity and, almost invariably, his eyes gleamed with a knowing amusement. At least, Anne had learned to ignore that—or rather she had learned to look away from it, as she did now.

She saw Tucker leading a sleek, well-mannered mare from the stables. She had always wanted to ride, and excitement rippled through her. With it came a determination to hold at bay the turbulent feelings Buckingham raised in her. If she did not, the lessons she'd so looked forward to would turn into a nightmare.

Anne was to learn the truth of her intuition soon enough. Buckingham was as attentive to her as he had been to the children, with the addition that he seemed to touch her an inordinate amount. When he showed her how to accept a leg up onto the mare, he held her hand. When he showed her how to sit in the sidesaddle, he took her by the waist to settle her correctly, then adjusted each foot in the appropriate stirrups before he smoothed her skirts, lightly touching her knees in the process.

When he was done, he stepped back to give her a critical look. Anne felt as if every place he had touched was

buzzing slightly, as if he had set up a clamor in her, but she
forced herself to disregard it and await his verdict.

"Yes, that's good. O'Neill."

The Irishman tugged on the mare's reins at Buckingham's command, and Anne felt as if she needed to clutch
something to keep from falling. "Tighten your right leg
around the horn," Buckingham commanded. "That will
help you hold yourself on. Keep your toe back in the stir-
rup. You don't want to get your foot caught if something
untoward occurs. That's it. You're sitting nicely now."

Anne felt awkward in the odd position, but she was
pleased to be where she was. She really was doing it. She
was riding. When she became accustomed to the horse's
rhythm and did not need to watch her intently, she looked
around and felt a soaring sense of freedom at how high she
was. And independent, as if she could ride off into the sun-
set, whenever she wanted. The thought made her grin just
as her eye, by purest chance, met her instructor's. He was
not with the children by the fence, but nearer to her to give
her instruction if she needed it. And he understood. She
could tell by the smile he gave her that he not only knew
how she felt but that he was glad for her.

Immediately, Anne looked down to the mare. She was
not so surprised to find she and the duke could communi-
cate without speaking—they had exchanged enough angry
glances—but it did unsettle her that he should seem so glad
of her pleasure. It was the look a friend might have given
her.

When her lesson was done and Buckingham came to
show her how to dismount, Anne found she felt strangely
shy. O'Neill gruffly complimented her efforts, saying in a
voice tinted with an Irish brogue, "Ye'll be ridin' in the
Derby before we know it, ma'am. Ye're pluck to the back-
bone. Ye weren't even a wee bit afraid."

Anne gave the head groom an easy smile. "Thank you,
O'Neill. I did, indeed, enjoy myself and in part, I imagine,
because I had such sure hands on the reins."

As he had been the one leading the mare, the Irishman
laughed unaffectedly, and it should have been the easiest

thing in the world for Anne to turn and include Buckingham in her joke as well. She found, though, that she could meet the approval in his eyes only glancingly.

"O'Neill's right, Anne. You are a natural rider."

"Thank you," she murmured, looking after the mare as O'Neill led her away. And then, desperate to fill a silence that threatened to unnerve her, she remarked, "But I wasn't properly introduced. I don't know what the mare's name is."

He played her well, Anne was to fume later. He did not answer at once, which roused her curiosity. When she looked to him, she saw the provoking twinkle in his eyes, but it was too late to look away. He was already saying, oh so provokingly. "Why, she is aptly named Lady Godiva." Anne stiffened abruptly, which only amused him the more. He grinned outright as he explained, "She had a lovely coat even as a filly, hence her name. But you needn't worry, Anne. I won't ask you to live up to it."

Anne was unable to resist the picture he had deliberately conjured, of a woman riding quite naked but for her hair covering her. Nor was she able to keep from flushing, and so she gave Buckingham a flashing look that should have flayed him. He laughed.

Gritting her teeth, she'd have left him there laughing all by himself, but her children came running to join her, exclaiming on her abilities and also forcing her to remember her manners as they gave their cousin their unsolicited thanks.

"Thank you, your grace, I have never had such a bang-up time!" was Alex's way of putting it.

Nell was more proper. "Thank you very much, your grace. You were very kind to us."

"You are both welcome," Buckingham replied. "And the pleasure was mine. You were both, no all three, excellent students. And, by the by, I've been thinking that 'your grace' sounds too formal between cousins. Perhaps you could call me Cousin Trev, as we are coming to be friends as well as relations."

Both of the children seemed to swell visibly with pride,

and Anne, smiling a little at their response, decided that all in all she was pleased by their pleasure. She turned to Buckingham, her gratitude heartfelt. "Thank you," she said simply.

He seemed to understand what she included in her thanks and, inclining his head, looked for once more serious than not. "As I said, the pleasure was mine."

Betta came then. Anne left the yard with her and the children, but not before she saw the girl glance about, seemingly idly, until Tucker came out of the stables. When she saw the groom, Betta turned pink, and abruptly looked away, her pug nose in the air. Anne shook her head and wondered if there were not something odd in the summer's air at Sisley, for Betta had good reason for her long-held aversion to Englishmen, and yet it did seem, from the determined way she ignored the lingering, grinning glance young Tucker gave her, that she had almost forgotten it.

Chapter 7

On the fourth day of the riding lessons, after watching the children work with the reins he had taught them to use the day before, Buckingham left his post by the paddock fence and turned back toward the house. "Cousin Trev is not staying for your lesson, Mama," Nell announced to Anne, for her mother was retying her hair ribbon, then added quickly, in a placating tone, "He must think you are doing very well."

Anne, standing on her tiptoes and struggling to tie off the bow, made only a vague response. "Hmm," was the extent of it, but in a soothing tone, for Nell had sounded concerned that she might be hurt by Buckingham's desertion. She was not, of course, though she had intended to ask him if he thought she was ready to ride outside of the paddock. The fenced area had begun to seem confining and the world beyond it correspondingly inviting.

Anne was not sorry Buckingham had gone, however. When he was present, he touched her too much—with his hands as well as his eyes. He never violated the boundaries of what was acceptable—Anne would have reacted strongly if he had—but he did test the permissible limits. If she walked with him, he took her arm in such a way that her arm lay along the length of his; or if he wished to direct her steps in some specific direction, he did not touch her lightly, but rather laid the full flat of his palm against the hollow at the small of her back; or when he wished to give her instruction as she sat upon Lady—as she called Lady Godiva—he would often take her hand in his and hold it, as if he feared he could not keep her attention otherwise. But what had caused her the most agitation had been the two or three times he had actually lifted her onto the back of the mare. The feel of his hands holding her there at her waist, nearly spanning it, their warmth and strength seeping through the thick material of the habit as if it were not even there, had remained with her all day. And night. She had awakened from a restless sleep thinking of it, remembering how close his strong fingers had come to the tight braid just beneath her breasts.

"Look Mama, Cousin Trev has come back, and he is on Jester!"

Jester was a strong gelding Buckingham often rode about the estate. Anne turned to look. She had not seen him ride since she had begun her riding lessons, and noted now with new eyes how easily he sat the large bay and how at home he looked mounted. Distracted—admiring him, she'd have admitted if pressed—Anne did not notice for a moment that he was leading Lady.

When she finally did see that he held Lady's reins, she looked up at him, startled. As he had pulled up no more than two yards away on the other side of the fence, she had no difficulty discerning the half-teasing, half-challenging gleam in his eyes.

"I thought you might like to test yourself with a ride outside the confines of the paddock," he said.

Nell cried out that she *must* go, seeming to see the ride as a test of Anne's self-confidence—and perhaps it was, though not, Anne knew, in the way Nell believed. It was not managing Lady that concerned her.

Buckingham had read her mind. Again. She ought to say . . . what? That she was afraid to ride with him? And was she, for that matter? What did she believe he would do?

Alex came riding over on Daisy to add his exhortations

to Nell's. Could she disappoint her children, Anne wondered, a reckless feeling sweeping her. She really did not want to ride tamely about the paddock another day.

"Yes, very well, your grace. I would like to see if I can manage Lady without a fence around us."

Anne said the words sedately enough, but her eyes gave her away. They sparkled with her excitement, and Buckingham's grin intensified. "Good girl," he said with an approval she noted despite herself. "I thought you would."

O'Neill gave her a leg up, and they left the stableyard with the children waving as hard as if she were royalty departing on a parade through the countryside.

The day was beautiful, with not a cloud in the light blue sky and the balmy air sweet with the scent of the wild roses growing along the lane Buckingham had chosen. On one side of the lane was parkland, with its gently rolling contours and thick patches of butter-yellow daffodils. On the other was a light wood of beeches and oaks, where purple wood hyacinths grew in the dappled light.

Anne took it all in with a pleasure intensified by the sense of freedom riding gave her. She might even have set Lady to a gallop, whether she quite knew how to or not, had Buckingham not been with her. But he was with her. Determined as she was to attend only to Lady and the beauty around her, still Anne was aware of him, of how straight he sat, how he controlled the bay with as little as a slight shifting of his thighs. And how he watched her.

When Anne felt a flush creep up her cheeks, she could no longer pretend to ignore him, but she did not give in with good grace. "Well?" she demanded, turning nettled, green eyes upon him. "Have you some further instruction after studying me, your grace?"

Buckingham's eyes, quite as blue as the cloudless sky above them, danced. Not only did he know she'd been aware of him, but also he had gotten her to admit it. "In fact, I was admiring your seat." When her eyes flared wide at his choice of words, he laughed. "Nay, now, you've no right to flash those green eyes at me. It is perfectly legitimate for a riding instructor to admire his student's seat. And I must say that you are as natural a rider as Alex."

Anne would not be mollified by his praise for her son. "Thank you, your grace," she said, her tone only slightly warmer than arctic. "But how do you know it is not Peter to whom Alex owes his abilities?"

Buckingham shook his head authoritatively. "Mayhap he got it from the de Montfortes somehow, but Peter himself was an indifferent rider. After all—" He caught himself as his eyes met hers. "Forgive me, Anne," Buckingham said at once, looking grim. "I spoke without thinking. I did not mean to raise unhappy memories."

"I did not think you did." Anne dropped her gaze. Peter had died after falling from a horse, but he'd not fallen on account of his equestrian skills, or any lack thereof. None but the men who had been there that night knew the full story.

She did not have to tell Buckingham, though. He guessed most of what she'd omitted. "May I know something, Anne?" he asked after a long moment. "If you don't care to speak of it, you've only to say so, but I have always wondered about Peter's death. He cared little for riding, but he was not so poor a rider as all that, and from the moment I heard, I suspected he had been drinking. He had a taste for brandy, but lamentably little head for it."

Anne looked out at the bright daffodils waving gently in the soft breeze. There did not seem any point in lying about what had happened that cold, rainy, fall night so many years before. "Yes," she conceded. "He had been drinking." Then she added, almost as if she could not help herself, "And the stallion he wagered he could ride was half wild." She felt Buckingham's gaze on her and flashed him a brief look. He was regarding her steadily, and the rest came out before she could think better of it. "He had just lost all the inheritance his great aunt had left him. His friend, the Viscount Peters, said he hoped to win the loss back with a wager on the stallion." Anne heard the bitterness in her voice. It was not much, just a tinge, but it was there, along with real sorrow for a young man lost before he had ever known his prime. "It was so . . . senseless," she said, glancing again at the man riding beside her.

His expression was hard. She thought he had heard that bitter note and faulted her for her sentiment. When he said flatly, "It was more than senseless. It was criminal. He left you with two small children and nothing to support them." Her eyes went wide with surprise. Buckingham's mouth flattened. "What did you think?" he said, reading her expression. "That I would blame you for Peter's wretched lack of judgment?"

"Why shouldn't I think it?" she returned, goaded by his tone. "Your family has blamed me for everything else."

"I am not my uncle, Anne," Buckingham said quietly. "You would do well to remember that."

But he acted for his uncle. Anne thought to remind him of that, but distracted, caught up in emotion, she inadvertently tightened her hold upon Lady's reins, and the mare threw up her head in protest. It took Anne a moment to settle Lady, but she did, and then, despite a strong desire not to, looked to Buckingham to see if he was put out with the way she handled his mount.

His expression was stern, but not for the reason she thought. "I find it easy to forget how new you are to horses, Anne. This is no conversation for your first ride out of the paddock, and I apologize for continuing it." Her eyes must have reflected her amazement, for he smiled a little. "You see, I do not claim to be infallible." He held her gaze a moment longer, looking as if he might say more, but then he seemed to decide against it. "Well, then, shall we concentrate upon riding? I will show you how to post, if you like. I doubt you'll be enamored of the gait, but I think you are ready for it."

Anne was not sorry to leave off discussing Peter or the short marriage that had brought her more painful memories than pleasant ones. She had revealed more to Buckingham than she had intended, and she wasn't certain why—or what the consequences might be.

Glad to have a distraction, even if only for a while, she concentrated upon learning the new gait. Buckingham had prophesied correctly, she did not much like posting. "I feel as if I am bouncing to death," she told the duke when she caught up to him.

His mouth quirked slightly as his eyes took in her flushed cheeks and the straight way she held her slender body. "However you feel, you looked controlled on your way to Hades, which is the effect you wanted. Now we'll climb this hill. At the top, there is a place to rest and a nice vista besides."

They trotted up the hill a way, then slowed again to a walk, Buckingham riding before Anne as the path had narrowed. Near the top, the trees began to thin, and Anne looked out. She could see Sisley. It looked like a magnificent jewel, for though it was an enormous house, it was stately, its large proportions carefully balanced and lightened by hundreds of windows and the tracery stonework that decorated its roof like a crown.

Because their pace had slowed, she had little to distract her thoughts, and perhaps because Peter had never quite left her thoughts, Anne found herself thinking of her exchange with Buckingham. Or rather she thought how Buckingham had been the one who had introduced Peter into the conversation, and she wondered suddenly if his seeming slip had not been deliberate. Perhaps, she thought cynically, he had wanted her to be thinking of Peter when she looked down on his home. Peter would have been born to something like it. Perhaps Buckingham's intent had not been merely to take her riding, but to drive home what her son would have if she but said the word.

The view from the top of the hill was even wider. As the trees there were interspersed with huge boulders, Anne could see thousands of acres of prime farmland stretching in all directions. The rents from those acres would be enormous, enough to support Sisley and the extensive grounds around it that were devoted to nothing but ornamental purposes, not to mention Buckingham House in London, and whatever other homes the duke had. His uncle was not quite so wealthy, of course, but Buckingham had made his point as far as Anne was concerned. Alex would forfeit a great deal by remaining with her.

It was a difficult admission to make, even to herself. Anne admitted it, but even so she thought the resentment she felt toward Buckingham was not unjustified. He had led her to believe he was taking her for nothing more than a pleasant first ride.

Anne's jaw was hard as a rock when she looked down to find Buckingham had not only dismounted but also had come to help her down. He raised his arms to catch her.

"I don't want to dismount," she said curtly.

Impatience flickered across Buckingham's expression. "I've no intent to ravish you, Anne," he said evenly, making his own assumptions about her reluctance to dismount. "It isn't my style. I prefer my women willing. And you *will* get down. You'll not be able to walk the rest of the day if you don't stretch your right leg."

Her leg had been aching for some time, but Anne was quite prepared to turn Lady about and ride back to the house—nay, palace—alone. Buckingham did not give her the opportunity. He simply plucked her off Lady before she could resist. Her leg was more cramped than she had realized. When she put her weight on it, it buckled and she fell against Buckingham, her breasts slamming against his hard chest.

He caught her to him, perhaps to steady her, though the light in his eyes had become suddenly knowing. "Do you want me so much, Annie, that you must throw yourself at me?"

"No!" She tore herself from his hold. But her leg had not yet recovered. It buckled again and she would have fallen had not Buckingham caught her.

"Dammit, Anne!" That lazy, wicked light had gone, along with the impulse to use her pet name. "You'll break your leg. You must sit and stretch the blasted thing before you make it bear your full weight. I can either carry you to that rock over there, or you may suffer my arm around your waist."

Anne chose to let him help her hobble to the rock,

though she held herself as far away from him as she could. At her sitting place, she shrugged him off ungraciously and, lowering herself down, began to massage her cramped leg.

Buckingham was not pleased. "You will look at me this instant," he commanded, "and you will tell me just how I have offended—"

"I know why you brought me here," Anne interrupted, her anger almost palpable.

"Oh? Well, perhaps you will enlighten me about the motive that has turned you sour as a lemon."

Anne gave him a look full of contempt, then turned and with a sharp movement of her hand indicated the vista below them. "You wanted to show me what Alex will have to give up in order to remain in my sullying company."

Buckingham made an impatient sound. "You have been seeing the world he would inherit from his grandfather from the moment you rolled through Sisley's gates nearly two weeks ago. I brought you here today because this is a favorite place of mine. But as you, and you alone, have raised the subject of Alex, I will respond. And first, I will thank you, madam, not to put your words in my mouth. I do not consider he has been sullied, as you put it, by his contact with you thus far. To the contrary, he has thrived. However, the question to be considered now, dispassionately if you please, is what kind of circumstances will allow a child as bright and energetic as Alex to continue to thrive. I submit that Sisley—or Darlington Towers, rather—will serve him a great deal better than the rooms I visited in Shipner's Lane."

Hester's dim, cramped rooms flashed through Anne's mind, but she told herself they would not live there after they left Sisley. With Rob's help, they'd find a cottage in the country someplace, one that had stables and a paddock, she added stubbornly.

"You are splitting hairs with me, your grace," Anne said, trying very hard to keep her tone level. "You know your uncle considers me a poisonous influence. And as to the kind of circumstances in which Alex will thrive, I can only say you've little understanding of children if you think trappings, even magnificent ones, important. Were he abandoned by those he loves, Alex would wither—even if he were given Sisley itself."

"He would not be abandoned," Buckingham responded with detestable calm. "He would see you still, and Nell. And he would come to know others who would care for him, too."

"Not like his mother!"

There was no question of the anger in her voice, but Trev heard as well the uncontrolled edge of panic. To his bemusement, he felt an overwhelming desire to cup her smooth cheek and tell her he would take care of everything—though just how, he was not sure. He agreed, ultimately, with his uncle. Still, he heard himself say carefully, "You are right, of course, Anne. We could never replace you in his heart." The darkness in her eyes did recede somewhat, which pleased him perhaps even more than he had expected, but Trev knew he could not in good conscience leave matters there and so he continued, "Nonetheless, you will have to admit, there is a great deal here and at Darlington Towers for him. As I said, we must all give level-headed thought to what is best for Alex. Have you considered consulting him, Anne, asking his preference?"

Anne regarded Buckingham narrowly. He had put that last to her quietly, almost as if it concerned him that he might upset her by the implication that Alex, if asked, might choose a pony over her. But Anne did not want his kindness. It made her feel weak, as if she might like to throw herself into his strong arms and let him make everything all right, which was likely the precise reaction he desired. While he wrapped one arm about her, he'd send her son to his uncle with the other one.

But the question . . . she turned away abruptly. The question was not, if she were honest, unfair. Looking again at Sisley and its surroundings, she considered whether she should grant Alex some say in the matter. Actually, Anne wondered what Alex might say if he were told at one and twenty that such a momentous decision had been made without even a nod in his direction.

There really was only one answer. "Yes," she said finally, looking from Sisley up to meet Buckingham's eyes. There was, she noted, looking for it, no flicker of satisfaction in them. "You are right. I cannot decide Alex's future without speaking to him first. But I do not think now is the time to do it. Alex would only be bewildered, were he asked if he wished to go to a complete stranger. When he's met his grandfather, and has a better appreciation and understanding of all that his choice would entail, then I will speak to him."

Buckingham studied her there on her rock. Her gaze was open, steady, even resolute, though her color seemed pale. "I cannot think of anything more fair," Trev said finally.

Anne nodded her head once. "Good then. Well . . ." She lifted herself up and tested her leg. When it took her weight, she looked again at Buckingham. "I wonder if I may ask for your forbearance, your grace. I should like to return alone. I . . ."

She shrugged, as if she had run out of words, or at least diplomatic ones. Her eyes looked dark and her mouth was tautly set. Trev experienced again an impulse to pull her to him and simply hold her. Instead, showing a consideration that surprised him, he gave her what she wanted.

"You are certain you will be all right?" he asked when she was mounted.

"I shall make my way back to Sisley, at least. It's rather hard to miss." Anne managed a faint smile, but there was something more animated in her eyes when she added softly just before she left, "Thank you, your grace."

Trev watched her until she was out of sight, a wry cast to his expression. He had made her grateful at last, but in the very last way he had wanted to do so. He had spared her his company, but it was a measure of how much better he had come to know her that he understood her desire to be alone.

She loved the boy. There was no longer any question of it in his mind. She would have had to be an actress of Siddons's quality, and not for a few hours on stage but every minute of every day, to have fooled him on that point. She did love Alex, and that was the difficulty for her. Loving him, she wanted the best for him, which meant she must give serious thought to sending the boy from her. For the first time, Trev appreciated fully what a wrenching thing that would be for her.

And so he had let her go, given her what he could, because he was not able to spare her the decision she would have to make eventually. Not that there were not compromises he could suggest to his Uncle John. When the old man had recovered somewhat and was not so afraid he would die at any moment, he might agree to leave Alex with her another few years. The boy would not suffer harm in her company. She would not sully him, as she had put it. Indeed, all in all, she did a fine job of acting the fetching lady.

He had watched her in the stableyard with the grooms, thinking to see some suggestion of coarseness, or at the least of the coquette she must once have been, but he had seen neither. Though the grooms followed her like puppies, even O'Neill, she never seemed much aware of their attention. Oh, she laughed with O'Neill, and was perfectly gracious with the others, but that was all she was. She had made, it seemed, a thorough study of how to be a lady.

The fetching part, of course, she had been born to. She did not have to pretend anything there. Trev's smile grew more humorous. She would, in short, make a splendid mistress, being beautiful and refined, and when she was his mistress, he'd shower her with everything Peter had so recklessly left her without. No pretty bauble would take the place of Alex, but surely she was enough like any other woman that a house of her own, perhaps, or a generous settlement on Nell, might ease the hurt of the loss she would suffer over her son.

Chapter 8

"Yes, my sister does live close to me, Mrs. Teasdale. Her home in Leicestershire is only a day's journey away, but I cannot say how convenient her proximity is. We have entirely divergent interests."

"Entirely?" Anne heard Hetty inquire, intrigued.

From the corner of her eye, Anne saw Buckingham's mouth quirk. "Entirely. While Maddy is consumed by a desire to see me married, I am equally determined to remain unattached."

Hetty took up the gauntlet at once, responding archly, "But what have you against marriage, your grace? I must say I found it a very satisfactory state."

"But you are a woman, my dear Mrs. Teasdale." Buckingham laughed softly. "And for a woman, marriage brings freedom from her parents, as well as all the societal restrictions attendant upon being a single girl. For a man, on quite the other hand, marriage brings only bonds."

"And children and abiding affection, hopefully," Hetty retorted.

Anne never looked up from the piece of roast beef she was cutting. Hetty had chided her for being virtually silent at dinner for the last few evenings, and with reason. Since Buckingham had taken her riding, her mood had been heavy. The momentous decision she would have to make about Alex, involving, she acknowledged more and more, loss whichever way she chose, accounted for most of her mood. She had even found herself railing bitterly against Lord John for refusing to make Alex his heir without restriction, though she had never before had the least thought that Alex had any inherent right to the unentailed estate.

But worry about her son was not all that had affected Anne. There was also the man sitting to her left. Sometimes he could be as gentle and careful with her as he was with Nell. He had not been under any obligation to allow her her solitude returning from that hilltop. Yet he had given it to her, and referring to more than her riding abilities, had asked her with genuine concern if she would be all right. At times like that, he tempted her to throw herself and all her burdens into his arms and to admit everything, even that she was cousin to the Earl of Edgemoore. But her softer feelings could vanish as if they had no more substance than smoke. When he made her unwillingly aware of him with a heated look or a lingering touch, she was reminded of the low opinion he held of her, and that very likely one of the reasons he had invited her to Sisley was to seduce her not only for his own pleasure, but for his uncle's purposes as well.

Little wonder, she thought, stabbing the piece of roast beef on her plate, that she had kept virtually silent for three evenings in a row. She scarcely knew whether to behave pleasantly or to lash out at him.

Nor was she interested at all in the discussion of marriage that Hetty had instigated. Of course he wanted to have his cake and to eat every last crumb as well. And what was worse, he would. He would play the carefree rake, enjoying women's favors without restraint until it finally pleased him to think of his own heir. Then, and only then, he would marry a docile, porcelain-like creature of unblemished reputation and malleable age, get her with child, and subsequently return, if he chose, to his old ways—discreetly, of course.

"Anne?" She looked up to find Hetty regarding her with a hint of reproach. "You have been woolgathering, my dear." There did not seem any point in denying it and so Anne simply waited for Hetty to continue. She did, a cajoling smile appearing on her sweet face. "We were discussing his grace's art collection, and I was just telling him how often you wrote of the art you saw in Italy."

Buckingham sat sprawled comfortably in his chair, managing to look rakish and elegant at once. He was observing Anne with a dry expression that indicated he knew very well she had not wanted to join the conversation, and was amused to see her being dragged into it by her aunt. He also seemed skeptical about her aunt's assertion. That odd thrill he so often prompted raced through her, and buoyed by it, she decided to prove to him how wrong his doubt was.

"Yes, I particularly enjoyed Florence," she said, forcing herself to keep a level tone. "To have such excellent sculpture in the very street was quite wonderful. But even the smallest church had its treasures. There were frescoes by a friar, Fra Angelico, I admired tremendously. . . ."

Anne went on and on, speaking of all she had seen in Florence and Rome. If Buckingham had been skeptical of the depth of her interest at first, he did not long remain so. His gaze sharpened, and he began to ask questions about specific works she'd seen, and then to tell her what he had seen, himself, when he had visited Italy. His opinions did not always coincide with Anne's—he preferred Michelangelo to Titian, for example—but he never dismissed her point of view as nothing more than female sentimentality, as she'd half expected him to do.

"There are some fine examples of Italian art here at Sisley," he said after they had been talking for a while. "Have you seen—"

"The piece by Donatello? That graceful David is his work, is it not?"

"Yes, actually, it is," Buckingham said smiling a little—though why, Anne didn't quite know. "My grandfather had the good fortune to come across it when he visited Italy. But I was going to ask if you'd seen the work by your favorite, da Vinci, as you admire him so much."

"No! A painting of da Vinci's is here at Sisley?" Anne asked in surprise.

"Yes, in the anteroom to my study. There is wonderful light there."

"Ah, well, Mrs. Goodwin did not take us to your inner sanctum."

Anne could see that her description of his study amused Buckingham. "Did she not? Well, I doubt it was any awe of me that deterred her. As far as I have been able to determine, Mrs. Goodwin is humbled only by dust. I imagine she neglected to show you to the anteroom specifically because she believes you've too much good sense to be interested in a foreign painter. As she has said on more than one occasion, a good Englishman is twice the worth of any one of those southerners. But as we are through with our dinner, would you care to put Mrs. Goodwin's taste to the test?"

Anne smiled at his dry characterization of his housekeeper. "Well, I am sorry to disappoint Mrs. Goodwin. She is an estimable woman, but I should very much like to see the da Vinci."

"Good then. I'll take my port in the drawing room, when Barrett serves your tea. Mrs. Teasdale?" Buckingham turned to Hetty as he rose. "You'll join us?"

He held out his hand, assuming she would, but Hetty shook her head. "I'll wait for the better light of day, your grace, for truth to tell I am feeling rather tired."

"Hetty!" Anne looked closely at her aunt. Hetty was leaning back in her chair and it did seem as if the energy she had displayed earlier in the dinner had left her. "Is it your breathing? I was so sure the country air would cure you of your attacks!"

"No, Annie! You needn't look so worried." Straightening in her seat, Hetty smiled. "Truly, my lungs are not bothering me. I overdid today, that's all. Nell and I gathered flowers and made a long walk of the work. I shall be fine tomorrow, but I think I will go up to my bed now. You go along and enjoy yourself. I should feel dreadful if you did not. Make her go with you, your grace," Hetty appealed to Buckingham. "Annie can be a very stubborn nurse."

"I shall do my best with your nurse, Mrs. Teasdale, but shall I have a footman escort you upstairs?"

It was, evidently, a rhetorical question, for Buckingham signaled to a footman before Hetty could respond, and she left the dining room a few minutes later on a strong, liveried arm.

"Is she really tired do you think?"

The question was ambiguous. Anne was not certain if Buckingham were asking whether Hetty had feigned her fatigue in order to leave the two of them alone, or whether she was masking real illness. Either one was possible, but it was the latter that concerned her.

"I don't know," she admitted.

"What is the breathing difficulty to which you referred?"

Anne explained, and to her surprise, Buckingham nodded. "I am not entirely unfamiliar with the condition. A relative of my brother-in-law has the same difficulty. If Mrs. Teasdale is not restored by her rest tonight, I will have our local doctor, Dr. Johnstone, out to see her."

Anne quietly gave him her grateful thanks. Perhaps he had been more suspicious than most would be of Hetty's sudden fatigue, but, she conceded, he likely had reason. After all, he could not but be one of the most tempting targets in England for ambitious mothers and their daughters, and it was possible, if not probable, that he had actually encountered the weary duenna ploy before. And besides, Anne was not entirely certain Hetty had not been playacting. Her aunt was a romantic by nature, and it was easily possible that she had decided Anne might win more from the de Montfortes than merely their goodwill.

"Shall we enjoy ourselves as your aunt wished?"

Buckingham held out his hand, but Anne wavered. She knew very well that Hetty's hopes, if indeed she harbored them, were absurd. It was not marriage Buckingham had in mind for her.

"Come," he insisted, his eyes cooling when she hesitated. "I have already told you I won't ra—"

Anne placed her fingers on his arm before he could repeat for the delectation of the footmen clearing the table that he would not ravish her, and regretted her weakness the moment they walked out of the dining room and turned left rather than right. "This is not the way to your study but rather to the library," she protested.

Buckingham inclined his head. "And thence to the gardens," he agreed blithely. "The dark of night is no time to appreciate a work of art, particularly if the night is clear and the reflecting pool full of stars." Anticipating her move, he swiftly trapped Anne's hand upon his arm before she could pull it away. "Why do you balk at taking a stroll in the gardens? I am far less likely to ravish you out on the damp, unyielding ground than in the comfort of my study."

It flashed through Anne's mind that he sounded as if he spoke from experience, and the subsequent image of Trevelyan de Montforte taking his pleasure of some beauty on the ground was so vivid and disturbing that she went mortifyingly red. That additional heat in her cheeks did little to calm her.

"I am not going another step with you anywhere! It amuses you to embarrass me or put me at a disadvantage somehow, and I am weary to death of it!"

It didn't surprise her that he did not let her go, but it did take her aback when Buckingham caught her by both arms. His touch was soft, though, as soft as the expression in his eyes. "You'll not go anywhere until you answer my question, Anne. Why are you balking at a perfectly pleasant suggestion? Are you afraid *you* may ravish *me?*"

Anne would not let herself smile at that, would not even let her gaze soften. But she had to fight so hard to keep her gaze stony that she'd no energy left to form an answer in the half-second he gave her. As if he were satisfied, Buckingham nodded. "Just as I thought. You haven't any reason for not going, and nothing better to do, besides. Well, neither do I, and I am not going to allow mere skittishness to keep me from the company of a beautiful and intelligent woman."

Anne gave an exasperated cry when he linked his arm through hers and began walking. Perforce, she had to walk too, or be dragged. "Were you ever in your life denied anything?" she demanded.

"No," Buckingham replied without hesitation. "Nothing I truly wanted." And then with the sudden grin that had the power to make her breath catch in her throat, he looked down at her and added, "Though you are proving a bit elusive."

Chapter 9

Anne went with Buckingham, feeling as if she were as foolish as a plump goose going off with a hunter—although she rather doubted the goose would have had its better judgment overcome by quite the same temptations. Frankly, that glimmering look and that remark on how elusive she was had set off a strange, almost irresistible excitement within her. Even as he half dragged her down the terrace steps to the gardens, lit by nothing more than a few torches and the faint silvery light of a quarter moon, she could think only of what might happen there in the darkness. She noted the difference between the soft silk of his coat and the hard strength of his arm. At least, she decided, she did not have to go arm in arm with the hunter.

Buckingham never acknowledged her effort to slip free of him. He simply put a hand over hers, holding her hand on his arm with the faintest promise of force, and when he spoke, it was of a subject certain to divert her attention. He told her how well her children were doing in their efforts to learn to ride and that he thought they would soon be ready to leave the paddock.

"Do you really?" Anne asked, her forgotten hand lying as quiescent beneath his as Buckingham could have wished. "Even Nell?"

"Nell's learned all she can in the paddock. The only way

she will gain in confidence is if she puts her abilities to the test. Don't worry, I'll stay beside her, and we'll only go down the drive at first."

"What if Merry shies, though?"

"That stolid creature?" Buckingham chuckled softly. "If Merry did anything so energetic as shy, I would be very surprised. Nell will do quite well, Anne. I would not put her to a test she could not master."

Anne looked up swiftly. "I do trust you there, you know," she said, taking them both by surprise. Self-conscious suddenly, she looked off into the night. "You have been very patient and careful with her, and I know I must fight an urge to cosset her, but she is such a tender thing that I cannot bear it when she is hurt or frightened."

"Nor would I care for her to be. As you say, she is a tender thing, although thoroughly engaging. But does she resemble someone in your family, Anne? She does not look like any de Montforte I know of."

Anne's hand tensed on his arm, giving Trev all the proof he needed that for some reason of her own, she quite deliberately had kept Nell's parentage a secret from him. "She, ah . . . she resembles a great aunt," Anne said, studying the dark shadows cast by the high hedges that bounded one side of the formal gardens.

"I see." Trev could have stopped there. That he did not, that he actually needled Anne further, he could not have explained, even to himself. "A great aunt? Mrs. Teasdale would be her sister, of course."

"No, no!" Anne turned her face up to him. Even by the faint light of the moon, Trev could see the anxious lines knitting her brow. "She was a great aunt on my mother's side. I saw her only once, but she had titian hair and brown eyes. And was a gentle soul, not at all prickly like me."

To Anne's considerable relief, Buckingham chuckled at that. She had thought she could account for Nell's different looks easily enough, but though she had seen no reason to trust Buckingham with the truth, she had found it unexpectedly difficult to lie outright to him.

"Do you see yourself as a hedgehog, then?" he asked,

clearly amused. "Is that why you haven't remarried, because you are too spiny?"

"Of course," she replied in the same light vein. "No man wants a spiny wife."

He laughed again, but in the ensuing silence Anne once more became aware of his arm beneath her hand, of his body, even, just a hair's breadth away, and of how he had lulled her into leaving her hand where it was. Before he could guess what she intended, she quickly slipped her hand from beneath his and made a play of busily adjusting the light shawl she'd worn to dinner.

For a moment, the only sound between them was the light crunch of the gravel beneath their feet. Anne stared into the night, tracing the light silhouette of a statue of Venus that stood in a niche in the hedge, but it was to the man beside her that her senses were attuned. She wondered if he were angry that she had freed herself from him. As the silence between them grew, she thought he must be.

But when Buckingham did finally speak, Anne found she had read his silence incorrectly. "What is the real reason you have not remarried, Anne?" he asked. His voice was low and velvety, seeming to envelop them in some private world where there was only the two of them.

"For a relatively simple reason, actually," she said, deliberately making her voice bright and sharp as she fought the effect he created, whether intentionally or not. "I did not care enough for those who asked, to accept."

"Are your standards so high, then?" he asked.

Anne thought it an idle question, but still she considered the eccentric Italian count who had asked for her hand even before her father had died; the merchant in Rome, who had offered marriage after her father's death; and the young English viscount, who had been a friend of Peter's and had proposed after Peter's death. She had refused them all, though they had each offered security of sorts, and each at times she'd needed it. But she had married once out of necessity, and knew what it was not to long for her husband's touch. "Actually, I haven't any rigid standards about the man himself," she said reflectively. "Only the requirement that I care deeply for him."

"Do you mean you must love your prospective groom?" Buckingham asked, then before she could answer, added with a sardonic laugh, "Do you wish me to think you a romantic, Anne?"

If she had missed the cynical edge to his tone when he had asked about her high standards, she did not miss it now. Quite gone was the low, intimate, caressing voice. Anne looked up at him. "I've no control over what you think of me, your grace." In her turn, she too, laughed with little humor. "I've learned that at least, but I'll not allow you to mock me, either. I answered you honestly, and as to the merit of my requirement, I do not think you've the authority to argue with me. Of the two of us, I am the only one who has experienced marriage."

There was a long pause. Anne waited, tensed for a cutting rejoinder. But Buckingham proved himself more subtle than that. "I concede you've more experience of marriage than I certainly. But love? Did you love Peter?"

Anne cursed herself. She had all but led him to the question, yet she had no clever or even diplomatic answer prepared. Her thoughts chasing themselves in her head, all Anne could think was that she had learned already how difficult it was to lie outright to him.

"No," she admitted finally, quietly, "I did not."

The words seemed to echo in the night. Hearing them, Anne thought too late of the ugly conclusions Buckingham was likely to draw. Abruptly she stopped, spinning to face him. "I was loyal to Peter! Though it was, I admit, a marriage of convenience, and I did not love him, I never betrayed him."

She could not guess at his thoughts. Though there was a torch nearby, it stood behind him, casting his face into shadow, and she had a sudden impulse to catch at his coat and shake him while she insisted again on her honor. The intensity of the impulse caught Anne off guard. Of course she wished to have Buckingham think well of her for Alex's sake, but the urgency of the need she felt to have him believe her was too great to attribute entirely to concern for her son.

Anne turned away in an instant, but he caught her hand. The feel of his skin on hers sent a shiver down her spine. "Where are you going?" he asked, not ungently.

She tugged against his hand, resisting the power of that softened tone. "There is no point in conversation between us. You mistrust me too greatly."

Buckingham did not speak until, with a groan of frustration, Anne accepted that he did not mean to release her. When she stood still, he tugged her in his turn, gently. She yielded again, because she thought she'd little choice. Their positions had changed slightly relative to the torch, and what she saw caused her mutinous look to moderate slightly. His too appealing mouth was set in a rather sober line.

"Your indignation is unwarranted, Anne," he said, when he had her full attention. "I have no reason to doubt you were loyal to Peter. No one has ever spoken against you after you married. As to your feelings for Peter, I am not surprised to hear you say you did not love him."

Anne did not respond at once but pulled against his hand yet again. That he believed her only made her feel more urgently that she wanted some distance between them. Buckingham released her slowly, as if to let her know he did mean to let her depart. The subject of Peter hung in the air between them. Anne told herself she did not want to discuss it further, only to hear herself ask softly, "Why?"

Perhaps she was surprised by her question, but Buckingham did not appear to be. He shrugged. "Had you been nursing some deep love for Peter these four years, surely you'd have wanted to speak of him, wanted to know what he was like as a boy, or where he had stayed at Sisley, or some such. But you haven't asked."

"Why did you ask, then?" Anne demanded, though she knew the answer.

He gave it to her without softening. "To see how honest you would be."

Anne began to walk at random, which happened to be toward the long reflecting pool that ran down the center of the gardens. Despite the briskness of her step, she railed at herself for not being angrier. He had been testing her, laying a trap. But hadn't she tested him in the same way? She had known why he asked a question whose answer he knew, and like her, he had told her the truth.

Trev walked beside her, thinking his own thoughts, and they did not include any further consideration of whether he should or should not have tested her. It was enough for him that he had wanted to hear her answer. As to his response to it, he supposed the slight but unmistakable lift he felt meant both that he had not been quite as certain of her answer as he'd thought, and that he was relieved he would not be obliged to compete with the memory of a dead hero for her affections—and consequent favors.

Yet, for all that he had the answer he wanted and had neatly accounted for his response to it, he found he was still curious about her relations with his cousin. It was unusual, that curiosity. He did not generally care two pence about the other men in his mistresses' lives—past, present, or future.

He fought the impulse. He had no reason to pry, not least because he had a good idea what sort of husband Peter had been. When they reached the reflecting pool, he was telling himself what he knew: how Peter had long displayed a tendency to act before he thought; how he had lost what little he had had left to support his wife and two children after his father had disowned him; how he had gotten drunk that night . . . but he did not know if Peter had gotten drunk most nights. He did not know if she had wanted to have Peter's child or how she had come to take on his child by another.

Trev stood just behind Anne. The moon's light danced in the shimmering water, but he saw how it gleamed in her dark hair, setting the silky mass alight. Below it, her neck looked slender, her skin light and soft, and he experienced an almost irresistible desire to close his arms around her and simply hold her.

"Anne, was he ever a good husband to you?"

The question hung in the night air, unbearable almost in the softness with which it had been asked. He stood so close behind her that Anne could feel the warmth of his body. It drew her as nothing had in her life. She had to clasp her hands tightly in front of her to fight the desire to turn into his arms and admit finally to someone what a disaster the marriage had been, how she had watched Peter turn from an amiable, even endearing boy, to a petulant, drunken burden when the consequences of his actions had proven far harsher than he'd expected. It was the night, Anne knew, that made her ache to confide in Buckingham. Its soft darkness isolated them from everything, creating the illusion of intimacy between them. But Anne knew better than to trust the illusion. There was no close affection between them, only Buckingham's desire for a woman, likely any woman so long as she was at hand.

Still, she had to force the words out. "There is no point in speaking of Peter, your grace. He, ah, did the best he could, and that was good enough."

Almost before she had finished, Buckingham's hands settled on her arms and he turned her. Anne felt like a rag doll, as if the battle not to speak of Peter had drained her of all her will. When she faced him, she could see even by moonlight the intensity in the eyes he had fixed upon her. "Peter was an amiable, generally sweet-tempered boy," he began, "but no one who knew him ever considered him either strong or dependable. I find it impossible to imagine that he was much of a support to you. And if ever you wish to tell me of it, I'll listen. Until then, however, do not try to fob me off with 'good enough.' "

He kissed her then, as she stared up at him, quite bemused. The touch of his lips was gentle, nothing at all frightening but rather a balm, somehow, for all the loneliness, for all the years there had been no one, and Anne was caught in a swirl of aching sweetness before any rational thought could intrude.

Her mouth yielded to his, her lips parting beneath his. Buckingham groaned and suddenly the kiss was different, intent, fierce even. A thrill shot through Anne. She wanted to hold him, to give back to him. She felt his chest hard beneath her hands, and suddenly, feeling how her hands trembled, she realized what she did.

"No!" The hands that a moment before had caressed his chest pushed him away, and she twisted her head to the side to escape his warm lips.

"Don't tell me you are a tease, Anne," Buckingham whispered, his hands against her waist. "I would be sorely disappointed."

Anne laughed, if the half sob could be called that. "Compared to what else you think of me, it seems little enough." His hands tightened at that, as if he meant to shake her or to pull her body closer to his. Terrified that he might yet persuade her against her will, Anne cried in earnest, "You must let me go! I erred foolishly. I repent! Oh, don't you see?" she demanded, drumming her fists against the hard wall of his chest. "This is all a game to you! Can I bed the widow by June or some such goal? While to me . . ." she did not finish but lashed out at him again with a stubborn fist.

Anne might have been a fly for all the attention Buckingham paid her blows. He wanted to hear the rest. "While to you . . ." he prompted, his voice something between a purr and a growl.

The velvety caress of it intrigued her, pulled at her, which in turn frightened her all the more. "While to me, dallying with you means the loss of my son! If I knew myself to be the doxy you think me, I could not stand before the world and say I'd the right to keep him. Please, let me go!"

She felt frantic and did not care if she had all but admitted she was susceptible to him. Oddly, she did not fear he would not release her if she convinced him she was in earnest. He had let her go in his study, after all. And so she was stunned when he said softly in reply, "Very well, but one more first."

But Buckingham did not bother to remark her shocked expression. He kissed her again, hard, taking her mouth with his and sending her senses reeling.

"You . . . rogue!" she spat when he stepped back from

her, leaving her to sway dizzily on unsteady legs, the loss
of him unaccountably, impossibly acute. "You . . ."

"Ah, ah," Buckingham warned lazily, reaching out to lay
his thumb upon her lips and rob her of breath. "It would
have been an insult to walk with you through fragrant gardens on a warm spring night without kissing you at least
once. As to the second one," she saw his smile flash white
and strong, "I *am* a rogue. But not entirely unconscionable,
it would seem. I shall let you go now, Annie, but if you
truly mean to go, then you had best do so before I forget
what few scruples I have and prove to you how little you
want to go."

Anne went, fleeing down the gravel path without another
word.

Trev watched her fly off, remarking as he did that it was
something he seemed to do rather often. But if there was a
rueful gleam in his eye, there was also a grim set to his jaw.
She had spoken no less than the truth, whether he cared to
hear it or not. An affair between them would make little
difference to him, ultimately, but for her the affair could
make all the difference. She could lose her son.

Not that she would relinquish Alex because of a feeling
of unworthiness. Though she might believe she would,
Trev thought when the moment came, her considerable
mother's instinct would take over. She would either deny
the affair, claim she'd been forced, or perhaps, appallingly
sentimental as it might sound, say that she had bedded him
for love. At any rate, she would justify herself. But Uncle
John would seize upon the lapse, however she tried to mini-
mize it. Once a whore, always a whore, he would claim,
and perhaps even look to Trev for confirmation.

Trev sent a stone skipping hard across the moonlit water.
Of course, he would never give that confirmation. He
wasn't accustomed to telling stories out of bed, for one. For
another, he did not believe Anne's bedding him had anything to do with how well she could raise Alex. If it did,
there were quite a few mothers he could name among the
ton who would have to give up their sons as well. No, the
point about Alex was she hadn't the money or position to

give the boy the place in life that he deserved, and when she finally accepted that, she would have to make some accommodation with her father-in-law.

But Alex had nothing to do with what was between himself and Anne. Trev sent another stone after the first. What was between them was the sweetest fire. He hadn't been certain he could release her—in fact, had not been able to without tasting her that second time. As to wanting a third kiss, there was no question he would take it and more. He would not be able to let her go without having her. It was that simple.

Suddenly, Trev laughed aloud in the night. When had there ever been anything simple about his relations with Anne? From the first, she had confounded him. He had once already announced to himself that he was giving her time. He'd meant a few days. Now? He didn't know how long it would take to win her trust, to convince her that he would not betray her to anyone at any time, not even his uncle. He could not merely tell her; she'd not believe him. He would have to show her—to woo her, in essence. Not that the task was impossible. She wanted him too, and eventually, she would come to him with those full lips softly parted again. And her coming to him would be all the sweeter for the anticipation. He hoped.

Chapter 10

"Just a moment more, Nell. There's still a bit of strawberry jam on your cheek, and you'll draw flies."

The little girl giggled, but she held still while Anne applied a handkerchief to her cheek. At Mrs. Goodwin's instigation, they had gone through the kitchens on their way to the stableyard, for the housekeeper had said she thought Cook had something for Alex and Nell. Cook had buns topped with strawberry jam—again, Anne suspected, at Mrs. Goodwin's instigation. The housekeeper had warmed to the children when, after she had supervised the production of their riding clothes, they had thanked her with, as she put it, "rare good manners for these days." The buns were only the latest treat she had produced for them. The day before they had been delighted by sugar cookies formed in the shape of animals.

"Are you not done yet, Mama?"

Anne looked guiltily at her daughter's immaculate cheek. She decidedly did not want to go to the stableyard, but she could not delay the inevitable forever. She'd make a dent in Nell's cheek.

"Oh, there you are, Mama! Is not Nell clean yet?" It was Alex, racing into the kitchen garden. He gave a curious glance at his sister's cheek.

"Yes, she is quite scrubbed now," Anne said, being scrupulously honest with her wording.

Alex spun about, prepared to race back the way he had come. "Good! Cousin Trev has not come out to the stables, but O'Neill says we will ride anyway and that you may ride with us, Mama, and that if you do, we shall ride in the larger paddock."

Buckingham was not at the stables. She would not have to face him, yet.

Anne smiled at her son, and gave the answer he'd been trying so cleverly to prompt. "I should like very much to ride with you and Nell."

Of course, she ought not to be disappointed that something had called him away. She had spent all the morning steeling herself to face him. To meet his eyes.

Nell took her hand and said something. Mercifully, Alex had not run off. He was running circles around Anne and Nell as they walked at a pace everyone but a five-year-old boy would have considered brisk. He gave Nell an answer to whatever she had asked. Anne heard the excited tone in his voice, but caught as little of his answer as she had heard of Nell's question.

She was thinking, despite herself, of the knowing gleam that would be in Buckingham's cursed blue eyes.

"Go, or I shall prove to you how little you want to go."

Anne bit her lip and prayed the breeze would cool her face. He would not have had to prove anything. She had already wanted his kiss. If she had felt resistance to the first kiss, especially, it had evaporated before she could recognize it. Just the touch of his mouth on hers . . . she had dreamed about him in the night. It passed all her understanding that after everything, she would dream about a kiss and more. She had put her arms around him in her dream, held him to her, lifted her face to him.

Never once had she dreamed of Peter's touch. Peter had not ever made her yearn for more, had never made her tremble. He'd never filled her with a sweet, racing, heat. It was not that Peter had repulsed her—he had not. He had simply left her more unmoved than not, and she'd assumed, ignorantly, that most women experienced as little passion as she had in the marriage bed, except perhaps a few wanton ones. She was not wanton. But she had wanted. She had only to remember how. . . . Anne squeezed her eyes shut. She did not think she could face him with the memory of how she'd clung to him—opened her mouth to him even—so terribly fresh in her mind.

Still fearing the duke might appear, Anne made a rapid survey of the brick court between the stables as O'Neill came to meet them. The Irishman was as congenial as usual. He brought out sugar from his pocket for Alex and Nell to give their ponies, and he told Anne it was a pity she'd not been born a male. As light as she was and with her natural abilities, she could have won the Thousand Guineas at Newmarket. Anne laughed, stating that she thought it was a Thousand Broken Bones she'd have won instead.

When they were mounted, O'Neill led them into a larger paddock. The children were learning to post and the Irishman pointed to the far end of the paddock and told them to trot their ponies all the way to the fence, turn them, and return at the same pace. Nell's pony spied some clover near the fence and balked when Nell tried to turn her away from the treat. To Anne's surprise, Nell never looked to her or O'Neill for help. She managed the recalcitrant pony herself, pulling hard on Merry's reins and giving her a sharp kick in the sides to get her going again. Merry was obedient from then on, and Anne acknowledged that Buckingham had assessed Nell's riding skills more accurately then she had.

He could be perceptive. She had never argued that. It was the sensitivity she'd not expected. *"If you want to tell me about Peter, I'll listen."* There was no real reason for his offering her a sympathetic ear—he'd have known from experience, she did not doubt, that she'd respond to his kiss without his offering to listen while she unburdened herself of the difficulties she'd met in her marriage.

He could be kind, then. But he could be a devil, too. He hadn't kissed her that second time out of any fine feeling for her. He'd taken what he wanted and, not incidentally, given her a lesson on passion. And now that his appetite had been whetted, he would try to take his pleasure of her again, but in the end when he had had his fill of her, he would report to his uncle she was every bit as reproachable as they had thought her.

She hated him. How could she not when he meant to take his pleasure of her and then betray her? Well, she would not be so easily undone. When she had proclaimed her strength against Buckingham to Rob, she had not known what weapons the duke had. She did now. And she was forearmed. Let that knowing light gleam in his eyes. She would not again be so overcome she forgot what harm his undeniable attractions could do her.

"They are rare fine children, Mrs. de Montforte."

O'Neill extended a calloused hand to help Anne down from the mounting block, and she gave him a pleased smile. "Thank you, O'Neill. They think very highly of you, as well, you know, particularly now you are 'allowing' them to groom their ponies themselves."

"It's an old trick, that," the Irishman said. "They'll know horses the better for workin' with them. I hope ye don't mind, ma'am? Not all mothers would care for it."

"You may be easy in your mind about me, O'Neill. I want my children to acquire a sense of responsibility. They'll be the more likely to care for me in my old age."

O'Neill threw back his head and laughed, but nonetheless Anne heard Alex's high, piping voice clearly. "Cousin Trev! Nell and I rode with Mama in the large paddock. O'Neill said we did well."

As if she were observing another person altogether, Anne noted how her heart raced when Alex announced Buckingham's presence. Although she had vowed to resist the attraction she felt for him, she'd never claimed there would be no attraction to resist. Wiser now, she knew that the thrill racing through her veins was not solely or even mostly a sign of fear. She knew it for excitement now.

It was a reckless excitement, the kind a man going into battle might feel. Anne turned, trying to control it, but her sight of Buckingham, looking so tall and broad-shouldered, his black hair ruffling in the breeze, only intensified the feeling. And he wasn't even looking at her. He was walking toward Alex and Nell with that fluid, loose-limbed stride that was uniquely his. Anne told herself that if anything was a sign of madness, surely it was that she found even the way he walked attractive. She almost prayed for him to look at her. She needed that knowing, insolent gleam, the one that had appeared when he'd raked his eyes over her at their first meeting.

Of course, he did not oblige her. He smiled at Alex. Anne tried to observe him coolly. He used that flashing white grin as deliberately as a carpenter would use a hammer. It was one of the tools with which he charmed. And then, as Anne watched, he bent his smile upon Nell, and the little girl, who had always been particularly shy of men, beamed up at him, and breathlessly affirmed that yes, she, too, had posted all around the paddock without incident.

"That is excellent, Nell. I am very proud of you, and you too, Alex. It is obvious you both listened attentively to O'Neill and did your best to follow his instructions." Anne looked on as Buckingham cocked his head slightly, as if he were musing, and both her children mimicked him, tilting their smaller heads to the exact same angle as they hung on his every word. "And though I am certain your effort does bring its own pleasure," he continued, half smiling, "I find I also believe a small reward would not be remiss."

A reward? When he had already presented them with their own ponies, lessons, and riding apparel? When just the other day, Mrs. Goodwin had appeared with another bundle of already altered, new-to-them-at-least clothing? Though the children's eyes went round, Anne's narrowed suspiciously, and she found herself meeting his gaze before she realized it.

"Ah, there you are, Anne," he said. She looked away. There had been nothing in his eyes. No, that was not right. There had been friendliness, but nothing, not even a lazy look to remind her of the night before. She looked back. He was smiling. There was nothing odd in that, but she had expected a rakish grin.

"Good morning to you," he continued pleasantly enough. "I've arranged a small treat for the children. Would you care to accompany us to the stables to see it?" As if she wouldn't go, Anne thought, staring hard at his too bland expression. Buckingham did not wait for an answer from her. He held out his hands to the children, who promptly latched on to him, and said, "We'll lead the way, if you wish."

Nell, oblivious to any tension in her mother, held out her hand to Anne, and the four of them proceeded across the stableyard, quite like a cozy little . . . but Anne would not allow herself to say family. Angry with him now, however unfairly, for behaving so contrarily to what she'd expected, she reminded herself Buckingham did not want her in his family—only in his bed.

She was repeating that grim fact to herself when he led them into the last stall in the stables, but when she saw the black puppy sitting on a mound of straw and heard the joyful cry Alex gave as he dove headlong for it, she wanted to stamp her foot in anger. He made it nearly impossible to follow her best instincts. Alex had often begged her for a puppy, but their situation had always been too unstable for her to allow him the simple treat. Now, thanks to Buckingham, Alex was giggling as the puppy exuberantly licked him on the face with a pink, wet tongue.

Nell giggled too, and stooped down to pet the pup's sleek back, but Buckingham moved forward with a basket that seemed to have appeared in his hand by magic. "Now you may like the puppy very well, Nell, and want to share him with your brother, but I thought this might appeal to you even more."

There was a cloth covering the basket. It lifted before Nell touched it, and when a calico head emerged, she gave a marveling cry.

"Look, Mama! Oh, look! It's a kitten!"

Anne knelt down by her, oblivious to the straw and dust in the stall. "I see, Nell. Ah, here she comes again. What a tiny beauty she is!"

"Is she really mine?" Nell asked Buckingham, when he knelt down, half resting on his heels beside her.

"Really and truly," he said, tapping Nell's snub little nose. "I only hope you will still thank me tomorrow. She appears to be energetic. And adventuresome. She's already halfway up your arm."

Nell's dimples flashed, but her tone was all fervency when she declared, "Oh, Cousin Trev, I shall love her forever! Thank you very much."

Anne looked away to her son as Nell buried her face in the little calico's soft fur. "Alex, have you thanked his grace for his gift?"

Shifting the puppy to his lap, Alex sat up at once. "Thank you, Cousin Trev! You're the greatest gun in all the world!"

"I am glad you are pleased, Alex." He was so close to Anne that his gleaming boot touched the hem of her habit, but he had yet to look at her. "You do understand, I hope, that you will be responsible for the pup's care?"

"Betta will help us!" Alex declared immediately. "She knows all about animals. She lived on a farm, you see, before Mama saved her life. May we keep the puppy and kitten with us in our rooms?"

It took Trev a moment to answer. At Alex's offhand disclosure that his mother had saved her maid's life, he glanced down at Anne, but she was studiously making the acquaintance of the puppy, and he got nothing more enlightening than a view of her flawless profile.

"As to where you will keep this pair," he said finally, "the answer will depend upon your mother. Mrs. Goodwin will not object to a kitten and a trained puppy in the house, if your mother does not."

Still avoiding Buckingham's eyes, she asked, "Is the puppy trained?" scratching the animal in question behind the ears.

"His former owner swore to it."

"Well, then, if Mrs. Goodwin does not object, I think this pair may live inside, though I imagine that for a few days, at least, we should take precautions against emergencies."

"That does seem prudent," Buckingham agreed on a dry note as he rose.

Anne resisted the impulse to smile at his humor. She felt too at sea for anything so friendly. He had been behaving so differently than she had expected, she didn't know whether he had thought nothing of the kiss, or was waiting to throw it in her face when her defenses were down. She did know, though, that she owed him thanks on her children's behalf.

Anne made herself look up at Buckingham, and noted his outstretched hand. "Come," he said, smiling slightly, though again she could find no smirk lurking about in his expression. "I owe you a viewing of the da Vinci. This late-morning light is the best for viewing it, and the children won't miss you while they are getting acquainted with their new friends."

This was it. The pets had been a means to divert the children and earn her gratitude. The invitation might sound perfectly correct to innocent ears, his tone might even be merely friendly, but when he got her alone . . . then he would remind her how weak she was, how very like the wanton woman he'd thought.

Just then, Betta came into the stall, exclaiming softly in Italian as Nell and Alex cried out and showed her what they had. Tucker followed Betta as far as the door, but when he saw the other occupants in the stall, he drew up short and turned red. Anne scarcely noticed the abashed groom. She finally accepted Buckingham's hand for her own reasons. She decided she had a good deal to say to him, particularly about her children.

Anne informed Betta that the kitten and puppy were to live in the house on a trial basis, then added, keenly aware of Buckingham just behind her, "I am going along to see a painting his grace has kindly offered to show me, but I shan't be longer than a half hour, I imagine. We can decide then precisely where these two will reside."

Buckingham did not remark on the time limit she had so publicly set, but when they attained the gardens, the shortest route to his study, he did question the pace Anne had set.

"Are we racing to the house? If so, I think I've an unfair advantage."

She didn't answer, only glared at him and kept on walking at precisely the same blistering pace.

"Well, if we are not racing, then I take it you have not forgiven me for those kisses last night."

He sounded so ruefully innocent, Anne thought she might scream. She did stop then, abruptly, and rounded on him, snapping, "Forgive you? I am virtually alone in your house and trapped here besides, as I've scarcely the wherewithal to leave. In short, I am at your mercy, what little of it you have! How can I forgive you?"

Now he would mock her, remind her she had not repulsed those kisses. Anne raised her chin in anticipation of the attack.

"I don't know, though I hope you will find your way to it eventually. And all you've said I acknowledge to be true." Anne stared, wondering of a sudden if it were really Buckingham talking. She was amazed he'd admitted being in the wrong. There was some humor mixed in with the steady regard, of course, but what amusement there was seemed to be self-directed. "I can't apologize," he went on, less surprisingly, "for I don't regret the kisses. I enjoyed them too much. But I'll not take advantage of your position here again. If there is ever anything between us, it will be because you, Annie, have said you want it."

There was no problem there, surely. If he did not creep under her guard with a touch, she would hardly beseech him to compromise her. Yet, for all that he'd said what she wanted to hear, he'd said it too readily. She did not trust him.

"What of the children?"

"The children?" he repeated.

He had every right to sound mystified, but she saw little point in saying she would not now or ever come to his bed—he'd only dismiss what he did not wish to hear. Besides, it truly was not about herself that she was primarily concerned.

"Yes, the children. Within two weeks, you have given

Alex and Nell riding clothes, fine ponies, and now pets, and I cannot help but wonder why you are being so generous after ignoring them all these years. Is your kindness this month's whim, or merely another way to win me to your bed?"

Anne did not have to wonder if she had flicked Buckingham on the raw. She had only to see the snap of anger in his eyes. "As you have delivered your opinion of me, madam, I believe I am entitled to do the same. And I submit that you are nothing more than jealous, because you are not able to give them these things yourself."

Anne sucked in a sharp breath and whirled away, leaving Trev to glare with little satisfaction at her stiff back. She had made him angry. Damn, but she could do it more easily than most, and he'd the devil's own tongue. Bloody hell, he thought, raking a hand through his hair, he was going to apologize for a second time in, seemingly, as many minutes to a penniless adventuress who'd nothing to recommend her but a great deal of beauty and a more than average concern for her children.

But as suddenly as she had whirled away, Anne turned to face him. Her green eyes were shadowed. "There is truth in what you say," she admitted, surprising him. "It does sting that you are able to give them their hearts' desires, while I cannot. But you must see that a part of that comes because how little I have to give is such an issue between us. It is not that I begrudge them—"

Trev caught the hand she waved in the air, silencing her. "You do not have to protest how little you begrudge them anything. You've an expressive face. I have only to recall how you looked when I told you I meant to find ponies for them. I apologize again. I have the devil's own tongue, but you must understand in your turn that I am not accustomed to having the worst possible construction put on my every action."

"But surely you see I would be remiss as a mother if I did not worry what the result of your gifts will be!" Anne exclaimed, simply anxious now. "To Alex and Nell the gifts are not merely items they have long wanted, but indications that you care for them. That, coupled with the address you must know you have . . . well, they idolize you, and though many doubt that children are capable of deep emotions, nothing could be further from the truth. Alex and Nell will be deeply hurt if you prove fickle and lose your interest in them as quickly as you've developed it. And I won't have them hurt! They have already suffered enough with the loss of their father."

Briefly, irrelevantly perhaps, Trev wondered if the simple fact that she had left her hand in his had chased away his anger. He liked touching her, Anne of the amazingly thick lashes he'd somehow overlooked before.

"I admit that I have noted your children are a considerable breach in your defenses, Anne." He smiled then, lopsidedly, unsettling the beat of her heart. "I am a rake, after all, but not such a one, I add in my defense, that I would attach Alex and Nell to me only to cast them aside when . . . I had no further use for them," he said. "They are not only my cousins, but young cousins without a father. I shall not abandon them, Anne, no matter what happens."

She believed him. She could not have said precisely why, but she did, and feeling as if a great weight had been lifted from her, Anne squeezed his hand tightly.

Buckingham laughed softly. "You test the bounds of my restraint with a look like that, you should know. And for having told you, I believe I am due an indulgence. I mean to be your friend, and as your friends call you Annie, so shall I."

It was Anne's turn to laugh, and though the gurgle was a trifle unsteady, even a little uncertain, still it was an acceptance of sorts. "I shall so indulge you, your grace. But, if I am not permitted to let you see my gratitude, then perhaps we should occupy ourselves otherwise. Shall we go to admire your da Vinci?"

Chapter 11

"Do come fishing with us, Mama! It is great fun, and you didn't come before."

It was true. Anne had not joined them when Buckingham had last taken the children fishing. That had been a little more than a month ago, and she had wanted to test just a little the extent of his devotion to her children. His response had been to smile and tell her they would bring her fish for the drawing that had been her excuse for not going. They had done it, too. All three of them had appeared in the garden some hours later, muddy but grinning widely as they held up a string of fish for which Alex and Nell swore they were as responsible as their august cousin.

"We'll help you, Mama. You needn't even bait your own hook."

Anne grinned at Alex. "Now you have said just the thing to persuade me. Very well, I shall go, but I shall have to change my clothes first."

"We'll tell Cousin Trev and Mrs. Goodwin, too!"

That was from Nell, who had the kind of mind that thought to inform not only the head of the party that there would be an additional guest but also the provisioner as well. The children dashed off as Anne hurried up to her room. Nell had lost all her shyness with Buckingham. She ran to him as readily as Alex did, even went to his lap in preference to her mother's on occasion.

She'd done it the day before, as they returned from an expedition to some Roman ruins near Aylesbury. Seeing powerful, rakish Buckingham holding her sleeping child ought to have been incongruously amusing. Anne had felt a catch in her throat and had had to look away before he could catch her staring mistily.

Not that he would have taken advantage somehow of her sentiment. He had been true to the word he'd given her the day after he had kissed her beneath the quarter moon. He had not made a single unsettling overture since then.

She had tested him on that avowal, too, though not by design. Buoyed by his assurance that he would not desert Alex and Nell, whatever might happen, she had not hesitated to go alone with him to his study. The moment he had closed the anteroom door, however, a dozen doubts had assailed her, and she had braced herself for some sly trick. But Buckingham had only shown her the painting, a beautiful thing of the Madonna and Child, and had talked about da Vinci's technical expertise, how well he drew, how smoothly he applied his paint, and so on. They had talked about other Italian artists, and of the different schools of Italian art, and in the end she had stayed with him two hours.

Anne tied the ribbons of her straw bonnet beneath her chin. The thing was old and wilting, but she supposed the fish wouldn't mind that she'd not had a new bonnet in years, and at least Buckingham would not think she was regretting the distance he'd kept as scrupulously as he had that day in his anteroom. Not once in the thirty or more days since had he laid his hands on her. Not once had he taken advantage of a warm, dark night to talk of Peter and then to kiss her witless. Not once had he watched her with one of those hot, intense looks that stripped her of what she wore, or penetrated it at least. There had been interest in his eyes on occasion—he was not a monk—but he hadn't seared her with it.

Anne even looked forward to dinner now. Buckingham still entertained Hetty with *on-dits* about members of the *ton,* which Anne admitted amused her as well, but now he and Anne discussed books and plays and especially the opera, for she had seen a great deal of opera in Italy. They even discussed Sisley, for Anne had discovered a fascination for the complicated workings of the estate, and Buckingham seemed pleased to explain it all to her.

"I won the toss, Mama! I get to hold the reins on the way to the Trent."

Anne smiled at the unnecessary announcement. As Buckingham and the children were already in the trap, waiting for her when she came outside, she could plainly see Nell ensconced in the duke's lap. Alex was settled in the back with the fishing poles and a hamper Mrs. Goodwin seemed to believe necessary for even the shortest excursion.

"I hope I haven't kept you waiting." Anne looked to Buckingham as Tucker ran forward to help her into the trap. Oddly, though it had been nearly two months since they had first met, and half that time he had been on the most circumspect behavior, his looks still had the power to steal her breath. She had only to look up and take in his black hair and startlingly blue eyes and her pulses raced—if anything she reacted more strongly, perhaps because she knew what to anticipate.

His teasing voice interrupted her reverie. "For your company, Annie, we were pleased to wait. Particularly as, you see, Cook swears she will not prepare anything for supper but our fish, and adding another fisherman to our party means we will be less likely to go hungry."

Anne laughed, but Alex looked around earnestly at her. "If I catch a big one and you do not, Mama, I'll share mine with you—although I'll want to give a bit to Tristan, too."

"I caught two last time, Mama," Nell said, though she did not spare a glance from the little-used lane that led to Buckingham's favorite fishing hole. "But I thought this time I would see if Isolde liked fish, too."

"I understand, Nell, but hopefully I shall be able to catch my own dinner," Anne told her. From the corner of her eye she was watching Buckingham smile, as he invariably did when the children mentioned the lovers' names they'd given to a cat and a dog.

"Of course Isolde will eat fish!" Alex exclaimed from the back. "Cats love fish, and besides, Isolde eats anything. She ate your ribbons, Nell."

"It was Tristan chewed my ribbons," Nell protested. "Isolde only made a hole in Mama's gloves."

Buckingham glanced at Anne, his brow lifted. "Only?"

Anne shrugged. "They were old and beginning to fray."

The trap bounced over a rut. As the seat was narrow, and Nell was sitting between Buckingham's legs, his thigh jostled Anne's. She looked away from him to the park and tried to appear as unaware of the contact as he seemed to be. But it was nearly impossible. It happened again and again, and each time all Anne could seem to think of was Buckingham's warm, hard thigh touching hers.

Strangely, the more Buckingham treated Anne as a friend, the more she was aware of him as a man. No, that wasn't quite right—she had been aware of him from the very moment she'd stepped into Hetty's doorway and taken note of him from the corner of her eye. But now that her guard was down, her awareness of him seemed only natural, no longer a cause for dismay. For example, she stayed where she was then, rather than make some excuse to ride in the back with Alex. She knew it was because she had never experienced such light, playful pleasure with a man before. Her mother had died before she was old enough to receive callers, and the jaded, expatriate world to which her father had fled had offered nothing at all so innocent or so light as being keenly aware of a man's inadvertent touch.

At the river, Buckingham lifted Nell down from the trap and left Anne to swing down by herself, quite as she had come to expect that month. As Alex and Nell had had their fishing lessons the duke supervised while they each baited their own hooks with bacon, and then he placed one of them on either side of the little cove that he vowed was filled with fish. The little river that meandered through Sisley, the Trent, was high, for there had been a good deal of rain in the last week, and so Buckingham cautioned the children to keep back from the edge of the bank. They nodded their understanding, but turned their attention to their lines so quickly, Anne thought it wise to repeat what the duke had said.

Then it was her turn to be readied. Buckingham was smiling at her, and all Anne could think of was how strong his smile was, and how his eyes seemed to shine when he smiled. He told her he thought she would find fly fishing more fun than the more inactive fishing the children were doing. She nodded gamely, though she'd no idea what he meant.

Anne did enjoy watching him tie her fly, though. His fingers were long, and she'd never noticed how graceful yet sure they were.

"It isn't difficult," he said, rising. "You hold your line here and flick your wrist." Buckingham repeated the movement, landing his fly in midstream. Anne noticed how solid his wrist was. While his hands were fine-boned, his wrist was strong. "Now you try."

He smiled encouragingly as he handed her the pole, and she smiled back, though she realized she hadn't the faintest idea what he had done. Even the pole seemed utterly foreign to her. He'd lifted it up, she thought, and did the same, only to have her line arc backward overhead and catch on a branch above her.

Both of Anne's generally endearing children hooted uproariously and Buckingham grinned. She laughed, too, but she was thinking that his grin was beguiling because of the way it lifted his mouth at the corners.

After the second time Buckingham had to tug Anne's fly from a tree limb, he changed his teaching approach. Placing himself behind her, he wrapped his hand over hers. To steady himself, he was obliged to hold her waist, but whereas before he might have wrapped his arm around her waist, now he touched her as lightly as possible, laying no more than the tips of his fingers on her hip.

"Now then, this is the motion," he said, as he lifted the pole and snapped his wrist. Anne watched the line arc over the river with a complete sense of unreality. The warmth of his body enveloped her. She was intensely aware of his fingers balanced so gently on her hip. She could feel the firm pads of each one through the muslin she wore and had an almost overwhelming desire to sag back against his chest and let him trail the heat that had pooled just beneath them up to her waist and . . .

"There, that's better."

His breath was soft and warm on her neck, and afraid he would hear how hard her heart was beating against her chest, Anne made herself move away from him. "Actually, I think I would enjoy watching you do this more than I wish to do it myself," she said, not looking at him. "As it is my first time, I'd be content with the easy fishing the children are doing."

When he nudged her shoulder, she nearly jumped. Buckingham smiled as if nothing were out of the ordinary, as if her cheeks were not flushed and as if her eyes were not uncertain, even shy. "Try once more," he said. "You'll get it."

Anne made a supreme effort to concentrate. He had said to pull down the line, flick the wrist . . . her line shot out in a flat trajectory and hit the water with a splat. Alex and Nell cried, "Better!" and Anne heard Buckingham say, "Good. Once more now." That time, she made the line arc, and promptly felt such an absurd sense of accomplishment, she laughed. Buckingham joined in.

She turned to him, eager to share her triumph, and saw something more than laughter in his eyes, something soft. Her heart fluttered, but in a moment the look was gone and Buckingham moved away. Gathering his fishing pole and bait, he chose a spot on a point just beyond Nell for his fishing place.

When Buckingham shed his coat, Anne glanced down the bank, unable to resist the sight of him in his shirt. The thin, white lawn hugged him tightly from the broad line of his shoulders to the much narrower line of his waist. She could see his muscles ripple lightly as he threw out his line.

Alex, mercifully, kept her from staring until she was caught. He cried out excitedly that he'd a fish on his line. Buckingham turned back with a grin to remind him to snag the fish by jerking sharply on his line. Doing so at once, Alex begged his mother to lay her pole down and bring him a net that was lying near her.

They looked very much alike, Trev thought, their glossy dark heads nearly touching and their faces lit with the same vivid smiles as they exclaimed delightedly over the sizable perch Alex had caught. Trev studied them, secure in the knowledge that Anne was too distracted to discover him. Over the last weeks, one of the unexpected pleasures he'd discovered was her laughter. She hadn't laughed half as much when she had been wary of him, and he hadn't realized how satisfying the rich, gurgling sound could be.

A wry grin quirked his mouth. Were anyone who knew him well to learn that he had contented himself for weeks with nothing more than a woman's laughter and the most cursory touches, whoever it was would doubtless protest that he'd been replaced by an imposter. Ah, but then, he thought, his grin deepening, no one would credit that he'd found an almost sensual pleasure in the pain of restraint. Certainly, he would have dismissed the notion as absurd before. From ignorance, of course. He'd rarely—in truth, perhaps never—been denied something he wanted.

But there was, truly, an almost exquisite pleasure to be found in holding his body inches from hers. When he'd given her the fishing lesson, he could have pressed himself against her. He had wanted to. It was agony to feel her warmth, smell the light lavender scent she wore, and not take her into his arms. He had felt the tension building in her. She was as aware of him, he knew. He had seen the pulse beating hard in the hollow of her neck, and it had been all he could do not to put his mouth over that pulse, bury his head there, pull her softly flaring bottom hard against him . . .

Trev had no notion how lost he was in his thoughts until a wild cry sent them scattering. Jerking around almost as if he were coming out of a dream, Trev saw Nell teetering on the edge of the bank, then realized it was the bank, itself, that was teetering. Evidently she'd been going to her mother and brother and had forgotten his warning not to walk along the river's edge.

The bank had been undercut by the rushing water of the river, and before he could move, it caved in. Everything seemed to happen with dreamlike slowness after that. Trev heard Anne scream, saw Alex shoot to his feet and lunge forward, prepared to plunge into the water after Nell. Anne caught him, but Trev didn't see what happened after that. He was plunging down the broken bank, sliding, searching the muddy froth, his heart in his mouth. When Nell's head bobbed to the surface, he launched himself forward, fighting the fierce current to get to her. Light as she was, the water swept her away, but he made a desperate grab and just caught her leg. Gripped by panic, Nell flailed frantically, as if she wished to throw him off, but he managed to pull her to him and heave her onto the bank. Then grabbing a tree root, he surged out after her.

Anne was there before Trev could do more than turn Nell carefully and push her soggy hair away from her face. "There, there, pumpkin. There, there. You'll be all right, thanks to his grace," Anne soothed, falling to her knees by the child. Although her voice was carefully reassuring, her expression was not so brave when she looked to Buckingham—Anne clearly needed reassurance herself.

Though the little girl was retching and whimpering, he did not think her badly hurt. "She swallowed a good bit of the Trent, but I believe she is more frightened than hurt," he said. Anne's bonnet had slipped off, and hung around her neck, dangling in her way. Trev untied it for her and tossed it aside, adding, "I'll fetch the blanket Mrs. Goodwin sent with us for our picnic. When we have her wrapped, we'll take her home."

Anne nodded, and looking up at Buckingham gratefully, suddenly realized that he was as wet as Nell. His shirt lay almost transparent against his chest and his buckskins were scarcely decent. Immediately, she lifted Nell into her lap and buried her head in her daughter's wet hair. Clearly, she was, indeed, a candidate for Bedlam, if she could be distracted by Buckingham when Nell was trembling in her arms.

When Trev returned with the blanket, he saw Alex was standing behind his mother. His first instinct was to remove the boy, for he was certain he'd have been shooed away had his sister been hurt when they were children. Before he could, though, he heard Anne say to Nell, "You are breathing more easily now, pet. Have you the strength to reassure Alex? He is very worried about you."

Nell turned her head and, seeing her brother, lifted her hand as much as her strength would allow. The eagerness with which the boy clasped his sister's hand took Trev by surprise. He knew he would not have been as anxious about his sister at the same age. But then he reminded himself that at five, he had not yet known of death as Alex did.

"Cousin Trev told you to stay where you were, Nellie!"

Surprisingly, Alex's scolding did not adversely affect Nell. She nodded solemnly and managed to rasp out in a voice made hoarse by retching. "I forgot. I wanted to see your fish, Alex."

"It is very large," the boy reported without bravado. "But I'd have brought him to you. Shall I get him now?"

Nell nodded again and Alex bounded off. Unfortunately, he bounded directly onto his mother's hat, squashing it flat. Upset as he was already, the boy gave a strangled cry and looked as if he would burst into tears.

Anne promptly wrapped her arm about his waist and pulled him down beside her and Nell. "It is an old but very tough hat, my love. Hand it to me, and I'll show you how resilient it is. Watch," she instructed when Alex, sniffing, had handed her the battered, muddy bonnet. She promptly thrust her fist into the crown. The straw held, to Trev's surprise, and lifted into something approximating its original shape. Her fingers flying, Anne went on to straighten the brim. "See?" She held it out before Alex, restored to the extent that it was wearable, if only her children and very indulgent friends were present. "It was an old thing, Alex, and good only for fishing expeditions, for which it will still do nicely. Now, go and get your fish and we will take Nell to a nice tub and bed."

Chapter 12

At Sisley, Betta gave Nell a warm bath, and Mrs. Goodwin, herself, brought the child some warm milk and biscuits. Anne changed out of her muddied clothes and, joining them, found their ministrations had worked well. Nell had fallen fast asleep. Leaving Betta to sit with her, Anne went to Alex's room. He was sitting on his bed, his hands in his lap, looking at nothing. He seemed so small and forlorn, Anne fought an urge to swoop him up in her arms, but he had been taking a great deal of pride in his manliness of late—Buckingham's influence, no doubt—and so she only held out her hand to him and suggested they go for a walk.

From the window of the sitting room she shared with Anne, Hetty caught sight of mother and son walking together just as a knock sounded at the door. To her pleasure, it was Buckingham, who'd answered her summons. He had been to the nursery to check on Nell and had come to assure her the child had suffered no serious harm.

"I thank you for taking the trouble to come and reassure me yourself, your grace. I am relieved—and not only for Nell. They've all borne enough."

Hetty gestured with a nod to the window, and Trev walked over to stand beside it, looking out at the scene below. He found Anne and Alex at once. Another knock sounded, but he did not take his attention from the gardens. "I hope you don't mind," he called to Hetty over his shoulder, "but I took the liberty of ordering tea to be brought here."

"Not at all. I am delighted," she assured him, though she guessed he'd thought Anne would be there and had ordered the tea for her.

As Hetty fussed with pouring him a cup of tea, adding the single lump of sugar he liked, Trev watched Anne and Alex slowly make their way toward the rose arbor. Anne was holding the boy's hand, and seemed to be talking to him. Trev could not know precisely what she was saying, but he knew them both well enough by now to know that whatever it was, Anne said it calmly and directly while Alex listened carefully.

Trev was right. Anne was quietly talking about what had happened, reassuring him that Nell had not been seriously injured. She explained that the fear Nell had experienced had drained her and that was why she'd fallen sound asleep. Tomorrow, Anne assured him, Nell would be up and about, perhaps even riding, then allowed him a few minutes of silence to digest what she'd said and ask any questions he might have. When Alex said nothing, she took both his hands in hers and said, "I admit I feel rather drained as well, because I was afraid, too. Indeed, I don't think I have ever been more afraid than when I saw Nell slip into the river."

For a long minute more, Alex still made no response, until, without warning, he flung his arms around her waist, sobbing in a strangled voice, "I thought she would die, Mama!"

Watching from the window, Trev felt something tighten in his chest. He had told Anne no more than the truth a month before. The children were a breach in her defenses and, at first, though he'd liked them well enough in an offhand sort of way, and had fully intended to fulfill his obligations to them as their cousin, he had seen them as little else. But he'd spent a great deal of time with them in the last month, and to his surprise, Alex and Nell had proven to him that they'd their own pleasures to provide. It was gratifying to teach them some new skill. They were game to try anything and listened attentively. They also had a straightforward, unvarnished view of the world that amused him, but it was the moments when they showed their affection for him that he cherished most: Alex taking his hand one day in the woods, his clasp trusting and feeling unexpectedly good; or Nell climbing into his lap in the carriage only last evening and falling asleep there. He'd not been able to meet Anne's eyes, he'd felt so absurdly pleased.

Hetty came to stand by him at the window, and seeing Alex sobbing with his head buried in his mother's skirts, gave a murmur of approval. "It will do Alex good to cry. He's so very attached to Nell and protective of her, though she's the elder."

Trev watched Anne lift the boy into her arms and carry him out of sight into the rose arbor where there was a bench. She did not stagger, though his weight had to be a struggle for her, for she was slender despite her curves. "Alex would have jumped into the river after his sister, had Anne not caught him," he told Hetty. "Have the children always been as attached to each other?"

"Anne says they have," Hetty replied, reminding Trev that she had not been with Anne in Italy. His jaw tightened, as he considered afresh what it must have been like for her after Peter died. She had had no one but two small children. She never spoke of it, but now that he knew her, he could almost feel the desperation she must have experienced, and the loneliness. If she had hurt the de Montfortes, marrying Peter though he was so far above her, the family had its sins to account for as well.

"I suppose living in a foreign land accounts for some of their closeness," Hetty mused idly. Glancing up, she saw the grim line of the duke's jaw, and having no way to read his thoughts, supposed he was thinking of Nell's mishap. Brightening her tone, she added, "But Nell will be fine, as soon as she's rested. She is a tender little thing, but she's been influenced enough by Anne that she has some spirit, too."

"Hmm. She's fortunate in the mother she drew," Trev agreed.

Hetty did not remark his odd wording. She was far too pleased by the sentiment he expressed, and a look of considerable satisfaction flickered across her face just as they saw Alex come racing out of the rose arbor. "Now then," she said, feeling doubly pleased, "Alex appears none the worse for wear. A few tears and his mother's comfort and he's as good as new."

Trev agreed, but propped against the windowframe, a cup of tea in his hands, he waited to see Anne emerge. When she still had not followed the boy after a few minutes, Trev abruptly begged Hetty's pardon and exited the room. He did not explain where he was going, but she knew and her satisfaction became a broad smile indeed.

In the rose arbor, Anne stared into the distance. Her arms were stiffly braced by her sides, her hands curled tightly around the edge of the bench. She neither smelled the roses around her nor heard the soft, lazy drone of the bees attending them. Alex had recovered well after shedding his tears. She wished she could shed some and have the same result. But her tears seemed to have turned to lead in her chest. She couldn't even move, much less cry.

She could still see Nell falling into the water, her auburn head disappearing from view. Over and over she saw it, and when she closed her eyes to obliterate the dreadful sight, she saw poor Mary Redvers. It had been summer then, an Italian summer and stiflingly hot. Unable to sleep for the heat, Anne had been up, bathing her neck and face with tepid water, when there had come a banging on her door. She had roused Betta and the two of them had gone down together to find Peter there. Her father had been dead six months, and Peter had already asked Anne to marry him several times. She knew he fancied himself her savior and had refused him every time; that night she nearly slammed the door in his face, assuming he was drunk and had come only to importune her again, but something in his face had stayed her.

"Dear God, Anne!" he'd cried, and then to her astonishment had buried his face in his hands. Behind him in the street was a carriage. Anne had looked to it, but could see nothing in the dark. Finally Peter had gathered himself and haltingly told her the miserable story. He had had an affair some months before in England. The woman had meant nothing to him. He had told her that, Anne supposed, in the belief that she would want to have been his only love. Still, whatever his lack of feeling, the woman had conceived and at a time when her husband had been away. When he had learned of his wife's condition, he'd gone into a rage. Terrified for herself and her child, the woman had fled the house. Unlike Peter, she had been very much in love, and gathering what few valuables she could with the help of a maid, had set off to find him and throw herself into his arms. Her search had taken her the full five months she'd had left of her pregnancy, for Peter had visited several cities on the continent, and Mrs. Redvers had been slowed by her condition. She had gotten to Rome a few days before and only found Peter that evening. He had taken one look at the flea-infested rooms that were, by then, all she could afford, and brought her away with him. It was a generous act, but as was often the case with Peter, he had not considered carefully what he would do beyond it. He could not take her to the rented rooms he shared with several other young men; nor did he wish to take her to a hotel where he might be seen with her. He never explained why the second option was impossible—Anne never knew for certain whether he wanted to spare Mary Redvers scandal or himself the wrath of her husband. At any rate, Mary was alarmingly close to her time, miserably distended, pale, crying with fear, and all he could think to do was bring her to Anne.

The poor woman never left the bed Anne made up for her that night. She went into labor in the early hours of the next morning, struggled pitifully in her weakened state for a day and a night, and then died quietly an hour after Nell had been born. But she survived long enough to grip Anne's hand—not Peter's—and to beg her with surprising intensity to care for her child. Anne had returned the grip of that pale hand with equal force and sworn, tears streaming down her face, that she would cherish the child. Indeed, in some strange way, she already felt as if Nell were hers, for she had been with Mary for the entire labor, including the birth, as Mary had clung to her so desperately. With a tiny baby to care for, she finally gave Peter the answer he desired. A week after Mary Redvers was buried, Anne married Nell's father, because he swore he could support them and because she had sworn to care for Nell to the best of her abilities.

Anne buried her head in her hands. Dear God, but it did seem that everyone around her withered and died. Her mother, her father, her husband, even Mary Redvers—all were gone. And Nell had nearly followed them. She could not have borne it.

Trev found her like that, with her head bowed. The faint tightness he'd felt in his chest when he had watched her and Alex from the window was nothing to what he felt now. For a moment, he did not move at all, paralyzed by a very real fear that he would jerk her up into his arms.

Anne sensed his presence, though, and lifted her head from her hands with a start. Her eyes were dark with strain, her expression drawn, but Trev did not think he would ever forget what happened then, when she saw him, for her expression softened at once.

"What can I say to you?" she asked, eyes so wide and shadowed.

"You needn't say anything, Annie."

"But you saved Nell's life," she said in a ragged voice that tore at him.

He could not keep himself from holding out his hands—or for holding his breath for the second it took Anne to accept his offering. She rose from the bench to slip her hands into his.

It wasn't until she felt Buckingham's hands upon hers that Anne realized how much she'd wanted to touch his solid warmth. Nor could she have imagined that that small touch would not be nearly enough. It seemed to her later that she never stopped, but came off the bench and straight into the strong circle of his arms.

"She nearly died."

It was no more than a muffled sob, for Anne had buried her head against Trev's hard chest. He held her tightly, and lowering his head, kissed the top of her silky head. There was nothing he could say. Had Nell gone under a second time, it was likely she would have drowned. He put his hand on the bare skin at the nape of her neck and began to knead it.

That sure touch where she was somehow vulnerable, broke some dam in Anne. Before she even realized she would, she began to cry.

"Shush now," Trev said softly, ruffling her hair with his breath. "It's all right, Annie."

"But for how long?" she asked, sniffing miserably. "You'll not be there in the future to save her, and she'd have died but for you."

Trev leaned back and caught Anne's tear-streaked face between his hands. "You do not truly believe you'd have failed Nell, do you, Annie of the fiercely maternal spirit?" Using his thumbs, he wiped away the fat tears on her cheeks, but though his touch was gentle, the look he gave Anne was intent. "You'd have jumped in after her. I know it, if you do not. If you couldn't swim, you'd have caught a log, or you'd have made yourself swim. You would have, Annie. You would never have failed her."

Anne couldn't have said whether she believed him or not. But she couldn't doubt that he believed in her, and when he lowered his head to kiss her, it seemed the most natural thing in the world for her to lift her face to him.

Trev kissed her to comfort her. He kissed her, even, to underscore his respect for her dedication to her children. But the moment her lips softened beneath his, all the desire

he'd held in check for weeks flooded swiftly through him.
Giving succor flew out of his mind as he felt her yield.

Anne strained toward him, her heart swelling. She
could not seem to get close enough to him. And his
mouth. Dear God, it felt so good on hers, so hot and
searching and right.

Her heart was pounding. She wanted nothing more than
to . . . Dear Lord, what was she doing? Alex! A stab of
panic went through her. She wrenched her mouth from
Trev's and slammed her hands at his shoulders.

"No!" she cried. She felt undone, bewildered by the intensity of her response to him, feeling shamed somehow,
that she could feel this way in the midst of her fear and pain
for Nell, and even her sorrow for poor Mary Redvers. "I
was afraid and lonely!" Anne lashed out, stoking her anger
to erase the lingering traces of passion. "You've taken advantage of me when I am weak, you wretch!"

"Annie!" Trev tried to catch her hands. He had meant to
comfort her and now she was frantic.

Anne twisted wildly, *"No!"* she screamed, her voice
shaking. "I want to go."

He released her, and she ducked away, running out of the
arbor.

Trev balled his hands into fists and felt all the worse as
he'd nothing to hit. He had not meant to take advantage of
her. He had meant only to give her comfort. Damn and
damn again! He had not forgotten himself so since he was
a boy! But he had never waited a month to hold a woman
again, a woman he saw every day to boot. Surely she
would understand that. When she was not so distraught,
she would remember that it was she who had come into his
arms; that it was she who had been straining toward him,
her lips soft and trembling. She had put him to too great a
test. It galled him to admit it, but it was true, and when
she'd had time to reflect, she would acknowledge that and
perhaps forgive him. Surely she'd realize that he had not
thought to take advantage of her when she was weak. He
was a good deal more honorable than that and had certainly tried to prove it to her in the last month.

But he would give her time to gather her thoughts. Later, when they were both rested and calm, they would sort the problem out. He trusted she would want to. She wanted him. Of that, at least, he was certain.

A little later, Trev strode into the Hall, calling for Barrett. He was going to Melbury for the rest of the day and possibly the night, but first he stopped to write Anne a note.

Chapter 13

"Dear Anne,

"I regret upsetting you more than I can say. I came to you intending only to give you comfort. That more occurred is entirely my responsibility. You are a remarkably desirable woman, but I am a man full grown and capable, when I remember it, of control. Forgive me? I am afraid I will insist you do, but I shall give you until tomorrow to do it. For the nonce, I shall give you some peace by removing myself to Melbury for the evening."

"Yours" and a large "B" were scrawled at the bottom of the note.

Anne's mouth tightened. How like him that was: to "fear" he would insist upon her forgiveness. Every time she read the note, she wanted to rage. How blithe he was, how charmingly repentant.

After he had taken such advantage! He himself had remarked—lightly, of course—that her children were a weak spot in her defenses. And when he had seen that she was weak as a kitten with gratitude to him? He had acted instantly.

A small voice within insisted that he might, indeed, have come to the rose arbor with no other idea than to give her comfort. She doubted it, but it did not matter. His "comfort" had come to seduction in the end, whether he had planned it or not. Practiced rake! He had seized his opportunity soon enough. He must have known how the simple act of kneading her neck, his fingers touching her bare skin, loosening the tension she'd not even realized was there, would affect her. Dear Lord, even now she could not think of it without feeling shivery and odd.

She hated him. He had made her go to him. And she had!

Anne balled up the note and threw it hard against the wall. If he'd stepped through the breach, she'd welcomed him. Eagerly. She'd become exactly what he wanted her to be—malleable and aching with want. And he knew. He knew!

Anne's cheeks flamed, and she flung her hands up to cool them. But her fingers brushed her lips and she jerked her hands away as if her lips were still sensitive. The windowpane would do.

The pane was cool, for it was raining. Perhaps that was part of her problem—she hadn't been able to get out of the house. Imagine, she thought, smiling bitterly, that she should find Sisley confining. How quickly she'd become accustomed to luxury. And to Buckingham. Dear God, she had walked into his arms of her own will.

Anne rested her forehead against the windowpane. If only she'd been able to ride that morning. She could gallop now. She had never done anything more exhilarating, and looked forward to it every morning. When she rode with him, of course.

No. She simply could not think of him anymore. If she did not leave the room, she would uncrumple that note and read it again.

Betta had the children. After luncheon, she had volunteered to take them to the stables to curry their ponies. Anne half smiled, thinking that, for one who did not ride, Betta was often to be found in the stables. But thinking about Betta and Tucker called to mind Tucker's master. Abruptly, frustrated that all subjects seemed to lead to him, she decided it was time she, too, escaped the confines of the east wing. She would go to the library, she decided, for something meatier than the children's books she'd read all morning.

Anne had no fear of encountering Buckingham. She had heard nothing to suggest he had returned from Melbury. What had he been doing there overnight? Suddenly, the answer seemed all too clear. He'd claimed he was going to Melbury to give her peace, but perhaps what he'd really sought was a willing female for the night.

Anne tossed her head at the thought and stepped into the library, taking care to close the door behind her. Should Buckingham return, she didn't want him to take her by surprise.

He did, though, despite her precautions. She was halfway to the bookcases when she saw the pair of boots, casually crossed at the ankles, hanging off the end of a Roman couch. Her glance traveled the length of the couch to the arm, and there he was, sound asleep.

Hardly daring to breathe, she carefully shifted her weight on her feet, intending to move back toward the door. But her gaze wouldn't leave him. His hair was tousled. Gleaming black, it feathered across his brow. And his eyes were closed. Without their force and with the mussed hair, he looked . . . not boyish. He could never be that—his features were too strong and compelling, and he was still the most handsome man she had ever seen. But in sleep his mouth was relaxed, more sensuous even. . . .

Anne was not certain when Buckingham awoke. It was entirely possible he'd been awake several minutes, watching her through his lashes. All she knew for certain was that as she studied his mouth, she saw the corners lift.

"There you are," he said, eyeing her with a softness that might or might not have been a result of just waking. She stood still, watching him come to life. He stretched lazily and, despite every considerable reason not to, Anne's eyes drifted down along the hard, full length of him. "I wasn't certain when you would get here, but I thought on a rainy day you inevitably would." Levering himself off the couch, as if it were the most natural thing in the world for him to have settled down to nap while he awaited her, Buckingham·grinned. "Your expression suggests, my dear Annie, that you are one of those people who disapproves of naps, but I protest that I've reason. I met an old friend in Melbury yesterday, and one thing leading to another, I got little sleep last night, though I did manage to accomplish my aim. I found a gift for you."

Desperately determined to resist him and disturbed by the vivid image of him carousing the night away with a friend, Anne once more sought refuge in anger. "You needn't explain yourself to me, your grace," she informed him and watched with an unsteady burst of satisfaction as that too appealing grin faded abruptly. "I am sorry I interrupted your rest. I can well imagine how much you need it. As to a gift from you, I will not accept—"

He cut her off curtly, all the endearing sleepiness gone from his face. "I apologized to you. And I do not apologize often."

"I am so very honored by your exception in my case, your grace!" Anne's eyes flashed golden-green with her indignation. "But I cannot say I am much persuaded by the sincerity of your apology when you first insist upon forgiveness and then attempt to buy it with some little something from Melbury! Now, if you'll excuse me . . ."

She was pushing down upon the door handle when Trev slammed his hand against the door with such force that she jumped. He did not touch her, but Anne could feel every inch of him poised, taut with tension, over her.

"I kissed you. It's true." His voice was low but so mocking it sent a shiver down her back. "That is the shocking crime I've committed. But you welcomed that kiss. And that's the real rub, is it not? You responded as any woman would, and you are furious with yourself, but you won't acknowledge your part, dammit!" Buckingham's curse scorched Anne's ears, and she caught her breath, afraid she might touch him inadvertently and unleash the tension radiating from him. "You prefer to have me shoulder all the blame. I had thought better of you, madam! I had thought you more honest than that."

Trev paused, breathing hard. He wanted to shake the

starch out of her, but he couldn't be certain where he would stop if he laid hands on her. Even now, the burnished sheen of her dark hair cried out for the touch of his fingers. With a sudden oath, he pushed himself away from her. "Don't move!" he growled. He strode purposefully across the room to a chair near the window. Leaning down, he swept up a round box and, returning to Anne, thrust it unceremoniously into her hands. "It is not some little something from Melbury to buy your forgiveness. It is a cursed bonnet and a pair of gloves. And you will take them. I owe them to you. They are a replacement for the gloves ruined by the cat I gave Nell, and for the hat I ruined myself, when I carelessly threw it on the ground to be trampled and muddied. If you find them loathsome, you may give them to your maid. Every time she wears them, you can revel in how low your opinion of me is. Good day, Mrs. de Montforte. Don't let me keep you."

He flung himself about, dismissing her. Anne did not hesitate. She slipped from the room, the box held tightly in her arms, feeling as shaken as if she'd been the loser in a boxing match, and yet Buckingham had not laid a finger on her. He'd assaulted her only with home truths.

They had done their work, though. Somewhere in the middle of the scene, all Anne's fury had drained from her. Actually, he had spared her a few barbs, she admitted, flinching as she set the pretty pink hatbox carefully down upon her bed. He might have said he'd been a charming companion for weeks, attending to her children and her aunt with every consideration, and to her without once demanding a return. He could have even been so cruel as to point out that she'd hardly been aloof all that time, that, more than once, it had been she who found some paltry reason to reach out and touch him. He could not but have noticed.

Anne clenched her hands into fists, but she fought an urge to drum the frilly feminine hatbox. Damn him, he had been too noble even to point out that, had she resisted his kiss, he'd have stopped it. She had lashed out insultingly, but the worst he'd bitingly told her was that she had disappointed him.

Ah, but that little undid her. He had made her feel cowardly, less than a mature woman, though he'd said she had responded like any woman would to him. Those had been his words, but he'd meant like every woman did, no doubt. Whores and saints alike responded to him. She was no different. Anne grimaced at the box. She hated those other women, hated being found like them, though she supposed she could take comfort from the thought that at least he did not find her uniquely wanton.

No, he thought her unfair. Mean-spirited. Less than honest.

He'd never before dismissed her as if he didn't care to see her again. He had called her Mrs. de Montforte. Perhaps he would not call her Annie again. Perhaps he would even leave Sisley. The Season was nearly over, but he could join the *ton* in Brighton. He'd leave her in peace, her resistance noted, her conduct unblemished.

Anne sank down by the hatbox. The bed dipped with her weight, and the box slid toward her. When it bumped her thigh, she took it onto her lap but eyed it guardedly.

She wanted too much to know what he had picked out for her. It was not a good sign, nor that at the thought of his leaving Sisley she'd wanted to cry out. And had a brief vision of her life seeming as flat and dull as a glass of champagne left out overnight.

Anne bowed her head, resting it on the box. She wanted to look inside, and she wanted his good opinion again, and she wanted him to stay. She wished . . . she wished for the possible. She wished them to be friends again as they had been. She wished the torn fabric between them restored, she wished the alarmed clamor inside her silenced.

With a groan, Anne suddenly plucked at the ribbons on the box and carefully lifted off the first, smaller box beneath them, the one with the gloves. It was the bonnet she wanted to see, and lifting it out, bit her lip. Buckingham had struck a perfect note. The bonnet was lovely, and yet, it was not so elaborate that she was humbled, for it was of straw like her old one and meant for the country. That was all his concoction had in common with the other, however. While hers had been of coarse straw, unlined, flat-brimmed, and ornamented with a single ribbon that had been fitted through the crown to form the hat's ties, this one was of supple, fine straw and lined with a light rose-colored silk that narrowed at the sides to form the ties of the hat as well. The brim was nothing so boring as merely flat but dipped in the middle and flared slightly at the front sides to make a heart-shaped frame for her face. At the back, the brim had been cut high to leave room for the soft knot in which she generally wore her hair when she went outdoors. The final touch was the soft, fluffy ostrich plume waving on one side of the crown. Anne flicked it gently with a slender finger, then set the hat on her head.

It fit perfectly. Either Buckingham was lucky, or he had bought hats for females before. If she hadn't much question as to which was the more likely proposition, Anne was pleased to have Betta slip into the room and settle how she looked in his bonnet.

Betta did so unasked, for she clasped her hands together and exclaimed delightedly, *"Bella, signora. Ah, que bella!"*

Anne smiled, almost feeling beautiful, but the little maid's next words brought a very different expression to her face. "Do you go to the village with his lordship and the children, signora? His lordship did not say so."

Whitchurch was the tiny village but a few miles distant from Sisley. It boasted only a few shops, but in one sweets could be purchased and in another the kind of cheroots Buckingham sometimes liked after dinner. As a result, Buckingham took the children down whenever he and they wanted to get out of the house but inclement weather kept them from some more sporting outing.

"I have changed my mind," Anne said to her maid, before she could think better of her sudden decision. "When do they intend to leave?"

Betta gestured to the boy's frock coat and girl's tiny spencer hanging across her arm. "The duke sent me for these wraps."

"Is it raining still?"

Betta shook her head as Anne glanced distractedly at the window. "The children wish to take the curricle, and his lordship feared they might take chill from the damp air."

"Well, then, perhaps I'll need my shawl. Do you wish to go as well, Betta? There should be room for you on the seat of the curricle."

Betta turned, a saucy grin warming her somewhat plain face to prettiness. "*Si*, signora."

Anne chuckled, causing Betta's flush to deepen. "So Tucker *is* driving. Well, let's be off and not keep . . . the gentlemen waiting."

She had almost said "our gentlemen," a telling slip of the tongue. Whatever Tucker might be to Betta, Buckingham was certainly not Anne's. Nor would he ever be. A friend, though, he could be that—if she had not completely put him off by blaming him for being ruled by the same desire that had ruled her. He had been so very good for a month, leaving it to her entirely to say what she wanted from him and when. She had given him no credit for that, frightened by the overwhelming desire she'd felt. But that desire was for her to manage. She'd know now not to go into his arms for any reason . . . unless—no, she could only have him for a friend. That was all.

Chapter 14

Anne stopped to ask Hetty if she wished to go into Whitchurch, too, but the damp day did not suit Hetty, and she was immersed in one of the penny gothics Buckingham had purchased for her the last time he had gone down to the the village. She was not so engrossed in her book, however, that she did not notice Anne's new bonnet. It was, in fact, the first thing upon which she commented.

Anne was pleased that she could hold her aunt's twinkling gaze steadily as she made her explanation. "Buckingham got it for me to replace my straw bonnet after he tossed it upon the ground for Alex to step on and ruin."

"Well, it was kind of his grace to replace your bonnet, and I must say he did choose one perfect for you," Hetty replied, still looking rather arch.

"Would I be so very hard to adorn, then?" Anne teased, but when her aunt's mouth pursed in an unhappy line, she patted Hetty on the cheek. "The bonnet is no mark of special favor, Hetty. He knew I was upset about Nell and wished to cheer me. It was thoughtful of him, but no more. We are not acting out one of your penny gothics for you."

"No, perhaps not," Hetty allowed reasonably. "Still, the duke does think well of you, Annie. You know he does. Lud, he has missed the last half of the Season, and though he may like Alex and Nell and me very well, I doubt he has stayed so long at Sisley on our account. Don't you think it is time to tell him of the connection you have to Edgemoore and ask if he will not intercede with his uncle for you? I admit I am beginning to feel as if we are deceiving him."

"No, Hetty, I don't think I shall be forthcoming yet." Anne looked away, distracted. Hetty had picked a poor time to voice her changed opinion. Anne's mind was half on Buckingham, wondering if he would leave Sisley, or ask her to do so. "I still do not know whether Lord John will be more hateful or less when he is fully recovered. If he is more, I may still need an obscure corner in which to hide."

"You cannot believe that Buckingham would allow his uncle to abduct Alex!"

"It is his uncle I do not know, Hetty. And the man who wrote that ugly letter stripping his son of all family could possibly abduct Alex."

"But Annie, I am certain Buckingham would not allow him to do such a thing!"

"I agree," Anne said slowly, "but that is only so long as he is here. And though he has stayed a good while, I've no guarantee he means to stay until the matter with his uncle is settled."

"But you will have to tell Lord John eventually, I am certain," Hetty said. "And what will Buckingham think then?"

"That I had good reason for what I did. Hetty," Anne said, a warning note in her voice, "there is no reason for Buckingham to think anything of my connection to Edgemoore. For example, it will not prompt him to decide I am marriage material. No, you must listen to me, or you will be sorely disappointed. Buckingham will not ask for my hand, regardless. For one, as he has, himself, said to you, he has no desire to marry yet. But even did he discover such a desire overnight, I'd not be a candidate for the position of Duchess of Buckingham. I've too uncertain a past. Papa's house in Italy was only a shade above disreputable, and after he died, I lived alone, though I was only seventeen. I've never had a Season, Hetty. Good Lord, I've never even been presented at court! No, he could not want me for his duchess. Be content, please, that we . . . ah, may be friends."

Hetty bit her lip, lest she observe that an appearance at court could be arranged easily enough. It was obvious to her that Anne was in an uncertain mood. The color in her cheeks indicated excitement, but the tense grip she had on her reticule suggested a goodly degree of anxiety. Perhaps she was afraid to hope for so much. Hetty could understand, but not being similarly afflicted, she meant to return to the subject at another time. She thought it very possible Buckingham would marry Anne if he knew of her mother's connections. It was obvious they were attracted to each other, and he had gone off so readily to give her comfort in the rose arbor. Yes, she would harbor her hopes, but she would not belabor Anne with them just then.

The brief visit with Hetty had not calmed Anne. While her aunt was entertaining, not so secretly, hopes of her marrying Buckingham, she was worrying whether he was even speaking to her. And what would he think of her in the bonnet? Would the effect disappoint him? Had he even considered how she would look in it? Or, perhaps he would not even look at her—or care what the effect was, if he did. Perhaps he would be too angry, still. Perhaps he would dismiss her with a freezing look and say as she was going, he would not. Perhaps he had already taken himself off to his study.

"Mother! Cousin Trev said we might stop at the Hart and Hare for tea. Please, may we?"

"Mama! You've a new hat. It's very pretty."

Anne smiled as Alex and Nell called out to her from the curricle. At least she had one of her answers. Buckingham was there. He was leaning back against the carriage, presumably waiting for her. Also, presumably, he was watching her, but she could not have said for certain. She hadn't yet summoned the courage to look to him.

"I've no objection to stopping at the Hart and Hare," she told Alex. "And I think the hat is very pretty, too, Nell. His grace made me a gift of it."

"Now you have two! The one I squashed for fishing and this one for other times."

In another situation, Anne might have chuckled at Alex's pragmatic tone. But she'd chosen that moment to look at Buckingham.

His eyes were so blue. They gave her the same start they always did. "Thank you, your grace," Anne said, registering that at least there was not freezing disdain in his eyes. "It was very thoughtful of you to bring me another hat. And your choice is lovely."

He kept her waiting a minute as he flicked his gaze over the pretty, plumed concoction. Anne was not aware she'd caught her breath until he looked back at her and she saw the smile teasing the corners of his mouth. "The hat is nice. But I should say it is the wearer who is lovely. As for the two together . . . it is a very generous reward."

Relief flooded her, making her giddy. She was afraid she was going to grin stupidly at him. They were friends again. He had not nursed his grudge. "You are very kind," she said softly, aware of the children's eyes upon her.

Perhaps it was the children who kept Buckingham from doing more than holding her gaze as he inclined his head and held out his hand to help her into the curricle. Anne took it, and looking up saw that Tucker and Betta were settling themselves on the curricle's seat, while Nell and Alex were looking down at something on the seat between them. Seeing the others were distracted, Anne hesitated, looking swiftly back to Buckingham again. What she had said was not nearly adequate, and meeting his blue eyes, she added simply, "I am sorry. And I am grateful you are as magnanimous as you are."

Trev looked down into her so thoroughly chagrined green eyes and thought to himself he could not wait much longer for her to see her way into his arms. Knowing how she would react to his thoughts, were she to learn them, he couldn't help but grin. "If you really looked at yourself in that bonnet, Annie, then you would know that even had I been inclined, I could not have remained angry beyond the first sight of you. I didn't know a plume could be so tantalizing. Now up with you, or the children's game will be undone."

With that mysterious remark ringing in her ears, Anne took her seat in the carriage, but though she smiled at her children and wondered with half a mind what sort of game they played, with the other half, she wondered if a plume really could be tantalizing. And how.

"All right, Tucker. We are ready," Buckingham called to the young groom seated beside Betta, the reins in his hands.

With a flick of his wrist, Tucker started them off, and Anne's curiosity about the children's game was immediately satisfied. The slight lurch of the curricle brought a dark head nosing out of the folds of Nell's skirts.

"You are bringing Tristan?" Anne asked.

"He had such a good time in the stables, we thought he would enjoy the trip!" Alex explained with the brightly reasonable attitude that Trev had long marked as being not only exceedingly effective with adults, but even a cause for admiration on their part.

However, his mother was, as Trev had also had cause to note, made of stern stuff and not unacquainted with her son, besides. She frowned, whereupon Nell spoke up. "He would have been so lonely had we left him, Mama. And we decided that the trip would be broadening for him."

Trev could see the edge of Anne's soft mouth quiver. "You thought the trip would be broadening for him," she repeated as if she were giving Nell's remark serious consideration. "Well, I suppose it will be, if Tristan sees something in the woods and jumps out of the curricle to chase it. He'll learn a good deal about the woods . . ."

"But he won't jump out!" Alex exclaimed with excited assurance. "Cousin Trev fashioned a collar and lead for him."

Anne turned a slow gaze upon Trev, who made no effort at all to fight his amusement. "You fashioned a collar and lead for him?" she asked, and took his widening grin as a confession. "I see. Then I suppose you will be willing to carry Tristan, when he proves he is not old enough to follow us down Whitchurch's streets on a lead?"

"Actually, I had in my mind designated Tucker for that honor," Trev replied with lazy amusement. "The boy needs some way to prove himself, and Betta does adore the pup."

Anne could not fight her smile at that. He had not only noticed that there was something between Betta and Tucker, but he also was willing to abet it. "Well, I can see you have given this matter serious thought, and I suppose I should commend you rather than object. Besides," she added with an owlish look, "who would want a narrow dog?"

Buckingham laughed aloud. The children responded by immediately holding up Tristan so that he might admire the view over the side of the curricle. "He sees those ducks in the river!" Alex cried, seeming as proud as if his puppy had created the ducks.

"There are swans over here!" Nell pointed, and they both lifted the little dog that he might bark furiously again.

Anne rolled her eyes to Buckingham. His were warm with amusement and completely unrepentant. "At least it wasn't Isolde they wished to bring."

"I suppose you would have fashioned some sort of lead for her, too?"

"Well, I do like for my livestock to be broadened."

Anne laughed, shaking her head. "What a thing to say! I cannot imagine where she heard it. But I suppose you are right, and we are lucky."

"Oh, there's no question I, at least, am lucky."

From the way Buckingham was regarding her, Anne did not think he was referring to the kitten. Her breath seemed to catch in her lungs, but before she became so hopelessly entangled in his blue gaze that she couldn't look away, she made herself do it. Mercifully, there was a farmer's cart rattling along ahead of them, and she could alert the children to this new marvel for Tristan to see.

Trev watched her, noted the faint blush on her cheeks, and smiled to himself. She had given him credit earlier where none was due. He was not magnanimous at all. He had not given up his anger out of some nobility of spirit. The moment the door had closed behind her, most of it had vanished as completely as if it had never been. He hadn't wanted to send her scurrying away. He had wanted to watch her open his gift. She hadn't had enough new things in her life, and he had wanted to see her pleasure. Frustrated, he'd stalked from the library only to encounter Nell and Alex in the hallway, eager to tell him that they'd curried their ponies, that the puppy had gone with them and enjoyed himself in the stables, and that it was no longer raining.

The news of improved weather had triggered the thought that he could at least escape the house, and with the children before him, it had been natural to include them in the outing. He hadn't really set out to plot against Anne's defenses. He hadn't even instructed Betta to tell Anne they were going. But he had thought she might, and she had, with the result that here was Anne, penitent and flushed and beautiful in the bonnet he had known was the one the moment he saw it.

In Whitchurch, they completed their various errands and then adjourned to the Hart and Hare for tea. That is, Trev and Anne ordered tea. The children went off with Betta to the kitchens, where the inn's host, Mr. Dafney, ever eager to please his ducal patron, happily promised a dish of milk for Tristan.

In the silence the children's departure left behind, Trev shot Anne a considering glance. She was studiously settling her gloves in her lap, matching finger for finger in a way that indicated she was either a slave of excessive order or nervous. At the sight he gave up any thought of mentioning the kiss or their disagreement. He had thought to assure her that he had not taken her response to him as evidence of a depraved nature, and perhaps even to add that he had long since come to the conclusion that whatever she'd done in the past in the way of selling her favors, he believed she'd done it because she had had absolutely no other way to put food in her mouth. Indeed, he could have told her he found her unique among the substantial number of women he had known in that she had not once tried to secure something for herself from his considerable wealth. He had fully expected she would. He had not thought how, precisely, but he would not have been the least surprised had she mentioned offhandedly that her clothes were not quite up to Sisley's standards, or that she feared the servants would carry tales about Alex's pitifully turned out mother, or that, alas, she'd only a locket to adorn her bosom when she wore an evening dress.

The irony was, of course, that he'd have been delighted to heap her with jewelry and clothes and bonnets and anything else she wanted. But it wasn't the time to tell her that. She would truly bolt then.

Leaning comfortably back in his chair and catching Anne's uncertain gaze, Trev idly raised a subject that had nothing in the least to do with the two of them, or her position at Sisley, or Alex, or anything else difficult.

"For some reason or other, studying Betta's back this afternoon on our way into town, I was reminded of the offhand reference Alex made—it must have been a month ago—to your having saved her life. Would you care to tell me the story?"

"Oh, well," Anne murmured, sounding as surprised as she felt. She had been feeling on pins and needles about his bringing up the kiss and her subsequent tantrum, and she had another apology prepared. She was not so small as not to know she should give a long one, but she was small enough to be vastly relieved that she would be spared admitting, face to face with him, that she had not resisted, had even welcomed the kiss that made her senses swim. Or that she had a sneaking suspicion some of her anger was due to the knowledge that she could not have more.

She might have wished he had raised another topic for conversation than the one he had, but relieved as she was, Anne did not feel up to quibbling. "It is not much of a story, really. I was visiting Naples with my father and went for a walk just after dawn one morning. It was a respectable part of town, and I thought I would not encounter anything unpleasant, particularly as the hour was so early, but I heard cries coming from an alley, and when I investigated, I came upon a group of young Englishmen attacking an ob-

viously defenseless young Italian girl. She was Betta. She'd
only come to the city for work a few days before, and to
save the pitiful amount of money she had, had chosen to
sleep on a sack in the alley, where by the purest mischance
they had stumbled upon her. They were quite drunk, of
course," Anne said, her green eyes turning dark. "And
shouting encouragement to one another. That is how I knew
they were Englishmen and of the upper classes. I imagine
they believed, as some Englishmen abroad do, that the for-
eigners around them, particularly the poor ones, are little
better than dogs. They were vile, grabbing at her, tearing
her dress . . . and so on."

"What did you do?" Trev asked. His face had gone hard.
He could too easily imagine the scene, down to the vicious-
ness of drunken young men far from the constraints of
home. "They must have turned on you."

"They did." Anne nodded. "But I have a loud voice, and
I used it to scream fire in Italian."

Trev studied her a long moment, then said quietly, "Remind me to have you nearby if I need someone who thinks
quickly."

Anne inclined her head in acknowledgment not only of
his words but of the steady look in his eye. "I acted out of
necessity, of course, else I'd have had to stand by and
watch them . . . hurt her, and myself as well. Nor was I certain what the results would be, but mercifully, windows
were thrown open and heads popped out all down the alley.
The scene became almost comical then, for it seemed as if
twenty people shouted and screamed at once—not a few of
them venting their ire at me for waking them—but Betta's
attackers evidently did realize the game was up, for they
fled."

"You never learned who they were?"

"I did learn the name of one of them," Anne admitted. "I
saw him a month later in Rome at a reception at the English
embassy. I spoke to an assistant at the embassy about him,
but the man said there was nothing to be done, for while his
father had sent him from England for something he had
done here, the bully's father sent him sufficient funds that

he was able to bribe the Italian officials to look the other way, whenever he was in difficulties. In short, the man's father sent him to Italy to do as he pleased. I'd have insisted more strongly that something be done about him had I known he was making his own inquiries about me. I had not realized he recognized me, but he had, and, discovering my name and address, came to my home one night."

"What?"

Buckingham tensed, looking as grim as Anne had ever seen him. "Nothing calamitous occurred," she assured him hurriedly. "Peter and I had married a few days before, and Peter returned in time to chase him off."

Trev marked that even as a husband of only a few days, Peter had been away from home until late at night, but he didn't give a damn about Peter just then. "Did he hurt you?" he asked in a harsh voice.

Anne shook her head. "No, no not badly at all."

"Not badly at all! He did hurt you! What is the name of this fine specimen of English manhood?"

"It doesn't matter." Anne reached out to touch his hand lightly. "Truly, you needn't look so. He received his just deserts. He was killed in a brawl at a seaside tavern only a few months later. I am sorry to say I was glad to hear the news."

"Yes, I imagine you were. I know I am. I only wish I had been in the tavern."

Buckingham said it with a brutal harshness that hinted at a violence Anne would normally deplore. But not just then, not when the fierce light in his blue eyes blazed on no one's behalf but hers.

Chapter 15

"I think we've enough flowers now, Nell." Anne glanced down at the peonies and irises Nell had carefully placed, one by one, in her arms. "Any more and I shan't be able to carry them."

"But Cousin Trev said he likes peonies, Mother, and I have only a few."

"Ten, actually," was Anne's wry reply, but she relented when Nell's small mouth firmed into a stubborn line. "Very well. You may gather a few more, but remember, it will soon be time for tea and you wish to have the flowers in place to surprise his grace when he comes into the room."

"Why do you still call Cousin Trev his grace, Mama? He told Alex and me his family needn't be so formal."

Mercifully, Nell did not wait for her answer but turned away to cut another peony. Acutely aware of a sudden heat in her cheeks, Anne murmured, "Ah, well, strictly speaking, the duke is not my family. Oh, look, Nell, there are some blue irises to go with your purple ones."

Anne watched her daughter trot to the patch of stately blue irises with relief, thankful she had successfully diverted her. What had possessed her last night? she wondered faintly, her face flushing yet again. But she knew what had possessed her. She could see him clearly. Using—or nearly using—his pet name had been the least of

what had happened the night before. And she wasn't sorry.
Or even so embarrassed. God help her, it was excitement
more than anything that raised her color.

They had played cards. There was nothing unusual in
that, or that Hetty had gone up to bed while Anne stayed
on. She had done it often, though not since he had kissed
her again. He had done nothing like that in the week since,
but a barrier had been broken. They both knew how strong
was the attraction between them—and knew the other
knew.

Still, they did not speak of it outright, nor did they touch.
But Anne did remain in the library against all reason, taking a glass of Madeira while Buckingham sipped his
brandy. After a few hands of piquet, her partner had
abruptly declared the game boring.

"There's no thrill in this," he said flatly. "Even if I win, I
only win a matchstick—or two, if I'm lucky. Lud, Barrett
must have thought we were mad when we requested he
bring us a basket full of matches."

"Barret's no fool," Anne remarked, eyeing Buckingham
a little suspiciously. They had played for matchsticks before. "He understood quite well that I've nothing to wager
but your matchsticks."

Buckingham was lounging in his chair, looking very
comfortable, for he had removed his coat and his cravat as
the night was warm. She could see the smooth skin just
below his throat where his shirt lay open. She could also
see the gleam in his blue eyes as he murmured, "You do
have something to wager."

"What, for instance?" Anne demanded, wary of his tone.

"Your hairpins," he said.

"My hairpins?"

"Hmm." A smile edged up a corner of his mouth. "The
ones you have in your hair."

"You want me to wager the hairpins I have in my hair?
But—"

Buckingham was not interested in objections. "You
would wager as many or as few as you wished, and if you

lost," he explained in an ever so reasonable tone, "you would remove them."

"And if I win?" Anne asked, though she knew she should have rejected his suggestion out of hand.

Buckingham shrugged and she watched his shirt tighten over his broad shoulders, knowing, in turn, that he was watching her. "Hairpins cannot be worth more than a penny apiece. I'll wager pennies."

"So then, if I win, I win your pennies," Anne said, finding her voice a touch too low, "while if you win, you win my hairpins?"

"Yes," he said, and when she didn't answer, but regarded him steadily a long minute, he added softly, "I swear I won't touch it."

Anne's heart raced so that all she was aware of was the pounding inside her and the man seated across the small table from her. "You sound very confident, your grace," she said, and if all she could seem to think of was that he wished to see her hair down, still she was able to add, "Who is to say but that I may have enough of your pennies to buy a dowager's cap?"

He laughed. As well he might, she knew full well, for he had won already. When they resumed play, they were both more intent, and Anne realized he had played her like a trout. He had hidden his skill. For every hand Anne won, Buckingham won two, even three. Within an hour, her glorious dark hair was free, gleaming richly as it spilled down her back and her shoulders.

His voice oddly rough, he said, "If silk could be polished, it would look like your hair."

Anne could not reply at all, silenced by the heat in his eyes as he stared at the tumbling mass. She rose. She knew she must. She could scarcely breathe. True to his unspoken vow, Buckingham did not stir a muscle, only followed her every movement with heavy-lidded eyes.

As she reached the library door, some unconquerable impulse made her turn to face him. "You planned this, Tr . . . your grace."

He heard her slip, and something flashed in his eyes, but

all he said in that same rough voice was, "Yes." Then, after a heartbeat, he said quietly, "Swing all of it forward over your shoulder in a single fall."

He was not smiling or cajoling now. His expression appeared almost strained, as if he were angry—only his eyes burned with something far more potent than belligerence.

They burned with a heat Anne knew with an ungovernable thrill that she stoked. Fully aware what she did, her heart pounding at the danger of it, and the dizzying sweetness, Anne gave a flick of her head and sent her hair tumbling over her shoulder in a dark, burnished, rippling fall. She met his eyes for a brief, almost startled instant, and then she turned swiftly away, her hair flying out in a wide arc, whispering, "Good night," as she did. He said nothing, only stayed where he was, as if the sight of her hair all wantonly loose and flaring out had knocked the ability to speak or even move out of him.

"Now, I think we've enough, Mother."

Anne blinked, coming out of the intense memory only slowly. In her arms there were at least a dozen more peonies. She hadn't felt or seen Nell hand her even one. Just catching a groan, she realized she couldn't go on as she was much longer. She couldn't tease them both like that and expect nothing to happen. It already had. She'd taken down her hair for him, and she did not repent it.

"Yes, poppet," she said, burying her face in the fragrant flowers. "We've quite enough. Come along. Mrs. Goodwin said she'd leave us vases in the drawing room."

"Are you sure Cousin Trev will like flowers for his birthday, Mama?"

They had only found out a few days before from Mrs. Goodwin that Buckingham's birthday was that very day, a Thursday, and the children had been thrown into a quandry about what to do for him. Finally, Nell had recalled that he'd once said he could not live anywhere where there was not the magic of spring and flowers, and so had decided to decorate the drawing room with as many flowers as she could. For good measure, she had also pressed a columbine she had found in the woods, and made a frame Anne had shown her how to fashion from braided ribbons. Alex had also considered his cousin's tastes. "Cousin Trev likes to read. He must—he has ever so many books. I will write him a poem about fishing, as he likes to fish, too." The project was more easily decided upon than produced. Alex was even then laboring over his ode with Hetty's assistance.

Anne did realize something was unusual as she and Nell made their way to the south drawing room, where it had become the custom for everyone to gather for tea, but she assumed the muffled sounds merely came from an unusual number of servants, because she knew Mrs. Goodwin and the children had planned a particularly festive tea in celebration of the duke's birthday.

Had she and Nell met Mrs. Goodwin or Barrett, they'd have been forewarned, but as it was, the first Anne knew that unexpected guests had arrived at Sisley came when she and Nell strolled through the drawing room doors, their arms full of flowers and their clothes better suited to a flowerbed than a formal tea.

Anne pulled up short in the doorway, her gaze ranging in a startled blur over a sea of unfamiliar faces until at last she found Buckingham. He was at a table, pouring himself a brandy, unusual in itself, as he did not normally take brandy so early. Perhaps he felt her gaze, for he looked up suddenly. To Anne, it seemed an eternity before he reacted, but of course it was in the next moment that, fully taking in her and Nell holding their flowers, his cool, remote expression softened abruptly.

"Welcome, Spring," he said, almost smiling.

If Buckingham did not give a damn about all the pairs of unfamiliar eyes either trained upon Anne, or shifting from her to him, particularly after that greeting, Anne certainly did.

"I beg your pardon, your grace," she said, as formal as he had failed to be. "I did not know you had company. Nell and I had thought to . . . decorate the room."

"I wonder why," he teased, but then shrugged off the remark. "Well, at any rate, come in and divest yourself of your flowers and meet my guests."

"Oh, but we are not—"

Buckingham peremptorily interrupted Anne's excuses. "We understand you've been mucking about in flowerbeds, and that we've taken you by surprise. Anne de Montforte, this is my sister, Lady Monteith." Anne knew her eyes flared wide. His sister! She looked like the woman in the Reynolds portrait—elegant, attractive, and at that moment at least, distinctly cool. "And this is Mrs. Sunderland and her daughter, Miss Phoebe Sunderland, and over here is my neighbor, the ever-reprehensible Anthony, Lord Edwards."

"I say!" Lord Edwards objected, but he did so indolently and with a wide smile as he rose.

Buckingham went on without a pause, "Ladies and Tony, I should also like to present to you my young cousin, Miss Nell de Montforte."

Laying a gentle hand on Nell's back, Anne urged her to perform a curtsy, which she did quite satisfactorily, given the flowers she held in her arms. Buckingham's sister, who possessed her mother's light coloring but the de Montforte blue eyes, unbent enough to smile gently at Nell. But when she returned her gaze to Anne, her expression chilled again. Her thin nostrils flared slightly, and her eyes narrowed as if she appraised but with distinct displeasure. The other two ladies, the mother and daughter, did not even smile at Nell. Anne noted then that the girl, Phoebe, was of marriageable age.

"Ah, here is Mrs. Goodwin," Buckingham announced as Lord Edwards approached Anne and her daughter with the only friendly expression to be seen in the room. Buckingham kept his eyes on Anne. "She can take your flowers so that you may join us for tea."

"I would not dream of offending your guests by sitting down to tea in a dress with grass stains decorating the hem, your grace." Buckingham stood near his sister and Anne could plainly see Lady Monteith's delicate eyebrows lift, but she disregarded that look of surprise as firmly as she ignored Buckingham's suddenly lowered brow.

"But you will return, I hope!" Lord Edwards had reached

her. He was not so tall or attractive as Buckingham, but his smile was warm.

Anne assured him she would, returning his smile though she found it an effort. Then with a sweeping glance over the company, she murmured her excuses and left with Nell and Mrs. Goodwin.

"We won't have our party for Cousin Trev now, will we, Mama?" Nell asked in a small voice.

Anne had to admit that likely they would not. Nell looked crestfallen, and Mrs. Goodwin took it upon herself to suggest that his grace would appreciate having Nell's flowers in his study and bedroom just as much as he would have in the drawing room. "He'll see them even more often."

When Nell brightened, Anne sent Mrs. Goodwin a grateful smile, and the housekeeper leaned toward her to confide, sounding somewhat put out, "Lady Monteith's arrival was a surprise, I can tell you." As Mrs. Goodwin was no gossip, Anne guessed it was on account of the disappointment Lady Monteith had caused the children that she was moved to hint at her displeasure. "It seems her ladyship and her party were on their way to Grangley Hall, Lady Monteith's home in Leicestershire, when Mrs. Sunderland's companion fell ill. As Sisley was closer than either London or Grangley Hall, Lady Monteith thought it best to bring her here."

Anne noted the dryness in Mrs. Goodwin's tone. Evidently, the duke's housekeeper mistrusted the excuse. Even Anne knew Lady Monteith was forever parading marital candidates before Buckingham, but would Mrs. Goodwin have guessed that Lady Monteith had another reason for descending upon Sisley? Rather sinkingly, Anne thought it likely. The housekeeper was no fool, and Lady Monteith's appearance was clearly due as much to her determination to examine the disreputable widow ensconced with her brother, as it was to present Miss Sunderland to him.

Though she had little relish for the prospect, Anne did return for tea, dressed in an apple-green muslin that at least set off her eyes. It was nothing to the luxurious clothes of the other ladies, of course. They wore silk, and in Miss Sunderland's case, such a rich weave of silk her blue afternoon dress shimmered with silvery tones each time she moved.

In fact, the girl would have been attractive even without the sumptuous dress. She had light blond hair that had been coquettishly styled in fat ringlets pinned high on one side of her head. Her skin was as fair as her hair, her face delicately pretty, and her figure girlishly slender. Young and elegant to the tips of her dainty fingers, Miss Phoebe Sunderland looked a likely prospect for Duchess of Buckingham, and if she appeared to know it, judging from the flirtatious glances she slanted through her fluttering lashes at the duke—and the lofty angle of her nose whenever she happened to forget herself and stare at Anne—Anne forgave her. It was obvious her mother and Lady Monteith had primed her.

With distinctly varying degrees of subtlety, both ladies took advantage of every possible opportunity to turn the conversation to Phoebe. As Anne listened to Mrs. Sunderland proudly describe one of the many successes the girl had enjoyed that Season, she decided the tea was one of those salutary experiences that one may not much care for, but on account of which one, hopefully, improves.

The tea called her to order, showed her she had been drifting along for over a month as if there were no tomorrow. She had warned herself, but in truth had not paid herself the least heed. Not the least. The night before she had taken down her hair for Buckingham. She had wanted to do it. Her pulses had throbbed at the look in his eyes. And she had known where she was heading. She simply had not made herself face it. The tea forced the issue. She was on her way to his bed, unmarried. She had told Hetty he would not marry her. Now, looking at Phoebe Sunderland, she saw the truth of her words in the flesh. He would never marry a disreputable widow. He would wed Phoebe, or some other innocent, unblemished, delicately reared girl like her.

Anne would not forget the point, but neither did she care

to dwell upon it just then. She'd not keep her chin high if she did, and lifting it on the thought, found Lady Monteith regarding her. Caught, Buckingham's sister seemed to believe she had no choice but to acknowledge her brother's questionable guest in some way, though it was by then some quarter of an hour after Anne had slipped into the room.

In a cultivated voice that was little warmer than the frosty look in her de Montforte blue eyes, she told Anne, "I was very sorry to hear of Peter's death. I did not know him well, you understand. He was older, and you know how boys disdain girls when they are young, but he was my cousin, of course."

Anne inclined her head a fraction and said quite as coolly, "Of course."

The spare reply brought a sharp look from Lady Monteith. Anne returned it steadily. However sorry the woman had been to hear of her cousin's death, her sympathy had not then, nor did it seem now, to extend to his widow and children.

"Yes, well," Lady Monteith continued, coloring faintly but unmistakably, "it was a shame. He was so young."

Anne could not see what she could say to that, and so she made no reply at all. The silence drew out a fraction longer than was comfortable. Lady Monteith's color heightened further, and then Lord Edwards stepped into the breach, shifting the subject by asking Anne if she had lived in Italy long. "Eight years," she replied.

"Eight years!" Mrs. Sunderland exclaimed. "Why you must have been a child when you went." Then, perhaps unhappy that she'd brought attention to Anne's relative youth, added more righteously, "I would never allow a daughter of mine to travel to a foreign land. There is no telling what might happen."

A very great deal, Anne thought dryly, thinking of all that had happened to her. But aloud, it was of her mother she spoke, again with calm dignity. "Sadly, my mother had died before my father decided to quit England for Italy's warmth. And men are often more adventuresome than women, I think."

The latter statement softened Anne's first remark, but Mrs. Sunderland colored nonetheless, and apologized, if stiffly. "I do apologize for bringing up unpleasantness. I didn't know."

"Of course, not," Anne said reasonably. "And as to Italy, I enjoyed living there in many ways."

Lord Edwards, who had taken a seat beside Anne, asked where she had visited, for he had been to Italy, too. He was an amusing man and made Anne laugh at some of the contretemps into which he had fallen because he knew little of the language. "But do you speak Italian, Mrs. de Montforte? Surely, after eight years, you must."

"I did even before I went, actually. My father taught me, for he had studied romance languages at Oxford and in Italy did some translating for the embassy."

"Did he? Then you must know my uncle, the ambassador to Italy—"

"Lord Audley?" Anne finished, looking at the elegantly dressed gentleman beside her with a smile that made her face glow. She was not aware that Lady Monteith stirred abruptly in her chair or that Miss Sunderland's mouth turned down. "Yes, I knew him and Lady Audley very well, actually. They were both exceedingly good to me, and their removal to St. Petersburg came as a great loss."

"Poor Drusilla could not bear Russia!" Lord Edwards laughed. "She left only a month after they arrived, saying that while Italy was bearable because of the weather, Russia was unbearable on the same count. She may come to Wentworth for a visit, actually, for she's having her own home redone and says everything is at sixes and sevens."

"I should like to see her very much," Anne said. "I gave Lady Audley Italian lessons, though it seemed we laughed more than we made conversation."

"She liked you, then," Lord Edwards observed, looking as if he understood why. "Dru can be cold as an icicle with anyone she considers to be encroaching. Do you remember,

Maddy," he went on turning to Lady Monteith, "how Dru . . ."

Anne did not listen. She had caught Buckingham's blue eyes upon her, and his gaze was enigmatic, veiled even, as it had not been in a long time.

Chapter 16

Anne did not care to linger in the drawing room after the tea. While the others turned toward Buckingham as they rose, she made for the door. She had decided to claim some indisposition while Buckingham's guests remained at Sisley, for she could account for his veiled, remote look in only one way. Seeing her beside Miss Sunderland, he had recalled all the reasons he believed her to be unfit company for an innocent, gently reared girl, and Anne had too much pride to go where she was not wanted.

"Oh, Anne?"

She was only a step away from escaping. But she turned, as did the others, she noted, to see what Buckingham wanted of her.

He had stepped around the Sunderland women. They both looked rather comically nonplussed. Anne lifted her brow. "Yes, your grace?"

"Should I come to the nursery now? Or am I presuming in thinking there is a need?"

He was smiling crookedly. And Anne wanted to cry out in frustration. Where she had been cast down, wishing his tonnish guests—and him—to perdition, now she felt herself smiling back at him. She was no more in control of herself, she thought, than some helpless flower. If he watered her with attention, she smiled. If not, she wilted.

She'd have liked to deny him, if for no other reason than to put distance between them. She would disappoint the children if she did, though. And, besides, Mrs. Sunderland was regarding her with narrowed eyes.

"To the contrary, your grace. You are not presuming at all, and it is very kind of you to suggest going up. Alex and Nell will be delighted."

"I'll meet you there, then," he said. "First I must see Tony off. He deserves the courtesy for having provided Maddy escort from London. It could not have been easy."

There was a chorus of response to that, from both Lady Monteith and Lord Edwards, but Anne did not stay to listen to the good-humored bantering. She'd had enough of the ladies in the party.

Not, she realized, that she should be surprised by their condescension. As she made her way to the nursery to warn Nell and Alex of their cousin's imminent arrival, Anne sighed, but not without a touch of bitterness. Likely she should be grateful that Lady Monteith had not refused to be presented to her at all, given what the woman must believe of her.

It was an insupportable thought, and Anne forced it away when she reached the nursery. The children would have known something was wrong had she not, and when Buckingham received his pressed flower and his poem about a fish that was as big as a wish, she even managed to smile. For his part, Buckingham seemed amused by the children's efforts, particularly when Alex was not content merely to read his poem but had to enact it.

Still, more than once Anne caught the duke watching her thoughtfully, and when he asked to have a word with her after his birthday celebration, she assumed he meant to tell her, gently, of course, that he would prefer she did not join his sister and her friends for dinner. They went to the sitting room that Anne shared with Hetty.

Buckingham shut the door behind him and went directly to his own point. "You look somewhat strained, Annie. Did Maddy offend you?"

Anne could not credit how quickly a lump was able to

swell in her throat, but damn Buckingham, he looked as if he regretted that she'd been hurt, when it was he who had forced her into the situation.

"If I look strained, it is because I was forced to do the polite with a woman who thinks of me as you and I know your sister must. I will not join you for dinner."

"You will allow Maddy to believe you doubt your table manners?"

His blue eyes held a cool challenge. Anne met it with her chin up. "She saw I managed tea without dropping my cup. But what of you, your grace? I saw that look you gave me as I sat among your refined guests. Have you not decided that you do not care to expose an impressionable young girl to such as you believe me to be?"

Buckingham came off the door he'd leaned back against after closing it. To Anne it seemed he crossed the room in a single stride, and she never saw coming the hand that caught her chin in a not particularly gentle hold.

"I believe you to be many things, Annie, but not one of them ruinous to a young girl. As to the particular girl in question, in fact, Miss Phoebe Sunderland could only profit from an association with you. Her trenchant remark about the watercolors by Turner was that they were bright. If Miss Sunderland objects to my having a beautiful woman of wit and intelligence at my table, then so much the better. Do you understand?"

Anne couldn't trust herself to speak. The lump in her throat had swelled to painful proportions. He would have an answer though. He was waiting for it, holding her captive, his eyes probing hers. She slowly nodded. On the instant, he lowered his head and kissed her hard upon the mouth.

He did not give her time either to push him away or to respond. The kiss was over almost as soon as it had begun. Buckingham had dropped his hand from her face before it even occurred to her to protest his actions.

"When did you teach Lady Audley Italian?" he asked quietly, frowning.

Anne stared, her mind seeming to have been wiped

blank. The kiss had been unexpected, but it was the fierceness of it that had disrupted the working of her mind. Finally, though, she did register that he'd asked, not did you teach Lady Audley Italian, but when. She had not been certain, after that look, that he had believed what she had said to Lord Edwards.

"I gave her lessons after Peter died." Anne retreated to the window seat. He could appropriate her lips there as easily as anywhere, but at least she would not have to feel her pulses racing for so little reason as that she had caught a faint whiff of bay rum. "Actually, Lady Audley spoke Italian almost as well as I, and I believe she employed me only because she knew how difficult my circumstances were. She also bought hats I decorated," Anne added gratuitously, when she had seated herself. Despite Buckingham's assurances that he preferred her to Miss Sunderland, she felt a perverse desire to have him know just how different her life had been from the sheltered girl's, even if it had not been so indecently different as his uncle thought.

"Hats?" Buckingham repeated, looking baffled enough to make Anne smile slightly.

"I made a not inconsiderable living at it, actually," she said. "Betta got the chip hats for me through her own sources at ridiculously low prices. I had only to append a few ribbons and other ornaments to sell them at prices that were absurdly high. When Lady Audley was seen in them, they became quite the fashion among the English ladies in Italy."

Buckingham regarded her so long, Anne thought her little mercantile adventure had disgusted him. She was on the point of requesting to rest before dinner—and she would go, he had won there—when he walked to stand directly in front of her and say, "I think you are an exceedingly courageous and resourceful woman, Anne de Montforte. As well as being amazingly free of self-pity."

Anne thought that she ought to have learned by then not to anticipate his response. She rarely got it right. "I was lucky," she said, her voice perhaps a little unsteady. "Lady Audley was a gem, and I owe her a great deal."

Buckingham reached out to trace the high, smooth line of her cheek with his knuckle. "You're the gem, Annie. And I want you at dinner."

He bent down and pressed a kiss soft as down on her lips. It was over almost before she'd registered his touch and then he was gone from the room. Anne stared after him a good while. He had kissed her twice, as if he believed he could kiss her whenever he wanted. And she did not regret either one. How could she? Her heart swelled at the touch of his fingers, much less his lips. Yet she knew, sitting very straight there on the window seat, that had Buckingham made so free of Miss Sunderland's lips, he'd have had to marry the girl.

"Ah, here you are at last, Trev, fresh from the nursery."

Trev eyed his sister coolly as she turned to him. She had been tidying the vase of flowers Nell had put in his room.

"I am, and laden with birthday gifts. Here is my poem from Alex." He tossed a piece of vellum rolled lengthwise like a scroll onto the table she stood beside. "And this is my pressed flower from Nell." He took the little frame from his pocket and laid it down as well. "Those flowers you've just rearranged are from her also, but then you saw her in the drawing room shortly after you arrived without warning or invitation."

"I hope I can stop at my brother's home—my own childhood home—in an emergency," Maddy remarked stiffly.

Her brother only gave her a mocking look. "Indeed, Maddy, I would be devastated did you not come, in the event there *was* an emergency."

"Miss Lemon was made exceedingly ill by the motion of the coach, Trev, and if you do not classify a traveling companion turning a putrid green and losing the contents of her stomach as an emergency, then you are speaking from ignorance."

"A position in which I hope to remain," Trev allowed. "And magnanimous as I am, I shall permit this woman the remainder of today and all of tomorrow to recover, but she had best be ready to travel on Saturday, Maddy, or I shall go to her room myself."

"You want us gone so soon?"

"You may give up on that wounded look, pet. I've seen you switch it on and off too often. And yes, I do want you gone as soon as may be. Wretched, aren't I?"

He flashed her a grin as he took himself off to a table in the corner where there was a decanter of brandy. He didn't avail himself of it often, but he admitted he needed it then. Maddy's nostrils were quivering, never a good sign.

"You *are* wretched," she said. He laughed, poured his brandy, and inquired with a wicked look if she wished some.

She did not dignify the absurd query with a reply, seating herself without invitation in a chair beside the table. A breeze carried the scent of the peonies to her.

"Peter's children seem very taken with you," she said, reminded of Nell.

"Umm." Trev seated himself in the matching wing chair opposite her.

His sister eyed him askance. "Honestly, Trev! You have not only taken up the annoying habit of unintelligible replies, but you are sprawling in your chair like a country squire."

"Maddy, why are you here? Or did you come uninvited to my room to amuse me with an imitation of that dreadfully starched governess of yours—I can't think . . ."

"Crandall," Maddy supplied. "And I came simply to chat. I haven't seen you in an age, after all. You have been sequestered here nearly two months."

"Hardly sequestered," he said, and had the ill grace to grin at her over the rim of his glass.

"Very well, you've not been alone! For two months. Mine was not the only lifted brow in town, I can assure you. No one can remember you dancing attendance on one woman for so long. Particularly during the height of the Season."

Trev laughed. Maddy lived for the Season. "Well, what do you think of her? I know you came to Sisley to satisfy your curiosity, Maddy, not out of sisterly affection. Not that you don't possess it," he added when she bristled. "And not that you don't have a sweet young thing to parade before me."

"You don't care for Phoebe?"

"Discard that crestfallen look, my love. It will only give you wrinkles, and the chit is as interesting as a piece of chalk."

"And no competition for Peter's widow?"

"What do you think?"

Maddy kept him waiting, taking the time to arrange her skirts before finally she looked up and admitted rather reluctantly, "She took me by surprise."

"Ah, I find that interesting, but tell me, Maddy, did you expect her to fawn over you when the extent of your conversation was to express the sparest sentiments about Peter, and Peter alone?"

"Well, I am the Countess of Monteith, while she is no better than she should be! I certainly did not expect her to regard me as coolly as if she were Sally Jersey and I some upstart begging vouchers for Almack's. I admit she has looks, refined ones, even. And I shall go so far as to add that she apes good breeding far better than I'd expected, but after all, Trev, she's . . . common."

Trev's lids lowered, veiling his eyes. "Common?" he mused, studying the amber liquid in his glass. "Surely everything you've said would indicate not. As well as the proof of my own eyes. But," he went on, looking at his sister with a faint smile, "at the risk of crushing my reputation, I should perhaps tell you she is not my mistress, though not because I have not offered her the position."

"Oh."

Whatever response Trev had expected it was not a monosyllable uttered in a faltering tone. "You sound faintly alarmed, Maddy. I own I am surprised. Surely you don't fear that I might be slipping?"

"Only into matrimony," his sister replied, studying him seriously. "She must be playing for it, Trev! At the risk of inflating your vanity, I must say I cannot recall any other woman resisting you for nearly two months. She must believe, or hope, that you want her enough to wed her in the end."

"Nonsense." Trev heard his curt tone and did not add, as he'd been about to, that Anne was not so devious. It would sound as if he defended her blindly. "She had another reason for resisting me. She claims she is not the demirep Uncle John believes her to be, and not surprisingly, she fears that if she behaves like one, she will put the lie to her contention and give Uncle John the ammunition he needs to take her son from her."

"Whereas if you married her, she could have the son and Sisley," Maddy retorted. "She is using the boy to soften you, Trev. Good Lord, he is writing you poems for your birthday! She wishes to have it both ways, but mark my words, when she sees she cannot, when she accepts you'll not marry her or that Uncle John will not settle more on her than he's offered, she'll give up the boy in a trice."

Somehow it did little to appease Trev that he had once entertained the same opinions. "You judge her on exceedingly short acquaintance, Maddy. Having spent considerably longer than an hour with her, I am satisfied that she will not give up Alex next year, regardless of what inducements are offered or withheld. She holds the unusual belief that the boy needs affection and warmth more than he needs wealth." When Maddy snorted derisively, Trev asked, referring to her son, "Would you have given up Jack in the same circumstances?"

"Why, yes, of course," came the immediate reply, "if it meant he would be able to move in the proper circles for the rest of his life."

"You would have given him up to Uncle John at six years of age and seen him only once a year?"

"Yes, I would have." Maddy appeared resolute, but when Trev allowed the silence to lengthen, she waved a frustrated hand. "Very well, I don't know. How can I say, when I have never encountered such a situation? But if I did not wish to give him up, then I would look about for another way to open his father's circles to him, and one simple, I daresay even attractive way would be to marry his father's cousin, who not only inhabits those same circles, but also leads them."

"Thank you." Trev grinned. "I marked that 'attractive,' you understand—but you truly are flogging a dead horse, Maddy. Anne knows my thoughts on marriage, or imminent marriage anyway. And besides," he added, his sharpness fading the more he considered why it was impossible to believe that Anne was trying to lure him into marriage, "she is too intelligent to entertain the fancy that I can take a woman of her background for my duchess. Her father may have studied languages at Oxford, but that is the only distinction any of her ancestors has earned or been born to. Your fears are needless, and I might add reflect a surprisingly poor opinion of my own fortitude."

"Oh, Trev, you are only a man!" Trev laughed, but his sister was undeterred. "And she is beautiful."

"She is that," he agreed, but he'd had enough of Maddy's conjectures about Anne. "Did you learn what Mary Redvers's family has said about her fate?"

Maddy conceded to the change of subject, but only with a grudging look. "Yes, though it was not easy. There are deuced few people who knew her, but I ran to ground an elderly crone who is acquainted with her family and learned that their story is that she went to Italy for reasons of her health only, alas, to die there. Yes, she was even buried there. But there was no hint of a child or any affair with Peter. Are you certain the girl is hers?"

"Nell is Mary Redvers in miniature."

"What an odd situation it must have been." Maddy's blue eyes lit with an innate and active curiosity. "I wonder if Mrs. Redvers appeared before or after Peter had married. What does Anne say about it?"

"She has never divulged that Nell is not hers, and I haven't pressed her. I could see no reason to do so."

"No reason?" Maddy demanded in astonishment.

Trev shrugged. "You are the one who inherited a ferret's nose, Maddy, not I. She will tell me when she wishes. What of Mr. Redvers?"

. Maddy could not credit that her brother was truly so in-
curious. She could, however, see that he was not going to
discuss his reticence further. "Mr. Redvers has died as well,
of a bad heart, and I don't think my informant was being
ironic."

Trev gave her an amused look, but his subsequent nod
was satisfied. "That's good. There is no one to fight us for
her."

"Us?" Maddy's eyebrows lifted almost to her hairline.
"And you do not believe I should be concerned that you are
on the verge of losing your senses over this woman?"

Trev threw back his head and laughed. "You are a bad-
ger, Maddy! Good Lord, but you never give up."

"Do you love her?"

He masked his start of surprise, tossing off the last of his
brandy. When he looked up, his amused expression was restored. "You are a woman, Maddy, and notoriously sentimental to boot. I have no notion what you mean by love.
All I can say is that I want her, and as to the future, I cannot
but imagine that she'll grow tedious eventually. It is the
fate of every woman." Maddy, quite forgetting her age and
breeding, impudently stuck out her tongue. Trev grinned.
"Except you, Maddy, of course. You have the advantage of
being my sister, and therefore know when to cease and de-
sist so that you will not become tedious. Now, I've satisfied
your curiosity about Anne as much as I care to. You may
judge her further for yourself tonight at dinner."

Maddy stared. "She is coming! I could understand about
tea, Trev, for there she stood, but you mean to have her join
us for dinner? A woman like her?"

There was an amber drop left in his brandy glass. Trev
rolled it about for a moment. When he looked up, the emotion glittering in his eyes gave Maddy pause, stilling the
sarcasm on her lips.

"What kind of woman is she, Maddy?" Trev asked too
softly. "Shall we review what we know? When her mother
died, her father promptly fell apart at the seams, and to escape the creditors he managed to acquire in only a few
months, he hied off to Italy. Anne followed him out of a

sense of duty, but he drank himself to death anyway and left her with scarcely a penny in a foreign land where she had neither friends nor family. She was sixteen. What would you have done, Maddy? Starved to death for your honor? Or when Peter's death left her as impoverished as her father's had, but of course with two small children as well, both de Montfortes? What would you have done then? She did not take up her former occupation, though I can promise you men would have paid through their teeth for her. No, with her children's reputations to think of, she used the connections she had made through her husband, the one benefit of her marriage that I can see, to make an honest, if less lucrative living, and while she was at it, she raised two exceedingly fine children, children whose father's family had turned their wealthy but so righteous backs on her.

"Now tell me, Maddy, you who have been cosseted your entire life, who have not wanted even for a single ribbon, tell me you still believe you are too good to sit down to dinner with Anne de Montforte and treat her with courtesy."

Chapter 17

Anne knew the dinner schedule at Sisley. She knew to the minute how long to wait after the dinner gong had rung. For the sake of her pride, she would go down to dinner, but she would not spend a moment longer in the unpleasant company awaiting her than was absolutely necessary.

As she approached the drawing room, she heard with relief Lord Edwards's voice. She had not known whether he would return for dinner, and at that moment, alone in the hall, approaching a room that would be filled with women who scorned her presence, every friendly face seemed a godsend.

She also heard Barrett's grave voice announcing dinner, and at that Anne smiled just a little. She really had timed it to the second. Everyone was rising as she entered the drawing room, but only one person was looking toward the door. Her eyes locked with his.

The exchange lasted no more than a moment.

The others were not so distracted that Anne could lock gazes with Buckingham for the evening, but so little was still enough. The fierceness in the look he gave her helped her lift chin. He wanted her there. No, more than that, his blue eyes seemed to say, he needed her there.

"Mrs. de Montforte! Jove, ma'am, you are easy on the

eyes. I am surprised the Italians were willing to give you up."

Anne gave Lord Edwards a light reply and a smile, thankful for his pleasant welcome, particularly in light of Mrs. Sunderland's disdainful expression. Squaring her shoulders, and praying for an early evening, she followed the guests into the vast and elegant dining room.

Buckingham placed her between Lord Edwards and Lady Monteith. Lord Edwards was fine, but Anne would have preferred to sit by anyone other than Buckingham's sister. She did not care two pence what the Sunderland women thought of her, but she would have liked to be on good terms with Lady Monteith. The sudden realization that she wanted to be on good terms with his family, or one member of it at least, took Anne aback enough that she did not pursue the line of thought. Forcing a composed expression to her face, she thanked heaven for Lord Edwards.

He was quite as attentive as Anne could have wished, but he had another dinner partner, too, and midway through the first course turned away from Anne to do his duty by Hetty. In the lull that followed, Lady Monteith's aristocratic voice was unmistakable.

"Will you tell me of your children?" Anne turned to her slowly. The woman had avoided using Anne's name, but her tone had been almost warm. Looking closely, Anne found the expression in the woman's blue eyes had thawed slightly as well. She'd not have said Lady Monteith regarded her warmly, her look was too . . . tentative, surprisingly. "How old are they? Trev showed me the presents they made for him, and I thought them . . ."

Lady Monteith hesitated then, and Anne found she could not but smile. "Nell is six and Alex is five. And if you will promise not to tell them, I will confide that I found their works more quaint than anything."

"Well," Lady Monteith began, and then, to Anne's considerable surprise, she chuckled. "I've three children, ranging in age from ten to six, and I cannot say I would characterize any of the gifts they have made for me any differently. I remember in particular some embroidery of my eldest daughter's. I am afraid I exclaimed over the lovely bee she had made me when, unfortunately, she had attempted a flower."

They both laughed then, and if they sounded a trifle self-conscious doing so, still Lady Monteith talked on afterward for some time about her children and the scrapes they had gotten into, while not failing to ask more about Anne's. She did not make any inquiries about Anne herself, but Anne didn't fault her, she was so much more cordial than she had been at tea.

After a little, while Lady Monteith was rattling in full spate about some trick her son had played on her daughters, Anne slanted a glance at Buckingham. She sensed his fine hand behind Lady Monteith's change. He was watching them, but she had known he was. She had felt his glance on her. And when their eyes met, she had her answer. His expression was too bland by half. He had admonished his sister on Anne's account. She smiled at him from across the table, and after a moment, he inclined his head in acknowledgment.

Whether Lady Monteith's thaw would have lasted for the length of her stay at Sisley, Anne was not to learn. Hetty fell ill. Anne had noted during dinner that her aunt seemed subdued but had thought it was the company that had quieted her. The next morning, however, Betta came to tell her that Hetty was in her bed, struggling for breath.

From experience, Anne knew there was not much she could do but sit with her aunt and give her a tonic made from a mixture of comfrey and willow bark. Hetty did not breathe so much better after it, but she did calm, at least.

Buckingham came to inquire after her in the morning. It was at a bad time. Hetty was gasping painfully, and Anne was distraught. She supposed she must have looked what she felt, for he brushed her cheek softly and told her he was sending for Dr. Johnstone.

The doctor was a kindly gentleman, who admitted he had no magic cure, though he did offer the suggestion that some of his patients had found steam to help. Between them, Anne and Mrs. Goodwin set up a system to heat water in the sitting room, where it could be conveyed to Hetty still steaming.

Hetty was having her first treatment when Lady Monteith came to the room. Anne assumed Buckingham had sent her until Lady Monteith reminded her what Buckingham had once told her, that a relative of Lord Monteith's also suffered with his breathing. "It is my husband's uncle, and poor thing, little seems to help. He has tried the steam as well, though he covered his head with a cloth to hold in the heated air."

"Of course!" Anne said, feeling foolish for not having thought of it. "Thank you. You are very kind to have come."

Anne turned to go, but Lady Monteith laid her hand on Anne's shoulder. If Anne was surprised by that familiarity, she was shocked when Lady Monteith observed in a tone that was almost kindly. "You look tired, my dear. I know it must be difficult to watch another struggle for breath, but you mustn't make yourself ill. I hope you will take a respite and join us for dinner. Tony has invited us to Wentworth, and it is a fine old house."

Wryly, Anne thought she really must look a hag for Lady Monteith to unbend so, but she admonished herself at once. The woman was being extraordinarily kind, given what she believed. Anne thanked her again but shook her head. "I could not possibly go. It would seem I am as much a worrier as any old biddy. I would not enjoy myself for my anxiety."

Lady Monteith regarded Anne a long minute, though Anne had no idea why or what she saw. In the end, Buckingham's sister patted her on the arm again and said only, "Your concern does you credit, my dear. And of course it goes without saying that we all understand. Please know as well that we wish your aunt a speedy recovery."

Though Anne was kept busy attending to Hetty, she did consider in the odd free moment whether she would have liked to go to the dinner party. She did genuinely find Lord Edwards enjoyable, and Lady Monteith no longer put her in mind of an ice dragon come to save her brother from an encroaching and disreputable widow. On the other hand, there were the two Sunderland women with their lifted noses and matching pursed mouths. She could not have looked forward to their company, but in the end, when the time came and she heard the carriage roll down the drive, she knew she was relieved to stay behind, and on no one's account but Buckingham's.

She had grown accustomed to having him virtually to herself at dinner, to sharing what they'd done with their day—what of it they'd not spent together; to discussing freely any topic that arose, from affairs of state to the gossip in Whitchurch that the vicar's wife was a notorious flirt; to planning what they would do the next day.

As for after dinner, a hot current ran through her whenever she thought about the night before. She had not had time to grow accustomed to the sensual spell he'd woven around them both. But her conclusion was the same, nonetheless. She did not want to share him. God help her.

He was not hers, and never would be.

Anne stood at Hetty's window and watched the violet shadows of twilight steal silently across the garden. What she felt for him had crept up on her in the same, silent way. Sometime, somehow, as the summer had drifted along, as the attraction between then had grown until it seemed she could think of little else, something more had happened. He was not hers, but she wanted him to be. When she had not been watching, she had fallen in love.

They had both had their goals for this summer at Sisley. She had hoped to bring him around to her point of view about Alex's future, and he . . . he'd been gentling her, accustoming her to his touch. Nay more, he'd been teaching her to want it—and him.

Not because he wished to marry her, either, but that was old ground. Only that afternoon she had been looking into her teacup, and acknowledging that Buckingham could not possibly take for his duchess a woman with her questionable reputation. She had known it all along. She had told Hetty so.

And yet, she had allowed herself to fall in love with him.

Like a good many others before her, she supposed, and with the same prospects. Yet she did not truly believe she was like the others. He was her friend, and she did not think he had called many other women friend.

Friend, and so much more. She was deeply grateful she did not have to sit across the dinner table from him and behave as if he were no more to her than her children's cousin. Even now, with Hetty ill behind her, she was restless to feast her eyes on him, to drink in every detail, to mark the way his mouth curved, the crease of the lines by his eyes, the blue-black crispness of his hair, the strong, chiseled beauty of his face. And it did not help that she knew Rob would come soon, nor that when he did she would have to go.

Betta slipped into the room just as Anne caught her hand to her chest as if she could press back the sudden ache there. Looking closely at her mistress, Betta insisted in a torrent of Italian that the signora needed rest from the room of her sick aunt. After she bid her children good night, she was to take a dinner tray in her room—Betta had arranged for it—and then she should take a walk outside. Betta said she would lay out a light cloak.

Anne did not have the will to argue with Betta. Hetty had finally fallen into a doze. She couldn't do anything more for her tonight and she thought it might do her good to escape the dreariness of the sickroom. Perhaps she'd even outpace her heavy thoughts.

She did for awhile. The clouds that had created the colorful twilight had brought a warm, misting summer rain. Anne threw back the hood of the cloak and lifted her face to it, feeling oddly comforted by the fresh, soft feel of it. When she grew tired of standing, she walked to a small pavilion that stood at one end of the reflecting pool. In the distance she could hear an owl hooting and, closer at hand, smell the fragrant scent of night jasmine.

She also heard the diners return from Lord Edwards's house. The sound of the carriage horses trotting down the lane was unmistakable, but she stayed where she was, her cloak warm about her, and the sounds and scent of the night her company.

Without turning, Anne could sense the house going to sleep. Candles were snuffed and quiet stole over Sisley. When she turned and saw no light at all, when she could be confident she'd not encounter anyone, Anne bid farewell to the night and, it seemed in some odd way, to her summer as well.

Her room was dark. She, herself, had snuffed out the candle before she left. Nonetheless, she knew from the moment she opened the door that he was there. She could smell the scent of his cheroot, and following it, saw its tip glow in the dark. As her eyes became accustomed to the darkness, she could see he was sitting, facing the door, but he said nothing, and neither did Anne as she dropped her cloak and moved silently across to him.

Only when she stood so close to him that their knees brushed did she at last speak. "Is this why you installed me in this wing, Buckingham? So that you could visit me discreetly if you had guests?"

In the dark, his smile came as a lazy flash of white. "Actually, you have it the wrong way about, Annie. I put you in this wing so that you could visit me, despite Mrs. Teasdale and the children."

His voice was rich with the irony of it all, and smiling softly back at him, Anne took the hand he held out to her, closing her eyes at the sharp pleasure she felt at his touch. When he tugged gently, she sank down onto his lap and, seeking the comfort of his warmth, melted against him, laying her head on his shoulder.

For Trev, the evening had been an unmitigated trial. Tony, one of his closest friends, had been tedious, and the Sunderland women even more so. As to Maddy, the author of his discontent, he'd cast damning looks her way throughout the night. She had avoided those looks, of course, and he had been left to endure the interminable evening—and try not to think of where he would rather have been.

But he did, of course, between sips of Tony's excellent

claret. He thought of the tea when Maddy had greeted Anne as if she were less than a scullery maid. She had held her own, though, looking as cool and composed as a queen. He'd been proud of her, but he had not been about to leave the subsequent dinner to chance. Had Maddy not come to his room, he'd have gone to hers and made it clear that if she wished to eat at his table, she would treat Anne with courtesy. He did not ponder long on why it mattered to him. It was enough that it did, and more than enough that Anne had given him the look she had. Her heart had been in her eyes.

In another day, after Maddy and the Sunderland pair had left, he would have her to himself again. They would resume where they had left off . . . Anne leaning over the green baize-covered card table, her dark, shining hair tumbling loose, her eyes alight—and not with laughter.

The image was so powerful Trev called for more claret. But the desire for the several glasses that followed sprang from another source. Even as he thought of Anne and how it would be again between them, he had an odd, vague feeling of foreboding. He knew it was absurd. He did not believe in presentiments, and he blamed Maddy and the suspicions she had voiced about Anne's designs. But they were baseless. Anne knew full well he wasn't about to marry her, for any of a host of reasons, the least of them that she was ineligible by birth. He'd have married whomever he pleased, the Honorable Ten Thousand be damned, had he had the least interest in marriage. But he'd always believed marriage was for other, less fortunate, less wary men. She knew what he thought. She was not trying to seduce him into marriage, though God knew it was the age-old method women had used to leg-shackle men. But not her, she was not a coquette—it had taken him two months to get her to let down her hair. He was even beginning to wonder about those testimonials of his uncle's. He had never looked at the names of the men who had signed them, nor did he know the circumstances under which they'd been gathered, but even if every word in them was true, and she had whored, it was not because she was a natural one. Whatever she had done—if she had—she had done as a last resort.

No, she was not plotting to trap him into marriage, he told himself as the dinner wore on and he heard less and less of the conversation going on about him. Everything would be the same again. He was worrying absurdly. They would gallop until they were breathless. He would tease her, and she would laugh. He would toss Alex into the air, making him shriek with delight, and she would regard him as if he had conquered a city for her. He would give her another fishing lesson, too, standing behind her, almost but not quite touching her everywhere . . . and one night, he would take her hair down himself.

Yet, despite all his reassurances, the sense of urgency built in him. He wanted to see Anne, to touch her, to know she was still there, that nothing had happened, and when, finally, he was at Sisley again, he had not been able to force himself to play the polite host. Though Maddy had started toward the drawing room for tea and a final coze before they went up to bed, he'd bowed out, he hoped graciously, saying no more than that he wished to look in on Mrs. Teasdale. When he had found Betta with Hetty, he had made arrangements for the Italian girl to sleep with Anne's aunt, and then, without further ado or consideration, had gone to Anne's room to await her return from the walk Betta said she'd taken.

Smoking his cheroot, surrounded by her things and the hint of her lavender scent lingering in the air, he had felt content at last. He had heard her footsteps approach the door. She moved with uncharacteristic languor, and he'd known then that she felt the same odd heaviness as he.

He wanted to hold her. That was all, he told himself—until she sank down into his lap. He kissed her hair then. It felt like silk on his lips and smelled sweet. He buried his face in it. She felt so warm. His blood began to thud painfully heavy in his veins, or perhaps it had been thudding from the moment he felt her soft, rounded bottom nestle against him. Still drinking in her scent, he began slowly to remove the pins from her hair. He knew she might balk at any time, but when he ran his fingers through the silky weight of it, she shook her head, as if she were savoring the freedom of having it loose. And then, while her hair swished over his arm, she turned her head and kissed him, openmouthed on the neck, whispering softly, her warm breath tickling him, "I missed you."

"Oh God," was all he could say. It was no more than a groan, but it touched something in Anne. Her arms went around his neck, and then Trev was kissing her with almost punishing force.

There was a moment when Anne considered what she was doing. After holding out against Buckingham for nearly two months, she was yielding. But she knew he no longer thought her a lightskirt. He'd made his sister, the daughter of a duke and a countess by marriage, treat her courteously. He could not think so poorly of her. And as to her succumbing, she knew Buckingham well enough to know now that he'd not think her despicably wanton. He would know she succumbed because she found him irresistible.

Which was the truth. She loved him. She wanted to hold him, to feel him, to taste him. The thought of spending all of her life wondering forlornly what it would have been like to lie in his arms was insupportable of a sudden. Perhaps it was knowing that their time together was coming to an end. She did not intend to become his mistress, no matter what he might think on the subject. But she would be his lover for a time, until Rob came. That little she could have, a short time of wonder to savor in the lonely years ahead.

Then fire licked through her, sending her spinning off into a world where she could not get enough of Trevelyan de Montforte, nor he of her. Anne couldn't think, nor did she care to. She wanted to run her hands down his back, feel his sleek skin, revel in the hard strength of him. Her breath came shallow and fast. She felt heated everywhere he touched, and yet, when they lay on her bed, bare skin touching and heating bare skin unbearably, he pulled back to look at her with eyes heavy-lidded from passion.

"You want me, Annie?" he asked.

If everything else had not, the huskiness of his voice would have sealed her fate. Even wanting so much that his voice was thick with desire, still he gave her a choice.

Chapter 18

The dew sparkled freshly on the grass and overhead the sky was still streaked with rose from the dawn. The hour was early. The air was cool still, but sweet with the scent of mown clover. Trev laughed aloud. It was a perfect day. He leaned down to pat Jester's strong neck. "She was everything and more, boy," he confided to the bay. "Everything. I had to resort to you, old fellow, or I'd have gone back to her."

It was the truth. The hour had been late when, sated at last, Trev had fallen asleep with Anne in his arms. He'd awakened once while it was still dark, only to feel her softness and draw her more tightly to him. When the light of dawn intruded into her bedroom, however, he had torn himself away from her sleepy warmth. The world would know eventually that Anne was his, but he knew she would not want the servants whispering about a liaison between them just yet, not while Maddy and her gossips were still at Sisley. He'd even gone to the extent of throwing back the covers on his bed and mussing the pillows. He never even considered getting into his bed, though, for he had never felt less like sleeping alone than he did that morning, with the taste of Anne on his lips and the memory of her soft, slender body curled against him. What he had wanted to do was return to her, and when he had begun to think just what he'd do there with her, he had abruptly stalked off to find his riding clothes. He would have his day—days—with her, but not this day.

Urging Jester to a canter, Trev began considering just how soon that might be. Maddy and the Sunderlands, thankfully, would be leaving this morning. Miss Lemon, it would seem, had recovered on schedule. Trev smiled to himself, thinking about afterward. Could he disappear with Anne for the afternoon? No, she would be nervous about the children, and rightly so. After dinner then . . . no, he had forgotten Mrs. Teasdale was ill. She would not come down at all. They could take dinner in his room.

Trev laughed aloud again, but the sound was strained. He did not know if he could wait those few hours. He had waited two months without anything like the same flaring of impatience, but he hadn't known what awaited him then. He had had an inkling. The air between them had crackled too sharply, he had been too aware of her, and she of him, for him not to have suspected lovemaking between them would be good. But how good, he'd not known. He could not have guessed how passionate she would be, or how her eagerness would set him ablaze. Dear God, he had feared he would hurt her in his need. Even as a boy, his first time, he had not felt anything like the intensity he'd felt with Anne.

He wanted to see her again. He wanted just to look at her. She would blush. He knew it. She would be shy. The thought made him grin after all they'd done the night before, but it was, in fact, another reason he wanted to see her. For all that she'd trembled with desire for him, for all that she had pleased him beyond all his expectations, she had obviously been untutored. She had not known everything there was to pleasuring, had been shocked more than once at what he had wanted to do. Trev was not so surprised that Peter had not taught her. For one, his cousin had been young, and young men were notoriously poor lovers. He'd likely satisfied himself in minutes and fallen asleep. As Anne had admitted there had not been a great degree of closeness between her and Peter, Trev was not surprised that she had not protested. She had likely been glad to have her duty done. He winced a little thinking of how Peter must have initiated her, but that brought him back to his original point. He could not believe now that she had had experience before Peter. She was simply too unskilled to have made her living pleasuring men.

When he returned to the house, Trev breakfasted, and then sent up a maid to inform Anne that he wished to see her in his study as soon as she could come. He intended, among other things, to ask her about what had really happened after her father died.

In his study, Trev waited impatiently. He had an estate book open on the desk before him, but he never looked at it. Leaning back in his chair, his boots propped on the desk, he sought to unravel the mystery of his uncle's testimonials, testimonials he now believed false. Why would four Englishmen have sworn falsely against Anne? Had they even known her? Had his uncle's agent influenced them, believing Lord John wanted a reason to denounce her? What had Peter thought? *Had* Peter thought? Bah! Now he was being cruel about Peter when his cousin was the one ultimately responsible for bringing her to him.

When the knock finally came at the door, Trev surged to his feet. Though he knew he was smiling like a schoolboy, he couldn't seem to control himself. But when he opened the door, it was not Anne who stood there, suppressing a blush. It was Barrett, looking oddly uncomfortable.

"Yes, Barrett, what is it?" Trev demanded, and though he knew his tone was abrupt, he could not help it. He'd expected to be holding Anne already.

"There's a visitor, your grace, for Mrs. de Montforte. He is the young man who was here before, Mr. Godfrey. I thought you would want to know."

"Yes, indeed, Barrett." Trev spoke without inflection, but he felt as if the ground had rolled beneath his feet. She had claimed the boy was her cousin, and he had every reason to believe her now. Still, he had seen her take money from young Mr. Godfrey, dressed in a robe at eleven o'clock. It was impossible not to be assailed by sudden doubt. Had she only played the innocent the night before, perhaps? Had he believed what he wanted to believe?

Trev strode off to meet Rob in the south drawing room, his face set so sternly the two young maids he chanced to encounter shrank back into the shadows. Rob was not so fortunate as they—there were no shadows in the magnificent drawing room into which he'd been shown. When he heard the door open, and turned from the window with its view of the drive and the park beyond, he hoped against hope that it would be Anne. But he saw what he'd feared. Buckingham himself strode through the door.

Though Rob had never met the duke, there was no mistaking the man. Buckingham had the good looks and enviable build he was reputed to have. Also the cool eyes and the sangfroid. While it was impossible for Robin to guess what Buckingham was thinking, he feared his own unease was all too apparent. It was impossible to remain calm when one was looking into a pair of cold eyes that belonged, he could not help remembering, to a man who was said to be the best shot in England—and looked as if he wouldn't be half bad with his fists either.

"Good morning, your grace," Rob began and, hearing the hurried deference in his tone, took a deep breath. He wasn't aware of it, but he also set his shoulders as straight as a plumb line and balled his hands into fists.

Trev noticed. Flicking his icy gaze over his visitor, he remarked the defensive gesture, and the resolute spine-stiffening as well. The boy was even younger than Trev had thought. It was likely, in fact, that he was not even Anne's three and twenty, which went a little way, at least, to balancing the concurrent observation that the pup bore no resemblance at all to Anne, with his red hair, hazel eyes, and somewhat square build.

"What may I do for you, Mr. Godfrey?"

"Well," Rob said, wishing the man's eyes didn't give such a strong impression of boring into one, "as I told your butler, your grace, I have come to see Anne de Montforte. I sent her a letter, saying I was on my way."

"She has not mentioned your letter, and I am afraid

you've come at a bad time," Trev told him. "Her aunt is ill."

"Aunt Hetty? Is she very ill? Anne thought the country air would help her."

Aunt Hetty. Still, Trev did not allow himself to relax. "Mrs. Teasdale is your aunt as well?" His tone might have seemed idle, but his gaze sharpened when Rob shook his head, and Rob discovered a certain eagerness in himself to clarify his purely familial relationship to Anne, if not to divulge how lofty the family.

"No, your grace. Mrs. Teasdale is related to Anne through her father. I am related to her on her mother's side of the family."

"You are her cousin, then?"

"Yes, your grace, I am."

Trev smiled. In the split second before, Rob had thought something abashed flickered in the duke's eyes, but the thought was so absurd and the subsequent smile so strong, he dismissed the notion as evidence of the fancifulness against which his strict Aunt Peg often warned him.

"I am pleased to make your acquaintance, Mr. Godfrey, and as to Mrs. Teasdale, I am happy to be able to reassure you. The country air has, in fact, seemed to do her good. This is the first attack she has suffered since coming here, and I am told that though she did have a difficult time yesterday, she is feeling much better this morning."

Buckingham with a friendly expression on his face was an altogether different man from the one who'd entered the room with steel in his eyes. Rob felt as if a great weight had been lifted from his shoulders. And not only was the duke regarding him with a friendly expression, but he also had spoken of Hetty with warmth, which seemed to imply that Anne had done it—she had brought the man around. He wanted to give a great whoop of joy.

Containing himself, Rob decided there was no harm in asking, cautiously of course, "I wonder, your grace, if you would tell me whether Anne's difference with Lord John de Montforte has been resolved?"

"It hasn't been yet, but it will be," Buckingham said with such off-hand assurance, Rob knew he spoke the truth.

"Oh, I am glad! After the both of us had worked and saved for so long to get her and the children back to England, it seemed the worst luck that her return might mean the loss of Alex."

"You helped her, then?"

Rob nodded. "Yes, my uncle owns a shipping business in which he has allowed me to invest in return for overseeing the cargo on each voyage."

Trev clapped him on the shoulder. Rob had the odd fancy that he knew how a squire newly knighted must have felt in the olden times. "Then I am in your debt, young man, for without you, I'd not have become acquainted with Anne or the children. Where did you stay the night, by the by? At the Hart and Hare in Whitchurch? And have you had any breakfast?"

"I am staying in Whitchurch, yes, and no, your grace, I was too anxious to eat before I came to see Anne."

"Well, come along then, and have some breakfast." Trev waved Rob through the door. "I'll send up word to Anne that you're here."

Rob noted that he had not previously been announced to Anne and likely would not have been had Buckingham not approved him, but he was not unduly concerned about that evidence of protectiveness. Everything about the duke suggested a man who would judge his callers for himself, no matter whom they came to visit.

As they approached the breakfast room, the two men could hear several feminine voices, and Trev briefly explained that his sister and friends of hers were visiting, but that they would be leaving that day. "I hope you will take their place." Actually, he did not hope it at all. To the contrary, he could not have hoped more strongly that Rob would disappear by late afternoon. The boy's presence would delay that dinner in his bedroom. Still, Trev made the offer and with every evidence of sincerity. He owed Anne that much.

As Trev had feared, Rob was only too pleased to accept

his invitation. Only in Rob's wildest dreams had he imagined remaining with Anne and the children in Sisley's luxurious surroundings. Excited and distracted as he was, Rob did not glance about at all the ladies at the breakfast table, only fastened upon the two nearest the door, and he had never met Lady Monteith or Miss Lemon, the providentially recovered companion to Mrs. Sunderland. Therefore, the young man was taken by considerable surprise when a woman exclaimed in a high, unpleasantly shrill voice, "You needn't present Phoebe and me to Mr. Godfrey, your grace. We met last year at his cousin's home in Yorkshire." Startled, Rob looked down the table and realized he knew the fashionable, broadly smiling woman. She was a friend of his cousin's wife. "How are Lord and Lady Edgemoore, Mr. Godfrey?" she queried cheerfully. Beside him, Rob felt as much as saw Buckingham go very still. "And how is it we have the pleasure of meeting you again here at Sisley? I did not realize you knew the duke."

"I did not until a few minutes ago," Rob divulged, his eyes on Mrs. Sunderland, but his senses attuned to Buckingham. There was something ominous in the man's stillness, but Rob had not the time to fabricate an excuse for his presence. "I came to call on my cousin, Mrs. de Montforte."

"Mrs. de Montforte is your cousin?"

Mrs. Sunderland made no effort to hide her astonishment. Her eyes widened ludicrously, and it was impossible for Rob to quash a spark of glee. The chinless witch had thought herself and her porcelain-brittle daughter above Anne.

"Excuse me, Mr. Godfrey." It was Lady Monteith. She looked curiously intent, he thought. But Rob had no time to wonder why, for she asked bluntly, "Are we to understand, then, that Anne is cousin to Lord Edgemoore as well?"

It seemed to Rob that even the room caught its breath, waiting. Feeling the eyes of everyone on him, most particularly the keen blue ones of the man behind him, he considered lying, but he discarded the thought as soon as it arose. He was a terrible liar and, finally, he simply could not see what was wrong with the truth. Buckingham had said the matter with his uncle was as good as settled.

"Yes. Anne's mother was the present earl's aunt."

Trev did not stay to hear more. He couldn't trust himself. Without a word, without a gesture, without even a stray glance, he left his young, so very well-connected guest standing where he was. He meant to go directly to Anne's room and confront her whether she was in her bed or not. He didn't only because he met Barrett, who had come to inform him that Mrs. de Montforte was waiting for him in his study. So much the better, Trev thought with grim satisfaction. The study was more isolated.

Anne had awakened to such a sense of contentment, she had closed her eyes and wished herself back to sleep. But the sunlight streaming in the window had not allowed her to shut her eyes to all the reasons she should be anything but content.

And yet, she was. Blissfully so. Merciful heaven, she had never guessed lovemaking could be anything like that. She had felt like a flame to his fire—or a wind to it, perhaps. She had wanted him so—she hadn't even realized how much—until she could not touch him enough, taste him enough, hear enough of him huskily whispering all those things, most of which he likely had not meant.

Her smile growing slightly ragged, Anne wondered suddenly if lovemaking was always so earth-shattering for Buckingham. That it had never been so for her did not mean much. Perhaps men were different. Or rakes. Perhaps the strange alchemy that existed between them existed between Buckingham and every woman. She had not the experience to know, but she did realize it was a bit late to worry about those other women. Indeed, she had gone to him knowing about them.

And she did not regret it. Had she not gone to him, she'd never have known what it was to want a man so much she cried out for him; so that she lost all sense of anything but him, his body and hands and the fire storm he created in her.

When Betta knocked on the door, Anne slipped under her sheets to give her cheeks time to cool, for she had thought of some of the shocking things Trev had done and persuaded her to do, too, to her pleasure. Betta would be bound to know something was up if Anne was blushing even before she'd had her tea. A quick glance over the edge of the sheet, when she was no longer rose-pink, assured her that Trev had left nothing damning behind in the room. He'd have had practice, she told herself, then reminded herself sharply that he had never said he hadn't. He also had not made any protestations of love. She had gone to him because she had wanted him for herself, for one night at least, and that she had gotten. In spades.

Anne grinned into the cup of tea Betta had handed her, only to glance up and find Betta eyeing her shrewdly. "The duke wishes to see you in his study, signora," the maid said.

To Anne's dismay, the simple announcement made her blush hotly again. Immediately, Betta's eyes went wide with interest. "It is nothing, Alberghetta!" Anne snapped. "His grace wishes to see me on Hetty's account, I'm sure. How is she this morning?"

Betta grinned. Anne could not possibly have held her gaze, though she did note as she looked loftily off toward the window, that Betta's grin had been pleased. Of course, the girl was Italian and did not have such a fine sense of propriety as the English. Anne blessed her for that, and for the discretion which, though she continued to smile secretly, kept her from any more overt reaction as she reported that Hetty had slept well and, after having had tea and porridge for breakfast, was dozing again.

With Hetty asleep, Anne saw no reason to delay meeting Buckingham. She wanted to meet with him for the first time in his study, away from the others. She knew she'd betray herself with another blush. But one thing she would not do was tell him quite yet that she would be leaving Sisley soon. She'd save that for when Rob came. Then, when she had the means to leave, she'd tell him that while she had been pleased to be his lover for a week—or two, if they were lucky and Rob slow—she could not become his mistress, living with him openly as such, taking his money for her living, his gifts, and eventually his congé. No, she couldn't bear that last, and she would make him understand. Somehow.

Somehow she would resist her own desire to succumb. Even now, knowing she could meet Lady Monteith or either of the Sunderland ladies at any moment, she felt like running to his study. She wanted to bury herself in his arms.

In the event, running would have availed her little. It was not Buckingham who awaited Anne outside the door of the study, but Barrett, who hurried to say that his grace had left for but a moment. Would she please await him, and did she care for tea while she did?

Anne said she would wait but that she didn't want for anything—except composure, she added silently. As she waited just inside the study door, she felt absurdly shy. And when she thought of all the reasons she had to be shy, she had to take a deep breath to steady herself. She simply could not melt the moment she saw him. He couldn't be counted on for restraint.

The thought made her giggle a little wildly, and she knew she was not at all ready when she heard the door open behind her. She spun eagerly, nonetheless—only to realize that he was not regarding her with even a modicum of the warmth she had expected. Dear God, she thought, her mouth going dry as her gaze focused on him, he seemed a stranger. A cold, contemptuous stranger.

Frozen, she stood dumbly waiting for she knew not what. Buckingham did not keep her in suspense.

"Your cousin is here," he announced in deadly tones. "You know, Rob, the one I thought your lover; the one from whom I believe you received a letter a few days ago. You timed it all nicely. Even circumstances over which you'd no control worked to your advantage. There were witnesses when young Mr. Godfrey was conveniently forced to divulge the name of your mutual cousin. You remember him, as well? The Earl of Edgemoore. He's a spineless toady, and I agree he's not much to claim, but I do think I'd have done it if my father-in-law believed I was unworthy to raise his grandson. In that case I would certainly have mentioned I was an earl's granddaughter. But divulging that fact didn't fit into your plans, did it, Annie? Better first to let me compromise you, and thoroughly," he added with such a sneer, Anne felt all the blood drain from her cheeks.

"What's the matter, clever Annie?" he asked hatefully, seeing her go pale. "Doesn't the thought of me thrusting into you make you blush hotly anymore? No? It's just as well. Maddy was right, damned if she wasn't. She said it was marriage you played for, and I will say you played your cards superbly. I never guessed. Never once—but you made one mistake dearest Annie. No one will ever trap me into marriage. I don't care how loudly or to whom you cry that you've been ill-used. You may shout it to your noble kinsman, for all I care. I'll simply say that you wanted what you got so badly I'd have felt less than a gentleman had I not scratched your itch.

"Ah, I see it took only plain speaking to put a line of color back in your cheeks. A pity I am no longer moved by the sight. Truth to tell, I find I cannot bear the sight of you at all. I am leaving this morning to go into Leicestershire with Maddy and the Sunderland pair. I will return in a week, by which time Mrs. Teasdale should have recovered well enough to travel. I expect you to be gone from Sisley by then. You and Uncle John will have to settle your differences yourselves. And so adieu, dear Anne. If you need it, you may take comfort from the thought that should you need a profession, you are as good as any whore I know."

He gave Anne a bow so faint it mocked her, then turned on his heel and left her standing there still frozen and quite painfully, damningly mute.

Chapter 19

Anne could not move. She felt bloodless, lifeless, her feet not even part of her. Yet, she was shaking, and she realized that she had clamped her arms around her waist as if to hold herself together.

"I'd have felt less than a gentleman had I not scratched your itch . . . Truth to tell, I find I cannot bear the sight of you at all . . . you may take comfort from the thought that should you need a profession, you are as good as any whore I know."

It was as if he'd left the words behind in the room to echo over and over again. *"Whore . . . whore . . . whore."* She clapped her hands over her ears and sank to the floor, curling up protectively, drawing her knees to her chest.

But the damage had already been done. He had already said those things to her. After she had opened herself to him as she never had to another person. Dear God, he had tasted her everywhere. Touched her and kissed her. His mouth . . .

She lowered her head, cradling it in between her knees, covering her face. She wanted darkness. She rocked herself back and forth.

She had hurt when her mother died, but her mother's illness had lasted weeks. She had had time to steel herself to the loss. As to her father, she could remember the man with the drooping mustache who'd come to tell her her father had fallen over in sudden death. He had looked so sad for her, but though she had been shocked, there had been a sense of inevitability, too. Likewise for Peter, though the shock there had been greater. He had been drinking almost as recklessly as her father had done, but he had been so young. She had had her babies, though, Alex and Nell. She had them still.

She must get up off the floor. She had her children. She was responsible for them. She had to uproot them again, but she couldn't think about having to tell them just yet. No, not yet, she promised herself.

They would have to go, though. She wanted to go. She wanted to rip herself out of Sisley.

Anger, finally. Anne felt her heart beat again. Hard. She hated him. He had hurled false suspicions at her before, but how different this time was! She stuffed a knuckle in her mouth and bit hard. She could not bear how different this time was from that first meeting. She had not known him then; she had not spent two months with him. She had not been waiting for him, sleepy and replete from his lovemaking.

She could not get away soon enough. Where would she— Rob! She'd forgotten Rob. He was having breakfast. She couldn't go to the breakfast room. She would not see *him* again. Ever.

A fierce determination to be gone from Sisley lifted Anne off the floor. Taking the back stairs, she encountered a maid whom she sent to bring Rob to her sitting room. There she gathered herself together. She'd have liked to lie to Rob, act as if nothing had happened, but she was not so good an actress. And besides, he'd have seen for himself in the breakfast room his host's reaction to her newly discovered status. She doubted *he* had bothered to mask his anger at finding she had deliberately lived in near poverty in London solely to weave a web of lies around him and his precious title. Anne very nearly hurled a small, handy Dresden figurine at the fireplace. She let go of the thing only because she feared Hetty might be disturbed.

Rob, when he came, looked as anxious as Anne had feared he would. "Great God, Annie, I am relieved to see you whole! I thought I could skate by even when that dough-faced harridan who is a friend of Charles and Helen's recognized me, but Buckingham's sister asked directly about your relationship to Charles, and I couldn't lie. Can you forgive me? Buckingham whirled from the breakfast room as if he had murder on his mind."

"You did nothing, Rob!" Anne seized her cousin's hands in hers and shook them slightly. "It was I who chose not to tell him about Mother's family, and it was he who chose not to ask why I did not, which is very like him. While I may be a stupid fool, he is an arrogant, insufferable man, and I shall be glad to be gone from here!"

"Annie! I have never seen you in such a mood!" And she had hoped to hide the extent of her agitation from him. Anne tried to smile, but Rob rushed on. "Did he hurt you? By God, I feared it. Before he left the room, he went so still that, oddly, all I could think was that he was set to explode. I'll make him pay, Annie. I will, somehow."

"No! Rob! He did not lay a hand on me. I swear it." Anne gave his hands a hard squeeze. "You know my temper. It angered me that coming to know me as well as . . . he has in two months, that he still did not give me the least chance to explain myself. But Rob, did you send me a letter recently?"

"Yes, telling you I would arrive today, though I had thought the hour would be later. Didn't you get it?"

"No." Anne absently pushed an errant lock of hair off her brow. So. There had been a letter. Still, he had not cared enough to ask if she'd received it. "I don't know what happened to it, but I can't think it would have made any difference." Perhaps . . . but no, there was nothing to be gained by thinking what she might have done. Anne looked to Rob and smiled, if a trifle raggedly. "This isn't quite the homecoming I had planned for you. I haven't even told you how glad I am to see you. Let's sit down, shall we, and forget this unpleasantness? I want to hear all about your trip."

Anne congratulated herself for being a better actress than she had thought. Rob made no protest and allowed her to pull him down on the couch beside her. "My trip was a success," he told her, glad to have some good news. "Our coal brought even more than we'd expected. We've more than enough for a cottage for you, and rooms in town for me, as well as a good bit for the next shipment."

"Rob, you are going to be a successful merchant."

"Yes," he grinned. "I do believe I agree."

"Well," Anne said, choosing her next words carefully, "as I said, I should like to set up my own house as soon as possible. Would it be too much, Rob, to ask you to go to Oxford to look for a suitable cottage so soon as tomorrow?"

"Tomorrow?" Rob stared at her. "I really have botched things with Buckingham."

"No," Anne said sharply. "I have already told you. I botched things, and he did, but not you, Rob. Now that's enough, really. I do wish to have my own house, and as I am familiar with Oxford, I thought the area around it would do nicely. It's not so far from here. Do you think you can find something in a few days and then come back for us?"

"I can try," Rob said. "But what if I am not successful in a few days? Should I continue looking or come back for you?"

Anne returned his gaze steadily. "Come back for us. We can let rooms in Oxford, if we must. It is the long holiday. There should be openings."

Rob looked at her anxiously for a long moment and then blurted out, "What of Alex, Annie? Buckingham said things with the grandfather would be settled, but now . . . ?"

But now . . . Anne could not believe that she had not thought about Alex; that Buckingham's break with her should be so terrible that she could think of nothing but that. She had known she'd have to leave Buckingham eventually. But not this way. Dear God, never like this.

Hurt swelled in her, but she forced herself to ignore it.

Looking up at Rob, she realized he was studying her with concern, and her first instinct was to reassure him. "Buckingham promised once that he would not abandon the children, regardless of what might happen. I hope he meant he would not see Alex torn from Nell and me. But his position is irrelevant, really. I have no intention of allowing Peter's father to take Alex."

Hearing her own words, thinking of the struggle that might well still take place, Anne discovered a fresh pain. Her night with Buckingham would be new and so very damning ammunition for Lord John de Montforte. She felt sick, thinking of Buckingham coldly divulging the particulars to his uncle. Oh, please, she prayed frantically, do not let him betray me so completely as that! Surely he would not . . .

"Anne, what is it? You have gone quite pale!"

Looking up, blinking, Anne found Rob's anxious face looming over her. She had sunk back in her chair without realizing it. "I . . . ah, felt dizzy for a moment. But I am fine now. Really. Perhaps I sat too long with Hetty yesterday."

"How is Hetty? I have forgotten to ask after her."

Anne managed a wan smile. "A great deal has happened; I think you may be forgiven. She is much improved. The bout was not serious. Perhaps you should go in to her now. I heard Betta with her a little while ago, but I doubt Hetty will remain awake long. She is still weak." When Rob looked uncertain, as if he were afraid to leave her, Anne forced another smile and pushed at his arm. "I won't run off. Go on, while you may. She doesn't know you are here. She'll be delightfully surprised."

When Rob knocked on Hetty's door, Betta answered, and greeted him with surprise, Hetty called out weakly, demanding to know who was there. Anne heard her give a soft cry of pleasure when Rob stepped into her room, then Betta shut the door and she heard no more.

She sank back in her chair again, as if a great weight were pressing her back. Would he tell his uncle? The question echoed over and over in her mind. No, surely he wouldn't. She hadn't even thought of the possibility, she trusted him so on the subject of Alex. She had been wrong to trust his feelings for her, but Alex was different. He liked her son, knew how important Nell was to him, and his mother, too. He would not betray Alex—unless he thought he would be doing the boy a favor to take him from such a wretched mother? Anne had to lower her head into her hands and breathe deeply. She must not panic. Buckingham was not evil. He would not tell tales to hurt her without thinking what harm he would do to Alex. She must trust him about that. If she did not, she would go mad.

She got up, needing to move to distract herself, but her pacing was interrupted by a visitor. Anne called out, expecting the maid she had left earlier with the children, but to her surprise and very little pleasure, it was Lady Monteith, stylishly turned out in a blue carriage dress, who opened the door and stepped hesitantly into the room.

Anne could not force herself to pretend any warmth of feeling. She did not hold Lady Monteith ultimately responsible for what had happened, certainly, but the woman had made a contribution, however small. She could have said, when she discussed Anne with her brother, "I have known her but a few hours, Trev. I cannot judge, though she appeared a respectable girl." Anne thought that would have been true, but Lady Monteith had not withheld judgment. She had rushed to assert her opinion, and planted a false seed.

"How may I help you, Lady Monteith?"

"I—" She looked away from Anne for a moment, as if she had lost her words. "I came to wish you farewell."

"Thank you. It looks as if you will have a good day to travel." Anne passed her, proceeding to the door. She wanted the woman gone, wondered how she could have come, thinking what she did. "I trust—"

"You can imagine that your cousin's arrival took us by surprise," Lady Monteith rushed to say, before Anne could reach for the door handle.

Anne turned and then slowly smiled with little humor. "Oh yes, I am well aware of that, Lady Monteith, and now . . ."

But Lady Monteith was a de Montforte, and a countess as well, and if she found she could not quite hold Anne's eyes, she was determined to say what she'd come to say. She interrupted Anne again. "My brother did not appear to be in the best of humors."

Anne made no answer, only waited for Lady Monteith to make her point.

"Oh, Anne!" Lady Monteith seemed to wilt before Anne's unbending look. "I judged you unfairly! I thought you scheming. I wish to make amends. I—"

"Please, Lady Monteith." Anne knew her voice was sharp as a razor, but she could not help it. "There is no need for this. I do not hold you responsible for your brother's actions. He is the author of them, as I am of mine."

"I don't blame you for wishing to see the last of me or any of us. I have never seen Trev in such a mood, actually. But that is one of the reasons I came! He would not have reacted so if he did not have some feel—"

"Lady Monteith!" It was quietly said, but not calmly. Lady Monteith broke off in mid-word and colored at the look in Anne's eye. "I shall spare you more of this interview, which cannot be any more pleasant for you than it is for me. There are, indeed, feelings between your brother and me. They are so ugly and repellent that if I never hear of him again, I shall consider myself fortunate. And now, I know you've a long journey ahead of you." Anne opened the door. "I do wish you Godspeed."

Lady Monteith bowed to the inevitable. "Thank you," she said, then stopped just as she passed Anne. "But, please, I have just been to the nursery. Your children are very dear. If there is anything I can do as cousin to Alex and Nell, I hope you will write to me."

"Thank you," Anne said, though from her tone and demeanor, it was obvious she would not write a word to Lady Monteith.

When she closed the door behind her caller, Anne fell back against it, all the starch drained from her. Only by clapping her hand over her mouth could she stifle a mad desire to laugh. The woman had been going to try to promote a marriage between her and Buckingham. She bit the palm of her hand. Too late, Lady Monteith! Oh, too late!

Anne went through the motions of living in the ensuing days. The children were not so disconsolate about leaving Sisley as she had feared. Buckingham had, apparently, gone to the nursery before he had left and prepared them. She never learned quite what he had said. When they spoke of him, as they frequently did, she learned to smile and count numbers until they were done. She played a variation of the same game whenever she found herself thinking of him, or about to. She conjugated Italian verbs. The trick worked well enough, but she had to do it so often, she remained in a daze. The nights, of course, were the worst. In the time between waking and sleeping, Anne was vulnerable, although her dreams were just as tortured. Her bed was an object of loathing to her. Scarcely able to look at it, she took to sleeping on the couch in the sitting room. Betta did not ask her why. Indeed, all the servants seemed exceedingly careful and attentive with her.

Even the footman who came hurrying into the stableyard one morning ducked his head as if he worried about the effect of the message he had for her. Anne gave him her best smile, having had enough of being pitied.

"Yes? Johnson, isn't it?"

"Yes, ma'am!" He seemed to gain strength at the discovery that she knew him. "Mr. Barrett has sent me looking for you, ma'am. It's Lord John de Montforte. He has come and wishes to see you at once in the south drawing room."

The young man, for he could not have been more than eighteen, was watching her. Anne saw his eyes, wide and uncertain, upon her, but she felt as if she were standing at a great remove from him. Peter's father had come. The coincidence was too great. Trev had betrayed her.

She felt so desolate suddenly, she was not certain she would not crumple there and then. To mask her reaction, she leaned down to flick a piece of dirt on her riding skirt. By the time she straightened, she'd found the strength to speak.

"You may tell Mr. Barrett, Johnson, that I will meet his lordship after I have changed out of my riding clothes. That will be in a half hour or so."

Chapter 20

Barrett awaited Anne outside the drawing room. She greeted him with a composed smile she had spent the half hour summoning. "Good day, Barrett. I understand my father-in-law has come. Will you take me to him? And bring in some refreshments in, say, a half hour or so?"

Barrett inclined his head readily. "I will bring tea, Mrs. de Montforte, but no spirits. His lordship suffers from heart illness, you know."

Startled, Anne looked at Barrett closely. He was not in the habit of providing unsolicited information, but already he was opening the doors to the drawing room, making it impossible for her to question him further. All the same, she considered she had been given a warning, and it added an unexpected element to her coming interview. In all her considerations, she had not once thought of Lord John as weak.

"Mrs. Peter de Montforte," Barrett intoned gravely, then, bowing, withdrew, leaving Anne to stare at last across the room into the reddened, belligerently set countenance of her father-in-law. If he was weak, it was only physically.

"So!" he bellowed in a voice loud enough to be heard in Whitchurch, "you are the wench Peter married against my will."

He did not rise, due either to infirmity or disrespect or

both. Anne might have flounced into a seat without his invitation, but as she crossed the room, she decided she preferred to stand and look down on him. She noted the mottled veins in his cheeks. They seemed to stand out more than was ordinary, but she had not been around many people of his age and health.

Her voice distinctly more controlled than his, she said to him, "Yes, I am Anne, the woman your son married."

"The doxy, more like!" he roared, his eyes lighting. They were blue de Montforte eyes, lighter than Peter's, though not so light as Buckingham's.

Anne moved closer, not close enough that he had to crane his head to look at her, but close enough that she could look steadily down into those fiery eyes. "I am not a doxy, sir, nor have I ever been."

Lord John's bushy white brows flew up and his face reddened further. Yet, for all his choler, Anne found him rather vulnerable looking. His shoulders were humped and his head jutted out from his body on a thin neck, and though the day was warm, he had a blanket tucked over his legs.

"My lord," she said quietly, "you arrived only a short while ago, and your journey must have been wearing. Perhaps we should discuss what is between us another day, after you've rested."

"You think to run out on me, do you? To abscond while Trev's away and escape me? I won't allow it! I want my grandson! I'll not have him raised by the likes of you. I've sworn testimonials from four different men saying that you whored with them."

Anne's temper could well have soared out of control at that, but the man's face had turned so red, she was more afraid for him than angry. For a moment, she considered simply leaving the room, but she thought that might upset him even more than having the interview over and done. Carefully, if emphatically, she told him, "The four men may have signed in blood, my lord, but it does not matter. I was innocent when I married your son, and I am still innocent of the deeds to which they falsely attested. Clearly, there is a mistake. Tell me the names of the men who have accused me."

"Eh?" Lord John jerked in surprise, his hands moving restlessly on his covered legs. "Mistake? There's no mistake! They swore on paper, and they're all English gentlemen!"

"I thought the mark of an English gentleman was his regard for honor and fair play."

"What are y'gettin' at?" he demanded, regarding Anne suspiciously.

"I am only trying to appeal to your sense of fair play, my lord."

"What?" he roared, opening his mouth and bellowing like a lion. "Have you the gall to imply I'm no gentleman?"

"I am not implying anything, my lord," Anne repeated patiently. "I am requesting you to behave like the gentleman you clearly are." Lord John stared at her, his mouth working oddly. Anne half feared he would either topple in a heap at her feet, or fling at her the glass sitting on the table beside him. Still, he was the one who had summoned her to him, and so she continued. "Even the rudest, meanest person in this land has the right to know his or her accusers, and the right to mount a defense. I am asking for no more."

"You're cool!" he sneered so scornfully Anne's concern for him receded significantly. "I'll grant you that—giving me a lesson in conduct! I can't imagine who you think you are, you Jezebel!"

"I know precisely who I am, my lord," Anne replied, and though she was unaware of it, her chin lifted. "I am Anne Elizabeth Manwaring Whitfield de Montforte. One of my grandfathers was the vicar of Tewsbury near Oxford, the other was the Earl of Edgemoore." Lord John jerked in surprise, which Anne had not expected. She had assumed Buckingham would have informed his uncle of her better-than-expected connections at the same time he had betrayed that she'd gone to his bed. When Lord John said nothing more, however, she went on with her recitation. "My father studied languages at Oxford, where he met my mother when she came with her family to visit her brother, who was also studying there. Her family was not overjoyed when the two of them married, it is true, but the Manwarings did not prevent the marriage, and she continued to see her family until she died at an early age of a fever. That is who I am, and that is my history. Even the branch of my family that is not so exalted as yours is quite respectable, for all that my father did lose his composure after my mother's death. But whatever my antecedents, I am, also, an Englishwoman, my lord, and as such I maintain that I deserve a fair hearing. You cannot be an impartial judge, as surely you will admit, but you can at the least allow me to know—"

"There, then!" Lord John abruptly raked his arm across the table by him, sweeping some papers onto the floor and nearly upsetting his glass in the process.

Anne caught the glass as it teetered, then knelt down to gather the papers that had been so ungraciously delivered to her. She did not recognize the first three names she read scrawled at the bottom, and she very nearly despaired of settling the matter to her own satisfaction, much less Lord John's. Conscious of the old man's hooded gaze upon her, she caught her breath as she looked at the fourth name. In a rush of satisfaction, she said, "I do know him!"

Lord John snorted. "Knew him well, did you?" he inquired poisonously.

Anne jerked her head up, breathless with fury that her father-in-law had put her and her children through such hardship on the evidence of a man so villainous his own family had sent him from England. But the rush of anger she experienced had pushed out of her mind how old and weak her accuser was, for all his rancor. And when he stiffened, looking almost alarmed by the light blazing in her green eyes, Anne closed them and breathed deeply for a long moment. When she had herself in control again, she rose and went to sit in a chair nearby. Oddly, when she did at last allow herself to look at her father-in-law again, she did not speak directly of the name slashing across the bottom of the paper she held stiffly in her hands.

"Did Buckingham ever see this name?" she asked, holding up the paper.

Lord John studied her, his eyes still cold as ever, but she saw uncertainty flickering in them, too. Finally, he barked, "No! Not that it matters."

So. Buckingham had not thought it important to question the identity of her accusers either. Of course, he hadn't known her then. "Did you ever speak to this man yourself?" Anne demanded, though she knew the answer, and knew as well that she was pushing the old man. She did not repent the small vindictiveness, though. He had cost her so much.

"I did not! I saw no need."

"Neither could you," Anne returned with a coldness she simply could not help. "He died only a few months after he attempted to rape a defenseless Italian girl of thirteen. Of course, you'll not take my word, but you needn't, either. The English ambassador, Lord Audley, the uncle of your nephew's neighbor, Lord Edwards, knew more than he cared to about the Viscount Reading. You may apply to him to learn the reputation of the man whose word you took because, I suppose, he slandered me."

"I'll not listen to this condescending, self-serving prat—" Lord John stopped in mid-tirade, dragging in a breath. His face had turned a deep red, and Anne crossed hastily to the table to move the glass she'd steadied closer to him. He took it and gulped deeply, but never acknowledged her action. When he was done, he slammed down the glass, as if to show he was not incapacitated.

"I don't care what you say about this man, this viscount!" he rasped out in a voice that was only half as loud, but still every bit as belligerent. "My grandson will be raised by people of impeccable reputation, and yours, madam, has not been half so pure since the day you came to live virtually alone with Trev. All the world knows you're his doxy! Ha! I knew you couldn't resist him or the prospect of residing at Sisley. Told him to compromise you, and he did!" The old man's rant had become a shrill, gleeful cackle. "I'll have the boy! He'll not be tainted by the likes of you. You can keep the girl. Trev wrote me that she's not yours at all but some by-blow of Peter's, but I don't want her. Can't abide females! All worthless—"

Suddenly Lord John arched sharply as if some unseen hand had grabbed him by his chest. His mouth flopped open and he made a stricken, gurgling sound as he clapped his hand over his heart. Anne spun and ran to the door, flinging it open. Barrett stood so close, it seemed he'd been about to knock. "Thank God you're here!" she cried. "His lordship is suffering an attack. Get his man! Hurry!"

Anne did not stay to see her order carried out. She ran back to her father-in-law. He had slumped sideways in his chair, and for a second she thought he had died, but then he gasped heavily, loudly, as if he were straining to drag in a breath. Instantly, Anne sprang forward and fairly tore his cravat from him. Mercifully, he began to gulp in air, and, heartened, Anne rushed to bring a stool for his feet, thinking he would breathe even more easily if he weren't cramped. He did not seem aware of her ministrations, and having no idea what else she could do for him, Anne took his free hand in hers. It was cold as death, and she began to chafe it as if she could warm him back to good health.

To her unutterable relief his man came then, and nodded approvingly at the pitifully few measures Anne had taken. Without a word, he calmly opened a case he'd brought with him and taking out a small bottle, poured several drops of a dark liquid into the glass on the table.

His movements were unhurried but efficient, and he soon had his master drinking whatever the tonic was. Anne saw no immediate improvement in Lord John, although she thought he did appear to rest more quietly after a few minutes. Carefully, she released his hand and placed it on the blanket. When he didn't stir, she gestured to his man and the two of them adjourned to the door where Barrett awaited them, looking deeply concerned.

"Dear Lord, that was very frightening!" Anne said to the valet. "I did not have any idea what to do, and I must commend you for your most reassuring efficiency, sir. I am Mrs. de Montforte, by the by."

The small, trim man flushed at Anne's praise. "Thank you, ma'am. I am Ridgley, and pleased to be of service."

"Should we send for a doctor, Ridgley?" Anne asked.

"It would do no harm," he replied, and Anne looked immediately to Barrett who nodded and hurried from the room. "I believe it would not be out of place for me to warn you not to get your hopes up, however, Mrs. de Montforte," Ridgley continued quietly, glancing toward his master. Lord John lay still, with his eyes closed and his mouth half open. "Though his lordship's condition improved after his great attack in April, his doctor warned him it had deteriorated again in the last month, and that he should not travel."

Anne wondered if Buckingham had realized how ill his uncle was. Surely, he would not have so excited the man had he known. "Is there anything we can do?"

"When he has rested a bit, I shall put him to bed. Beyond that and the tonic his doctor has prescribed, there is nothing that I know of, except that he should be kept calm."

"Calm?" Anne echoed faintly, aghast to think how far from calm her father-in-law had been, and how she, at the end, had been less then careful with him. Had she brought on his attack?

Perhaps Ridgley read her self-doubt. When Anne looked to him, she found him regarding her in an almost kindly way. "Perhaps it is not my place to say so, Mrs. de Montforte, but I believe it only right that I assure you that his lordship is not a calm man under any circumstances. He is also stubborn. He should never have come in the first place, but as he did, he ought to have rested before speaking with you."

"Thank you, Ridgley. You are very kind," Anne said, grateful for his reassurances. "As there is nothing more that I can do, I shall leave you to do what you must, but later, when Lord John feels better, please advise him that if he wishes to meet his grandchildren," and she put an emphasis on the plural, "they would be pleased to meet him. I shall want to be present, however," she added, her tone stiffening slightly.

Ridgley inclined his head. "I understand, ma'am."

As Anne told Hetty sometime later, it was a pity Lord John lacked his valet's good manners. "He'd have been dandling his grandson on his knee these several years past had he half the man's manners or sensitivity. Ridgley understood precisely that I wished to be certain that tartar does not spout some ugly nonsense to the children. He even sounded sympathetic."

"Of course he was, my dear," Hetty soothed from the chaise upon which she reclined, for as her strength returned, she had grown weary of her bed. "Anyone with sense must know the old man is mad. It happens to some as they age, you know."

Anne gave her aunt a half smile. "Some?" she teased, but her amusement could not last. Her experience with her father-in-law was too recent. "Merciful heaven! I shall have his attack on my conscience for the rest of my life, whatever Ridgley said. I was cutting toward the end, Hetty, after I learned he had blackened my name on no more than the say-so of that vile wretch who attacked Betta. I imagine the other three names were those of the other men with him. Curse that agent for not checking on his sources! He must have known his employer wanted only the worst information about me, and getting it, never bothered to ask the ambassador or any other of the English people in Italy about me."

"Or asked and chose not to convey their reports, knowing Lord John would not be pleased by them."

"Yes, I suppose that is possible," Anne agreed gloomily. "But the worst of it is that even after he learned the wretched character of his principal witness, Lord John did not relent about demanding Alex." Anne had revealed to Hetty what Lord John had accused her of in Italy—she had been too full of her discovery about her accusers not to do it—but she had not mentioned anything about Buckingham. To divulge what accusation the duke could make would involve admitting too much. But Buckingham's actions in regard to Nell did not involve anything that would sink Anne in her aunt's eyes. "Buckingham knew about Nell." At

Hetty's start, Anne nodded. "He wrote Lord John telling him she is not my child."

"And he never said anything to you, Annie?" Hetty shook her head, disappointedly. "I would not have thought he would do such a thing."

No, they had both misjudged him. Anne smiled thinly. "The irony is, Lord John cares nothing about Nell as she is a girl. Keep the brat, or some such, was his touching sentiment."

Perhaps Buckingham had known his uncle would have no interest in Nell. But if so, why hadn't he told her? Why hadn't she told him Nell wasn't hers, or of her mother's family? Anne shook her head as if to clear it of her thoughts; she was coming to doubt herself. She wasn't even certain any longer that Buckingham had told his uncle about her one shameful yielding to him. Lord John had not spoken as if he had come fresh from a meeting with the duke. And it did seem so unlikely that Buckingham would excite his uncle, risking the man's life merely to revenge himself on her. Anne rose to her feet and began to pace, though only minutes before she had felt too drained to move. She was making excuses for him, still trying to see him in the best light! She was mad. Although he had written his uncle about Nell, he had never bothered to inform him he'd discovered Anne was not a doxy, and that after spending two months with her.

"Oh, I wish Rob would return! It has been five days now!" she exclaimed.

"But, my dear, we cannot leave now, not with Lord John ill!" Hetty protested. "It would not be right."

Anne whirled about, unable to face Hetty's dismay. It was too much. She couldn't stay. She could not see Buckingham again. She would not. She had not invited the old man to Sisley. She had no responsibility for him. Except that he was her children's grandfather.

Hetty started to say more, but Dr. Johnstone came to them to report that Lord John was resting fairly well, and that he must continue to rest if he was to recover to any extent. "He must sleep and avoid excitement of any kind, for his heart is very weak. Unfortunately, I could see even from the few words we exchanged that he does not possess the temperament to rest."

Anne could not but agree, though she did not do so aloud. She carefully listened to Dr. Johnstone's instructions about administering the medicines he'd left in Ridgley's charge. After the good man had looked over Hetty as well, she invited him to stay for tea, and it was as she was serving him a cup that Betta burst into the room, wringing her hands, her face white with distress.

Chapter 21

"Signora! Signora!"

Anne caught the girl's hand to calm her, and at her touch, Betta let loose a torrent of Italian which Anne interrupted sharply from time to time.

"What is it, Annie? What has happened?" Hetty broke in to query, for she and Dr. Johnstone could not follow a word of the conversation.

A white line of strain edging her mouth, Anne turned to her aunt. "It is Alex. He cannot be found."

"Perhaps he has only gone for a walk—into the woods, say," Dr. Johnstone remarked, unknowingly echoing what Anne had said herself.

As Betta had, Anne shook her head. "His pony is missing. Betta went to the stables when she could not find him in the house, and Daisy, his pony, is gone."

"Surely one of the grooms must have gone with him, then," Dr. Johnstone said, but again Anne shook her head.

"Most of them were out, exercising Lord Trevelyan's horses, and the one left behind says he never saw Alex. Betta believes he was napping and is afraid to admit it."

"Well, even if he has gone for a ride, I cannot think you need look so worried, Annie." Hetty offered her assurance earnestly. "It is only a boy's lark, I am sure."

"I imagine you are right, Aunt Hetty." Anne essayed a

smile. "Still, I shall go and see if Nell knows more than we do. You will excuse me?"

Anne scarcely heard Hetty and the doctor bid her farewell. Anxiety clutched at her. It was not as if Alex could not have ridden, if he had wanted. Anne had told the children their grandfather had come and asked them to prepare themselves to meet him, but after Lord John's attack, she had sent Betta to tell them of it and tell them they could play as they wished. She had not gone herself. She had not wanted the children to see her as shaken as she had been. She'd taken a walk to calm herself, and afterward had gone directly to speak to Hetty, who knowing more, had been the most concerned about her interview with Alex's grandfather. Now she castigated herself. Why had she not gone to them herself? And where had Alex gone? Perhaps he had gone for a ride without a groom, but that was unlike him. He knew he was cared for and that his unexplained absence would cause concern. Biting her lip, Anne tried to remember if she had said or done anything to betray the reason for Lord John's visit and the threat he presented. She didn't believe she had, but she found it unsettling that Alex would disappear on the very day Lord John arrived.

In the nursery, Nell was sitting in a small rocking chair near the window, her favorite doll hugged tightly to her. Anne's heart sank at the sight. Normally, Nell would have been busy, dressing the doll, perhaps, or reading her a story, but she was sitting like an old woman, staring out at the view of sky and treetops the nursery window afforded, rocking steadily.

"Nell." Anne pulled up a larger chair beside the little rocker. "Alex is missing, and I am worried. Do you by chance know where he could be?" Nell did not look at her mother, but Anne saw her head move in a faint, scarcely perceptible nod. "Will you tell me what you know?"

Nell turned then, yet could not meet Anne's eyes. "Is is after four o'clock, Mama?"

"I don't know," Anne answered truthfully, forcing herself to patience, though anxiety tore at her. "I have lost track of the hour, I'm afraid. Did Alex ask you to wait to tell me anything until after four o'clock?"

"Yes." Anne's inspired guess brought Nell's eyes to her face. They were wide with confusion.

"Oh, darling!" Anne caught her hand and squeezed it. "You look so worried, Nell, and though it may be a bit before four, it is not many minutes before the hour, and besides, Nell, I really do not believe Alex would fault you for sparing me worry, now that I do know he's ridden somewhere on Daisy."

Perhaps it was Anne's logic that convinced the child, or perhaps the worry clearly etched upon her face. Carefully letting go her mother's hand, Nell searched in the pocket of her dress and removed a folded, somewhat battered piece of paper. "Alex did not want you to worry, Mama," she said in a small voice as she held out the paper.

Whatever Alex might have wanted, he caused his mother's heart to plummet when she read his note. It was written in the painstaking block printing he was working hard to master. "Dear Mama," it began, on a slanting line. "Do not worie about me. I have gone to find cusin Trev. He will not alow my grandfather to shout at you and take me away. Alex."

Even as panic flooded her, Anne felt a spurt of bitterness that Alex should have turned to Buckingham. He had made her children believe they could rely upon him. Now one of them had run off to him, though he was miles and miles away, and though he would likely betray Alex to the very man Alex sought to escape.

"Nell, what led Alex to believe your grandfather shouted at me about Alex?"

"We heard two maids talking while they swept out the nursery. You were with him, and they said our grandfather was mad." Nell's eyes filled with tears, and when Anne swept her into her arms, Nell began to sob. "They said he shouted at you viciously, and that you are a fine lady and mother, and that Cousin Trev would not have stood for it if he had been here. We didn't know what else to do, Mama. We were afraid he would hurt you and take Alex."

"But why did you not come to me, Nell?"

Anne tried to make the query gentle, though she wanted to shriek it. Nell sniffed. "We did not know if our grandfather would let you go."

"Then Alex left before he knew your grandfather fell ill?"

Nell nodded. "When Betta came, I told her . . . I told her Alex was with Mrs. Goodwin!"

At the confession Nell began to cry again. "Hush, Poppet." Anne stroked her curly head. "You ought not to have lied to Betta, and I know you'll never do it again, but you thought you had overwhelming reason this time. Just now, however, we must concentrate on finding Alex, for though he is a resourceful fellow, it is a long way to Leicestershire, and he is very small. Do you have any notion if he knew where to go?"

The child nodded. "Yes, our cousin Maddy came to see us in the nursery before she left Sisley." Nell sat up in her mother's lap. "She showed us on our map where she lives in Leicestershire. Alex knows he must go north until he reaches Rothwell, and then he turns toward the setting sun. Cousin Maddy lives only a little west of Rothwell, you see."

"Did he intend to go by the road?" Anne was glad she had thought to ask the question, for Nell shook her head.

"No. We thought there might be highwaymen, and so he decided to ride near the road but not on it."

When she was certain Nell had no more to confide, Anne left her with Betta and went to organize a party to search for her son. The household was abuzz with the news of Alex's disappearance, and Barrett, bless him, had had the astounding foresight to send for O'Neill. The head groom awaited her in the library looking so grave, Anne hastened to assure him that she did not hold him or any of his men responsible. "It is not your duty to watch Alex, Mr. O'Neill, and truly this isn't like him. He is frightened and determined to seek out Buckingham. According to Nell, Alex left sometime around one o'clock and is riding near but not on the road that runs north."

O'Neill volunteered all his grooms to ride after the child. "We'll fan out, Mrs. de Montforte, with some of us ridin' on the road and some on either side."

"That sounds like an excellent plan, Mr. O'Neill. But I mean to come as well. I know I am not the rider you and your men are, but I cannot be certain that Alex will come to you unless I am there."

Anne did not explain further, though she realized that given the eavesdropping, inadvertent or intentional, that had obviously gone on, both Barrett and O'Neill were surely as well informed of the purpose of Lord John's visit as the maids were. O'Neill never hesitated. Displaying an understanding for which Anne would ever be grateful, he accepted her presence with a brisk nod. "Of course, ma'am. I'll have Lady saddled and waitin'."

Barrett, for his part, assured her earnestly that the entire staff would send up prayers for the boy's safety. "Master Alex is a great favorite with everyone," he added, earning himself a smile he confided later to a distraught Mrs. Goodwin he would not soon forget.

After she had hastily donned her riding clothes, Anne hurried to Hetty's room. She was pleased to find Dr. Johnstone still there, and most grateful to him when he said he intended to stay. He did not say why he stayed, whether it was to be on hand for Lord John, Hetty, or God forbid, Alex, but Anne was glad Hetty would have his calm, reassuring presence, as would Nell and Betta, for she had had the maid who'd helped her dress fetch them so that she could bid Nell farewell.

As she gave Nell a kiss, Anne heard the sound of horses on the drive and cut her leavetaking short. She suspected it was only O'Neill's grooms, but she hoped it was Rob, finally returned from Oxford.

She had reached the final landing of Sisley's great oak staircase when a footman rushed to open the front door. There was only one footman, Barrett evidently was distracted with the two crises that had occurred on the same day. Anne paused, as if to concentrate all her attention and thereby conjure Rob.

She did succeed to a certain extent in her efforts. It was not O'Neill who stepped through the door, sweeping off his hat and gloves and tossing them into the care of his footman. It was the last man in all the world she wanted to see, and they were alone in the large, intricately carved hall. The footman had sped away.

He looked up and found her as unerringly as if she had made some movement and drawn his eyes, though Anne knew she had not.

There was no question of retreating. There was Alex, and her pride.

Buckingham took in the grim, unwelcoming set of her features. "Surprised to see me?" he taunted in a cool voice. Striding toward the stairs, he raked Anne with an unreadable glance. "I cannot think why. I warned you I would return within a week." Anne was certain he had given her the full week, but he did not wait for her to argue. "Yet, here you are, tripping down my stairs, ready to ride out with someone—though I find upon reflection that I am not at all astonished to see you are ensconced still."

He looked impossibly handsome, all black hair and blue eyes and strong, chiseled features. Anne clenched her jaw. She could not credit that his looks could affect her, startle her almost, not when he spoke to her so. Not after all that had happened, not after playing her friend and then her lover only to toss her aside as hurtfully as he could at the first test.

She wanted to hurt him as he had hurt her. All the ugly things he'd said came back to her. She tried to tell him that he and his uncle might have Alex's life on their hands, but she could only get as far as opening her mouth. To Anne's horror, she could not force speech past a great tightness in her chest.

"Have you come to think of Sisley as yours?" he mocked from the foot of the stairs. "Is that why you can't tear yourself away? Or did you think I might still be interested in you as my mistress?"

"*No!*" The denial tore loose from somewhere deep inside Anne and seemed to take a piece of her with it. "You've accomplished what you wanted."

"Oh?" he queried, smiling the cold, thin smile of a stranger. "That intrigues me. I wonder what it is that you believe I wanted."

Before Anne could tell him that his uncle had revealed his goals quite clearly, the front door swung open again. It was O'Neill. He looked first to Buckingham and inclined his head. "Good afternoon, your grace. Will you be coming with us, then? When I saw you'd come, I had Jester saddled."

"That was thoughtful, O'Neill, but I can't say, as I don't know where you are going."

He looked at Anne, his eyes narrowed, as if he expected some lie from her, but she had thought of her own question and blurted it at once. "Did you come from the north today?"

"No, actually, the east." He did not explain the surprising direction. "Why?"

"I'll be waiting outside, your grace," O'Neill said, flicking an uncertain glance from Anne to his master.

She began to stay him, to say they would go at once, but Buckingham spoke first, addressing O'Neill, though he never took his eyes from Anne. "Yes, that will do nicely, O'Neill." He saw Anne's instinctive reaction and started up the stairs, startling her into stillness. He had made the landing, was towering over her, his eyes holding hers, when the clicking of the door proclaimed O'Neill's removal. "Now you will tell me what faradiddle you've created to give you reason to stay at Sisley."

Faradiddle. He judged her even before he'd heard the charges, never mind her defense. "I hate you," she said, her teeth clenched so tightly she could scarcely speak. "You have stripped me of everything. Everything, perhaps even my son, and yet you act as if you are the one harmed. Well, you may lick your precious wounds without my insidious presence to vex you! I'll send word as to where you may have Nell and Hetty and Betta conveyed. That should please you—that and the company of your mad uncle.

Come to think of it, the two of you are a matched pair the way you rave on about naught but illusions."

Trev caught her by the shoulders and shook her, the movement so forceful her tall beaver hat slid sideways. Anne caught it before it fell, but she was powerless to shake off his hold. "You will tell me this instant what it is *you* are raving about. And I warn you, Anne—don't try my patience further. I would think nothing of taking you over my knee now. You are a liar and a strumpet—"

Anne struck him so hard the cracking sound reverberated through the entry hall, echoing over and over. For an endless moment neither of them moved. Trev held Anne still in a hold so tight it would leave bruises, and she stared back, white-faced with shock at the violence she'd committed.

She could not apologize, though, no matter how wrong it was to hit another. She was glad she had done it, no matter how he retaliated, and she lifted her chin, defying him to do his worst.

He read her gesture and smiled grimly. "You will pay, Anne, but not at this moment. Now, what I want is to know the whole—why O'Neill is riding out with you and when my uncle came."

Anne eyed him narrowly. "You really did not know he had come?"

"Had I known, I would not ask about him," Trev retorted curtly.

"He came this morning, and shortly thereafter we had an interview quite as unpleasant as you could hope. Unfortunately," she looked him resolutely in the eye, though she knew he would blame her, "Lord John became overexcited and suffered a heart spasm. He is not mortally ill," she hastened to add, when Buckingham started. "Dr. Johnstone has been to see him, and says he will mend if he remains quiet." Anne did not allow herself the luxury of sarcasm. The day was wearing on, but she could not go after Alex unless Trev released her. "While we were preoccupied with Lord John, Alex chanced to overhear a discussion about his grandfather's intentions. He took fright and fled. To you."

"To me?"

She smiled a bitter smile. "Rich, isn't it? He fled to the very man who wished to give him over to a grandfather so mad, he took the word of the Viscount Reading against his own son's wife." Anne looked defiantly at Buckingham, allowing herself to savor the surprise, and even repugnance, that flickered across his expression. "I see you know of Reading, your uncle's sworn source. As to Alex, Hetty and Nell know as much as I, and Dr. Johnstone is waiting with them in case . . ." Anne shrugged, unable to finish the painful thought. "At any rate, I want to be off. Let go of me."

But Trev did not release her. "You are not going anywhere," he said preemptorily. "You'd only slow O'Neill."

"But I don't think Alex will go to O'Neill!" Anne cried, panic raising the pitch of her voice. "He'll think his grandfather sent him and hide, if he can. Please! You can't mean me so ill as this!"

"Don't be absurd!" Trev snapped. "I am going. You will only slow O'Neill down."

"No! You want to take him!" Anne made a furious effort to free herself, but she only succeeded in causing Trev to tighten his grip.

"Where would I take him but here? Do you think I am afraid I cannot control the two of you together?"

Trev expected the ludicrous question to bring Anne to her senses, but she cried wildly, "I have to go! He may be hurt! He has been on the road for nearly three hours. Anything could have happened to him. Dear God, you could not be so cruel! I must go!" Her voice cracked.

"All right!" Trev agreed abruptly. She was frantic enough to follow alone, and the thought of her alone on the road was unexpectedly, but nonetheless decidedly, intolerable. "You may come, but if you fall behind, I will send you back with one of the grooms."

Chapter 22

Trev watched Anne's shoulders sag and her head nod, then suddenly she jerked, stiffening, and sat straight again. He had expected her to give up in weariness after no more than an hour, two at the most. She had never ridden even that long, but now it was nine o'clock. They had been riding for five hours, and if her shoulders were sagging, her will was not. If anything, he thought she seemed more determined with every hour. Certainly more desperate.

There had been no sign at all of Alex. They had asked at every house and cottage along the way, ridden the bridle paths in the woods, and inquired in both the villages they'd passed if anyone had seen a small boy on a pony. The answer had invariably been the same painful no.

Now the light was fading rapidly, and they were all tired and hungry. There was an inn ahead. It was not a large one, but it was clean. Trev had taken luncheon there once on his way to Maddy's. It would do for a night. He had spoken to O'Neill. Now he only had to tell Anne that her child would have to spend the night without her. Without apology, he knew he would rather have faced a squadron of crack French troops.

With a scarcely perceptible movement of his head, he sent two grooms into the woods on the left and another two riding through woods on the right. O'Neill and the last groom fell back. Trev noted that they avoided Anne's eyes. The knowledge that his men were loathe to disappoint her did little to lighten his task. He wished, in fact, that he could order O'Neill to do the deed. He thought she'd not resist O'Neill as she would him, for she was fond of his head groom.

Trev pulled Jester in beside her and said more abruptly than he had intended. "We shall stop for the night at the inn ahead."

Although he had expected the incredulous look Anne turned upon him it did not affect Trev any less. He felt something like the murderer her green eyes proclaimed him. "Stop for the night? But we cannot! We've not found Alex. What if—"

"There will be no moon tonight," Trev cut her off, his voice firm, though he did not find it any easier than Anne to think of Alex, all of five, alone in the dark for an entire night. "We will not be able to see the road, much less look for a small boy in the woods. We won't be able to inquire at any houses we pass, and come morning when we will have some chance of success, we'll be too exhausted to press on. We will stop for the night, Anne."

"You may stop for the night. I intend to press on."

The stubborn answer was too much for a temper severely tried by frustration. "Very well, you may go on by yourself, and if some miscreant chances upon you in the dead of night, I hope he leaves enough of you intact that Alex may recognize you." She gave a strangled gasp, and Trev swore. "Devil take it, Anne! I apologize, but we cannot go on as a group or alone. It will not be of benefit to Alex, no matter how hard it may be to take rest when we do not know if he is safe and sound."

She said nothing, only rode a little straighter in the saddle, as if to show him she could ride for ten hours more. Trev edged his gelding slightly in front of hers, should she take it into her head to try and gallop past him and the inn, but she turned in meekly enough when they arrived. She rode directly to the mounting block and dismounted unaided, but she could not walk without assistance. She had been in the saddle so long her legs buckled.

Trev caught her as she started to crumple. "Give yourself a minute," he directed dispassionately, though every muscle in him seemed to tighten the moment he touched her.

She nodded, refusing to look at him. Trev could feel her trembling, from weariness he supposed, but nonetheless, after no more than a precise minute, she stepped away from him. She stumbled on the step, but righted herself before he could catch her again. The innkeeper puffed out, and Trev bespoke accommodations for his party. Cartwright, the innkeeper, was all willingness to please, of course, and when Anne stumbled again, he clucked over her like a mother hen and took her arm. She suffered the innkeeper's assistance with a smile, though the pleasant expression did not last beyond the negative answer he gave when Trev asked if anyone had seen or spoken to a boy riding alone on a pony. In the light of the candle branches blazing in the inn's entryway, Trev saw the look of despair that crossed her face. His jaw tight, he turned to the innkeeper to explain their circumstances and secure nightclothes and a comb, at least, for Anne. She said nothing. He wasn't certain she could speak by then, and considered carrying her in his arms up to her room so that she might wash before dinner, but she was already following Cartwright, leaning heavily on the banister.

Trev went to speak to his men. He wished them to take watches in the stables that night and to leave a lantern burning, all on the very slender chance that Alex might be near and drawn to the inn. Afterward he found his way to the private parlor he had reserved, hoping he would find Anne already there. She was not, and when two giggling maids bustled in with the dinner he had ordered, and she still had not come down, he tossed off his claret and went up to her room. An odd knot of fear gripped him at the thought she'd somehow managed to ride off on her own. He opened her door and discovered the truth—after washing her face and hands and taking down her hair, she had fallen asleep on the bed, fully dressed but for her boots.

She lay on her side, her knees drawn up toward her chest, presenting her bottom in dusty skirts to him. He imagined she would have bruises there from the ride. They would be dark on the rounded, white flesh. A sacrilege. His eyes traveled over her thighs. In the skirts they looked only slender. In the flesh, they were sweetly rounded too. He knew the furrow that ran down her back, the creamy white of her shoulders. And her hair. It looked no different than it had that night—sable on a white pillow.

He had returned to Sisley early. Anne had been right to start in protest when he challenged her continued presence—he had said he would give her a full week to depart from Sisley, but he had been there on the fifth day.

He left her room, returning to the private parlor and his meal, but he scarcely knew what he ate. His thoughts were on the woman he'd left, and on his sister, too, for Maddy had played a small part in bringing him there. Not that she had said much. Indeed, wary of his mood, she had limited herself to a single question. In an inn where they had stopped for luncheon on their way into Leicestershire, after their traveling companions had left to refresh themselves, she had turned to him. It was obvious she had been thinking about Anne and could not restrain herself. The question had fairly burst out of her. "Why did she not tell you, Trev? What reason did she give?"

He could not give her an answer, of course. Oh, he'd defended himself bitingly enough that Maddy had said not a word more. He was good at biting when he was defensive. His father had had the same tendency. Trev could remember well enough being on the sharp end of his father's rapier-like tongue, and not always deservedly.

But what could Anne have said? What legitimate reason could she have given for withholding something so vital to her dispute with Lord John, not to mention to her relations with him?

Damn! He couldn't know, for he hadn't asked. Hadn't even, if he recalled correctly, ceased flaying her with his tongue long enough for her to volunteer some reason, or excuse.

When he had announced, early, that he was leaving
Maddy's, his sister had looked pleased. That partly smug,
partly hopeful smile of hers had whipped up his temper.
He'd laughed scathingly and inquired in the same tone if
she were now going to promote a known whore for his
wife. For good measure, when she had stiffened, he had informed her he was taking himself to London, not Sisley.

Perhaps he had even thought he was. He had taken the
London road for a time. A short time. Due east of Sisley,
he'd turned abruptly.

Yet the closer he had gotten to her, the angrier he had become. The exact moment of his arrival had been a bad time
for her to encounter him. Particularly as there had not even
been a footman's presence to constrain him. He had deserved the slap.

She had accused him of stripping her of everything. As
he had nothing tangible of hers, he presumed she had meant
her pride. He could sympathize with her fury, even that "I
hate you." He felt the same.

She had stripped him in her turn. He could hurl the same
accusation. She had played him for a fool! He hated her.

But there was the sticking point, for, in truth, he did not.

He did not want to want her as he did. He had not lasted
five days without her. Not a week! Siren. Witch. No
woman had ever drawn him so.

Nor inspired such a desire to protect her. Even thinking—knowing—her a jade. She had said the interview with
Lord John had been as unpleasant as he could hope. He had
not allowed her to see how he had gone cold inside at the
thought of it. He had never been the butt of his uncle's temper. He was Buckingham, an idolized older brother's first-
born. But he had heard enough other people describe the
old man's temper as savage. For over a month he had believed, when he had thought of it, that he would be with her
for the interview. Damn and damn again. She had gotten
the savage side of both their tongues in one day.

And to learn it had been Reading who had sworn against
her. How very strange that was. He had whipped the viscount once with his fists, when they had been boys at

school. It didn't bear thinking on why. Suffice it to say, Trev wouldn't have taken the man's word had he been on his deathbed.

Trev stiffened suddenly. Reading was dead, had died in Italy, and so rumor had it, in a common brawl. It was too great a coincidence. Surely, he had been the one who had led the attack on Betta. He had learned Anne's name. And when Peter had run him off from their house, Reading had found another way to exact revenge for her having broken up his cruel sport.

Trev swept up the bottle of claret, his grasp tight as if he were thinking of the Viscount Reading's vicious throat. At least he'd had the satisfaction of having beaten the man bloody. The thought made him smile grimly when he reached his room. It was almost enough.

And she'd other, greater heartaches now, anyway. He drank the claret he'd brought up with him, as he removed almost as few clothes as Anne had and lay down in his bed, all the while thinking about Alex. He wondered whose discussion the boy had overheard, and what exactly had been said to send him hieing off by himself to Leicestershire. He was a brave boy, and had a strong instinct to protect those he loved. Anne had had to restrain him physically from leaping into the river after Nell. And where was he? How had they missed him, for miss him they certainly had. The boy could not have outpaced them so on a pony.

Perhaps Trev dozed, but if he did, it was lightly, for he heard a door close quietly, and sat up, fully alert. He pulled on his boots and grabbed up his coat, for it was she. He knew it, and knew he'd been half expecting her to set out in search of Alex, though it was madness to do so.

She was quick and quiet. From the top of the stairs, he saw her slip silent as a wraith around the corner at the bottom, her boots in her hand. The front door was locked by that time at night, and opening it proved somewhat difficult. Outside, she had to slip on her boots. Trev caught her in the yard.

Hearing the inn door open, Anne flung a startled look over her shoulder. She knew at once by his size and the fluid way he moved who it was. She ran, though how she'd have gotten to a horse and mounted before he seized her, she could not have said. It was simply instinct that sent her flying.

He caught her from behind, half lifting her by her waist and pulling her tightly against him. "No more, Annie," he warned, breathing hard. "You have only to look about you to see how inky dark it is. If you ride out, not only will you miss Alex, but you will also break that lovely neck of yours."

Anne bit her lip, trying to resist to pull of his voice. It was too familiar, stirred too much, so rough and low. "What do you care?" she flung at him, her voice sharp with disgust for herself as much as him.

"What would I tell Al—damn it, Annie!"

She had jabbed him in the ribs with a pointy elbow. He exacted revenge, locking the offending arm with his and doing the same with one of her legs, so she could not kick him if she thought of it. She strained against him violently, but he held her prisoner.

"I have to go, Trev! I cannot bear it!"

The anguish in her voice was torture. Trev tightened his hold, pulling her into the warmth of his body. There was nothing else to do. He could feel his heart beating against her back; feel her bottom nestled in the cradle of his thighs.

She struggled again, though she must have known it was futile. When she surrendered, she sagged, beaten, against him. "He is so small!" She was crying. He could hear the tears in her voice.

"We'll find him, Annie. I swear it to you. We'll ride out at dawn. It won't be long now."

"Oh, Trev! What if . . ." She was turning into his arms. He loosened his hold just enough for that. "I have to go, don't you see?" It was a black night. He could see the shape of her face as she lifted it to him, no more. He could feel her breasts, though, full and firm pressing against him. "Please, Trev! I'll go mad!"

Anne clutched at his hard, strong arms. Desperate over Alex, she didn't think how different his hold had become, or hers. Yet, then, when freeing herself was not even in her mind, he released her. She stumbled slightly, his release was so unexpected. Trev caught her, but she could tell he was not attending to her. His head was half turned and then she, too, heard the footsteps pounding rapidly around the corner of the inn.

"Your grace!" It was Tucker, Anne could tell from his voice. Like her, he had recognized Buckingham despite the dark. His next words, breathless and triumphant, wiped out any thought but one. "It's Master Alex! He's here!"

Anne shot forward, taking Tucker so by surprise, he fell back a step. "Alex is here, Tucker? Where?"

"He came to the stables, ma'am. And he's fine."

She ran then, across the dark yard, picking up her skirts, her heels flying high like a young girl's.

Trev strode after her, reaching the stable door just behind her. He saw Alex turn. Seeing his mother, the boy gave a sobbing cry and ran to throw his arms around her with such a force that Anne rocked backward. But she held on. Dear God, but she held him to her so tightly, bending over him, murmuring his name over and over, that Trev felt his chest fill painfully.

Glancing about he saw Tucker watching, his fists balled tight, and O'Neill blinking suspiciously. Trev caught their eyes and, nodding toward the door, sent them outside. When he turned back, Alex had lifted his face from his mother's skirts. Tears streamed down his cheeks.

"Are you angry with me, Mama?" he asked in a tremulous voice. Anne could not speak for a moment. She could only shake her head and smile.

"But you are crying," Alex said in a small voice, and indeed there were tears slipping down her face.

"They are tears of the greatest joy, my own," she managed to say, finally. "I was very frightened for you, you see. But how could I fault you, when you acted for my sake, Alex? Only, my love," Anne dropped down on one knee so that she could look directly into her son's reddened eyes, "I must have your vow that you will never act on my behalf again until you have consulted with me. Together we shall come to a solution that is not so dangerous as your running off all alone. Do you agree?"

Sniffing back his tears, Alex nodded. "Yes. I was very afraid after night fell."

Anne could not speak at that, and she caught Alex to her again. He peeped over her shoulder and caught Buckingham's gaze.

"Cousin Trev!" he cried, his voice wavering. "But . . . but it was you I sought!"

"Yes, I am here, Alex. I returned early." Trembling with relief and elation, Anne nonetheless heard that. She swung her head around to stare at Trev. He'd come forward, but all his attention was on Alex. "I am very glad to see you, young man. I was also very worried, as was everyone at Sisley. I know that you did not mean to cause anyone anxiety, and most particularly not your mother, but now that you know you did, I firmly expect you never, ever to break your vow to her."

"No, sir." Alex's voice was small, but his fervency was unmistakable.

Trev nodded, a smile of great warmth breaking out on his face. "Good lad. And in addition to being a good lad, I imagine you may be a hungry one as well. Shall we see what the innkeeper can arrange at this hour?"

"Oh, yes!" Alex exclaimed with the sort of relief that only comes after a boy realizes he has received all the scolding he will get for an act that has proven to be foolish in the extreme. "I have not eaten since luncheon."

Cartwright, the innkeeper, had already been roused by one of his stable hands, and as it was the Duke of Buckingham who did the asking, he was delighted to serve ale to the duke's men, produce meat pasties and cider for the duke's young cousin, and brandy and a glass of Madeira, for his grace and the lad's mother, all at one o'clock in the morning. But that was Quality for you and besides, it did warm his heart to see the lady, fair lovely as she was, looking so misty-eyed and hardly able to keep from squeezing the boy's hand, even while he ate.

Chapter 23

Alex fell on his pasties with a nearly religious fervor. Two vanished in the twinkling of an eye, the third Anne thought she actually saw him eat, and by the fourth he had slowed enough to talk between bites.

He had ridden steadily for hours, most times through the woods but occasionally along the edge of the fields. Once or twice he had seen a farm laborer in the distance, but he had spoken to no one and skirted the villages. At first the riding was not so bad. From what Anne could gather, he had felt brave and cheerful, but as time passed he became hungrier and wearier. Falling into a doze, he nearly slid off Daisy and decided to take a nap.

"When I awoke it was dark, and I couldn't see. I didn't know what to do, but I was too hungry to sleep again and so I led Daisy to the road. By the time we came to the inn, I was tired again. I thought I'd sleep in the stable as there wouldn't be any wild animals there, then when I slipped through the door, Tucker was there. I couldn't believe my eyes, and I was glad, even if he did take me back."

"You needn't worry about your grandfather, Alex," Trev said, reading the sudden darkening of the boy's eyes easily enough. "He will not hurt you."

"The maids said he shouted viciously at Mama and that

you would not stand for it," Alex said, regarding Trev uncertainly.

So. It had been the maids he overheard, and her interview with his uncle as difficult as he had feared. "Your grandfather is very old, Alex. Perhaps he did not realize quite how he behaved, but you may be assured that he will not do such a thing again."

Anne was sitting beside Alex at the inn's kitchen table. The oak table was old and worn buttery-smooth from years of use. She had been running her finger along it, but she looked up then, once again surprised by something Buckingham said to Alex. Again, though, his attention remained focused upon her son, and with reason.

"He wants to take me away," Alex was saying to his cousin. There was question in his voice, and a quiver of fear. Anne laid her hand over his and squeezed it. Alex's gaze never wavered from Buckingham's.

"Yes, he does want to," Trev admitted straightforwardly. "But that only means we shall have to face him and convince him that taking you away would not be a wise course to follow. And we shall, Alex."

Alex nodded then, satisfied, and finishing his cider, turned to his mother. "I am sleepy now, Mama."

Anne was staring at Buckingham again, nonplussed, but Alex drew her attention away, and she rumpled his hair. "No doubt you are. It is after one o'clock. Come on, then. We'll see what sort of cot Mr. Cartwright has produced for you in my room."

It was evidently a very comfortable cot, for Alex fell asleep almost as soon as his head hit the pillow. When Anne straightened from kissing him good night, she found Trev standing in the connecting doorway between their rooms. She had not noticed the door before, and started.

"He had no difficulty falling asleep?" Trev asked quietly, looking beyond her to the boy.

Anne shook her head. "No."

She was aware that her blood seemed to be rushing too quickly through her veins, and knew Alex's safety had naught to do with the quickening in her.

"Would you care for a final glass of Madeira? I negotiated with Cartwright for it and the brandy—for medicinal purposes."

He sounded faintly humorous. But he was regarding her steadily. She lifted her chin. "I should like a glass of Madeira, yes, but I do not wish to be accused of trying to entrap you. Will I be?"

His light blue gaze never left hers. "No."

He went before her, turning back through the open doorway into his room. She could have slammed the door shut and shot the bolt. Anne thought of it only fleetingly.

Trev stood at a small, high table placed before the window. He had taken off his coat. His shirt was rumpled, as if he had slept in it, and lay open at his throat. Anne could see his shoulder bones, his skin sleek and taut over them. The next button, she knew, would reveal dark chest hair.

She pulled her eyes away from the V of bare skin just before he looked up to hand her a glass of pale, sweet wine. "Here's to Alex's safety," he said, raising his own glass of brandy.

"Indeed," Anne said, and took a swallow. Her eyes fell to his chest again, and the hard, lean strength of him. As she had had occasion to do before, she decried the unfair advantage his looks gave him.

Turning away from him, she saw that the room was small, but there were two chairs on either side of the table. She took the one nearest her room, settling into its depths, studying the wine in her glass. A long moment of silence passed before she spoke, addressing her glass. "Why did you not tell me you knew about Nell?"

Trev had seated himself on the bed directly in front of her, and the branch of candles on the table cast his shadow on the wall. From the corner of her eye, Anne saw the shadow start abruptly and was not surprised. Of all the questions to be asked, it was one he'd not have expected.

Still, he answered readily, his voice low and firm, "I waited for you to tell me."

Anne's eyes found his of their own will. There was surprise in her green ones, and a hint of chagrin, too. "I thought your uncle would take her as I'd no legal claim over her."

Trev shook his head. His legs were stretched out before him, crossed at the ankles. The toe of his boot was only a hair's breadth from Anne's. "John wants an heir. He doesn't have any desire for a girl."

"No," Anne agreed dryly, "He certainly hasn't, but I did not know before of his antipathy toward women."

Trev's jaw tightened. "Was he that bad? Was he vicious as Alex said?"

Anne bit her lower lip with her teeth. "It was not an easy interview, no, and as you may have gathered, the entire household knows just how poorly he regards me, and why."

"And takes your side, it would seem," Trev added.

Anne half-shrugged, half-nodded. "That is some consolation, I suppose, but I would rather not have put them to the test. I don't know what your experience of Lord John is, really, or what you consider vicious, but I do not believe he is entirely well in his mind. He is certainly physically ill. I thought at one moment that he had died."

She looked very grim. Trev said flatly, "He didn't though, and if he had, he'd have brought the attack on himself." Their eyes locked. The moment seemed to draw out endlessly, then Trev said roughly, "Why the devil didn't you tell me who you were?"

"I thought you knew who I am!" she shot back, but it was too flippant an answer. She looked away, letting go a long breath. "That is not fair." After a moment, she looked at Trev with a gaze somehow both stubborn and vulnerable. "I feared my father-in-law, you see. Though I did . . . come to know you, I still did not know him beyond the letter he wrote to Peter, and though he may be quite an unexceptionable person when he is not angry, when he is . . . I feared he might try to abduct Alex if we could not reach some agreement. If it came to that, I wanted to have a place where I could take Alex, someplace in England where your uncle would never think to look for us. As I haven't the funds to set up myself and the children independently, the only place of refuge left to me was Edgemoore. Charles would not be delighted to take me in, but I thought if I were truly at my last ropes, he surely would have to."

Anne was crying even before she was done, soundless tears slipping down her face. She could not have said why she was crying, there were so many reasons—not least, the tender look in the eyes of the man across from her.

"Oh!" she exclaimed, thumping her glass blindly down on the table and rising to flee.

She had gotten no more than halfway to her feet before Buckingham scooped her up into his arms and sat down in the chair, holding her in his lap. Anne buried her face in the hollow of his neck and sobbed, in real part because she was where she had thought never to be again. And crying, too. She seemed to cry on him so often, she could not imagine why he was not disgusted with her. But he did not seem to be. He was caressing her, kissing her hair, murmuring, "Annie, Annie," over and over. "It's all right, Annie. Shush."

"Oh, Trev. I ought to have trusted you. I know it now, but then . . . there was so much at stake for me . . . and I never thought of marrying you. Oh no, that's not true. I did, but I knew you would never marry me. I thought, oh, Trev, I thought to be your lover until Rob came. His letter never reached me. You've only to ask Barrett. I did not know he was coming that day. I would never marry you if you were forced to it. You would hate me, and I would hate that. Trev, you did mean what you said to Alex?"

Anne felt a faint tremor shake him. Sniffing, she angled her head to stare at him suspiciously. He was almost smiling. "You are laughing at me!" she accused.

His mouth curved. "I do not believe I have ever heard anyone say so much without stopping even once for breath. But did you mean what you said, Annie? You thought to be my mistress for a week?"

Anne shook her head. "No. Your lover for a week. I don't care for the idea of being your mistress. Too much company, I suppose." Trev laughed, but the look in his blue eyes was unbearably soft. Anne yielded to the impulse to smooth his black hair back from his forehead. "And I wasn't certain whether it would be one week or two. I didn't know when Rob would come, though I certainly did not expect him so soon."

Anne said it with such regret, Trev kissed her lightly on her forehead. "You inspire love and loyalty in great degree. Rob came to learn what had become of you before he'd breakfasted even."

"You spoke so long?" She rested her head on the chair so that she could look at him still.

Trev nodded. "We became fast friends until the Sunderlands sighted him. Ah, Annie!" All the ease went out of his face. "How can I make up to you for all I said then, and today—or yesterday, rather?"

"You—"

"Hush, now." He kissed her nose, but his expression was dark. "It is my turn, and I've much to atone for. Oh God, Annie." He drew in a ragged breath and shook his head. "I had come to feel so strongly about you. More strongly than I had ever felt about any woman, but so long as I thought of you only as my mistress, I did not have to think about what I felt. I knew the lay of the land, so to speak, and could negotiate it blindly. Then suddenly everything was topsy-turvy. You were an earl's granddaughter and quite innocent, I knew after our night together, of Uncle John's charges, and being so innocent and well born and unjustly made to suffer so much, you deserved marriage. I had known it for a long while, really, known that you did not deserve the casual treatment I had in mind, but to have to face it so directly, to know, too, that I'd added to your woes . . . I reacted like a fox in a trap, and I twisted things about. I knew all about ambitious women, willing to scheme to marry a duke. I felt betrayed and undone, and I lashed out. Can you ever forgive me, Annie?

But Anne asked, "Can you forgive me for not telling you?"

"Yes," he said unhesitatingly. "You are a lioness about your children. If you thought you were protecting Alex . . ."

"And I knew . . . know you cannot marry me, Trev!" Anne sat up to look at him urgently. "You must understand

that. I know my family cannot make a difference. My life . . .
I am too disreputable."

"Odd," Trev said softly, and took her face in his hands.
"I consider that you possess more integrity and more honor
and more loyalty than anyone I know, Annie. If those qualities are not foremost among those required to be the
Duchess of Buckingham, I cannot think what qualities
would be, except perhaps for intelligence, wit, and bone-
deep beauty. Your uncertain past be damned, Annie. What
is the worst you've done? You've decorated hats, a shocking indiscretion, to be sure, but nothing half so disreputable
as most of my reckless life. I want you for my wife, my
own. I could not live even five days without you."

He was pulling her toward him to affirm with a kiss how
he wanted her. Anne held him off, her hands on his chest,
her green eyes wide and shadowed. "Trev, I cannot ask for
this. You will hate me in time, become disgusted when no
one will receive me."

To her consternation, Trev sank back in the chair, chuck-
ling. "Pray they won't receive us, Annie, and perhaps we'll
have some peace! Ah, my own." He pulled her to him, kissing her lightly before he shook his head. "You will see for
yourself in time, but for now you may take my word that
society embraces nothing so readily as beauty and title, particularly in combination. Even the Sunderlands will fawn
over you, hoping for an invitation to Buckingham House.
And the rest will scramble over themselves to see if you really are so seductively beautiful as the gossips say, and
then, blight them all, they will return again and again, because you are beautiful and gracious and all else. Annie,
they'll not only receive you, they'll madden you with their
interest, besides which, you already have the approval of all
the important people. Maddy wants you for a sister-in-law,
and the servants are to a maid in your pocket. Oh, my own
love, say it now. I want to hear from your own lips that you
will be my wife."

The smile Anne gave him was slow, and entirely at odds
with the soaring of her heart. "Do you know, I find I rather

like you in this mood. I don't know that I've ever seen you importune—"

"Annie."

She laughed softly and kissed the palm of the hand he had placed on her cheek. "I feel as if I am dreaming. I love you so." She looked up then, her gaze turning full and deep. "Yes, Trev, oh yes, I will be your wife."